ALSO BY D.N. MOORE

Ballad of the Dead: A Modern Fairy Tale

The Blandford Fly and Other Tales

THE
BOY WHO LEARNED TO LIVE

D.N. MOORE

Avonlea
Publishing

This book is a work of fiction. Any references to historical events, real people, or real places are used fictitiously. Other names, characters, places, and events are products of the author's imagination, and any resemblance to actual events or places or persons, living or dead, is entirely coincidental.

Copyright © 2024 by D.N. Moore

All rights reserved, including the right to reproduce this book or portions thereof in any form whatsoever. If you would like permission to use material from the book (other than for review purposes), please contact **therealdnmoore@gmail.com**.

Audience: Ages 12 and up. | Audience: Grades 7-12
Library of Congress Control Number: 2024918712 |

ISBN 9798218495800 (hardcover) | ISBN 9798218540449 (paperback) | ISBN 9798218495817 (ebook)

Printed in the United States of America. Book design by Lorna Reid.
First edition, Avonlea Publishing, November 2024

ISBN 9798218495800 (hardcover)

Shelter From The Storm
Words and Music by Bob Dylan
Copyright © 1974, 1976 UNIVERSAL TUNES Copyright Renewed
All Rights Reserved Used by Permission Reprinted by Permission of Hal Leonard LLC

Girl From The North Country
Words and Music by Bob Dylan
Copyright © 1963 UNIVERSAL TUNES Copyright Renewed
All Rights Reserved Used by Permission Reprinted by Permission of Hal Leonard LLC

For

Annabelle
Emily
Jack

and those in your generation and the next who may need a reminder
of what living is really about

"All the world's a stage, and all the men and women merely players."

—William Shakespeare

THE BOY WHO LEARNED TO LIVE

AMBER ALERT

HAVE YOU SEEN THIS MISSING TEEN?

Oliver McNeil
Missing Since: September 3rd, 2085
Missing From: The 5th City
Age Now: 17
Gender: M
Race: White
Hair Color: Light brown
Eye Color: Blue
Height: 5'10"
Weight: 160 lbs

An Amber Alert has been issued for Oliver McNeil, who went missing from his home on the eighteenth floor of building 202 in City 5 last Friday night. He is believed to be on foot. Oliver requires psychiatric care and is without his medication, which makes him a danger to himself and others. If anyone has information on Oliver, call Dr. Makoyiwa, his primary care physician, at 400-1315. Thank you for your help to keep our community safe.

ONE

"Is this a black-and-white movie?"

My voice shattered the night air like a pickaxe on ice. I blinked and looked down at my feet. White sneakers against asphalt. Another blink. Dirty smudges on gray jeans. Blink. Out of the corner of my eye, a flash of yellow.

"Oh, maybe not." I blinked again, staring at my feet. "Unless someone put a filter on the world. Could be. Could be that."

I was vaguely aware that I sounded crazy. It was as if my mind had detached from my body and split in two. Or was it three?

Another slow blink and I lifted my head. A road stretched out before me, long and empty, rolling over hills until it disappeared in the darkness. The faded yellow line down its center seemed to vibrate.

I laughed madly. "Yellow! My favorite color! Just like sunshine."

The sane part of me wondered who I was talking to. It also wondered where I was and how I'd gotten here. At this point, however, the sane part of me was voiceless.

Another part of me had a bad feeling about that road. It led to something dangerous.

I turned to face the other direction, although that seemed to take hours. My feet didn't want to move when I told them to. That stretch of road was the same. Long, empty, and definitely dangerous.

"Hmm." My voice dragged out the "mmm" part for a very long time. "What do we do now, my dear Watson?"

My eyes were heavy. It was time for sleep.

*

When I came to, I was stumbling through water. It swirled around my ankles and pushed against my calves, making it hard to walk. I charged through the waves ferociously. Surely I could out-muscle a bit of ocean surf—but no, it pinned me back and I stumbled down to the ground.

"Stupid legs," I mumbled, lifting my head to look down at my feet.

I had been mistaken. This was not water at all. This was a tangled mass of barbed wire that had devoured me like a hideous monster with hundreds of teeth. "This *must* be a movie," I said, for although the wire was embedded in my skin, I could not feel a thing.

I blinked again, the movement so slow that I watched my eyelashes feather over the frame and float away again. This time the color in my black-and-white film was not yellow, but red. Thick, crimson lines that oozed down my arms and dripped off my fingers. I held my hand up and grew mesmerized by its bloody silhouette against the night sky. "And this is where our hero dies," I said in my best narrator voice.

But I knew full well that I was no hero.

Something suddenly jostled the wire and my legs bounced wildly. If I hadn't been completely numb, I probably would've cried out in pain. As it was, I could only stare dully at the pair of boots that crossed the metal and stopped directly in front of me. They were army-style boots, probably steel-shanked, and caked in mud from bottom to top.

The owner of the boots got busy. Bolt cutters snipped away at the wire. A pile of branches was dragged next to me. The movement was too fast for my eyes, so I lay my head back and said, "Where's the fire?" with a snort of irritation.

The voice that belonged to the boots was entirely unexpected.

"You have to get up," it said, and it was soft as first snowfall.

I forced my eyes upward. A cloud of auburn hair, thick like a lion's mane, framed a tiny, porcelain face in the moonlight. Quiet eyes stared down at me, expressionless. "You're a girl," I said, reaching my hand up to touch her face. "And you're so real."

She crossed her arms and nodded. "And I can't lift you. I need you to snap out of it for a second and get yourself onto this gurney."

My head felt like lead, but I slammed it over to face the layers of evergreen branches that she had fashioned into a makeshift stretcher. "I can't move my legs," I mumbled shamefully.

"Can you roll, if I help you?"

"I'll try."

"Good." The boots stepped over me and she crouched down at my left shoulder. "Ready?"

I looked up at her and blinked one last time. "Are you an angel?" I asked. My words were so slurred that it sounded like, "Are you GI Joe?" She probably had no idea who GI Joe was. I was the only kid I knew who watched old-fashioned movies.

I was expecting her to laugh, but she didn't. She didn't even smile. She pursed her lips and the corners of her eyes drooped down. "I can't believe they did this to you," she murmured, pressing my shoulder between her two gloved hands.

"Oh, I did this to myself," I said flippantly. "This is what I do. Constantly get myself into trouble."

She just shook her head. "What's your name?"

"Oliver." I had to listen to the sound of it on my tongue to make sure it was correct. It sounded right.

She slid her hand under my back, and I was surprised to find that I could feel her fingers, small but strong within her gloves. "Okay, Oliver. On the count of three, okay?"

*

I had to admire her for getting me out, but man, that gurney was not much of a ride. Even through the cotton wool of numbness, I could feel the jostling of the branches under me and the jarring of the rocks.

A couple times we hit a rut and I went over, face down into the dirt. She had to flip everything over and get me back on again. That was no easy feat. My limbs were like those foam pool noodles that are totally useless for anything but flailing around, and my body was like a rubber bumper. Somehow she always got me back on again, hoisted the handles up with a tiny grunt, and continued dragging me through the woods.

The tree canopy above me was backlit by the moon, and the silvery silhouette was hypnotic in its beauty. I had never seen anything like it before. I disappeared into the intricacies of branches against sky (gnarled and twisting), branches against the ground (brushing and dragging), and the steady footsteps of a girl who had just saved my life.

*

"He's from the city. Middle class."

It was spoken at a low whisper, but there was no mistaking that the voice belonged to a man. Older. Probably bearded.

I refused to open my eyes to check, though. My head had an intense throbbing to it, like a tiny elf had gotten in there and was hammering away at the inside of my skull. I knew that opening my eyes would bring the light, and the light would bring searing pain, like the little elf-man had turned in his hammer for a machete and was hacking away, up to his elbows in optic nerves and brain tissue.

"How do you know?"

That was her. My angel. You'd never catch me saying that out loud in a million years—ultimate cheese—but it was the only way I could describe her. That image of her face, waves of auburn hair, tiny chin, porcelain skin… it was the only thing I wanted to think about right now.

"You can tell from the cut of his hair, his shaven face." He was describing me. "Look at the size of his body. He's properly fed, but not overweight. Those are the shoulders of an athlete."

"What do you think he's on?"

There was a pause, and I could imagine him studying me.

"Could be diazepam. He looks about sixteen or seventeen, and anxiety's pretty common at that age… you said he was hallucinating, talking to himself, right?" The man's voice paused again. "He could be on a whole cocktail of stuff. We'll need to be careful."

"I just couldn't leave him there, Dad. It was probably the stupidest thing I ever did, bringing him here, but he would've died, and he looked so confused…"

At this point, my headache had gotten so bad that it wrung my stomach out and brought bile to my throat. I turned on my side, clutching my midsection while I retched. I couldn't remember the last time I'd eaten, or what it had been, but it tasted like acid coming up.

The fetal position felt really good. For just a moment, I was pain-free. I lay my head down, but there was no pillow. The surface was hard and made rustling noises when I moved. I still didn't want to open my eyes.

Then her hand was on my arm. I knew it was hers because it was so light, her fingers grazing my shoulder and her palm coming to rest against my back. The thought crossed my mind that this would be embarrassing tomorrow, knowing that I had lain there in a puddle of my own puke while she stroked my back like I was an invalid. My future humiliation was enough to pry my eyelids apart and lift my heavy head off the ground.

"What happened?" I asked, sitting up and wincing as the light hit my brain like an anvil.

She was crouched next to me, arms dangling over her knees, her hair a sunrise-saturated cloud. She still wore those dirty army boots.

"We were hoping you could tell us that," she said gently. Most people back home fired questions at me without pause, but she waited patiently for my answer.

I began massaging my temples with my palms. "I don't remember. I was walking down the highway, but I have no idea how I got there. I thought I was dreaming."

Her eyes flitted behind me, exchanging a glance with someone. "What's the last thing you do remember, before you woke up on the highway?"

"Playing a basketball sim." The squeak of sneakers on the floor, fluorescent lights, blue uniforms. Tightening my headset when it kept slipping off. The usual smell of the air conditioning in my room.

"A basketball sim?" She had her head cocked to the side.

I looked around the clearing, squinting through bleary eyes. God, it was bright out here. Trees loomed over me like overprotective giants, crowding out the sky and smothering the horizon. Even so, the sun was inescapable, blazing down in fierce slats wherever an opening could be found. What time of year was it? I hadn't looked out my apartment window in months.

"What is a sim?" she asked.

"Oh." My words came out slurred. "You guys don't have sims out here, do you." It was a statement, not a question. It was dawning on me that these people lived in the woods. How would they drag one of those machines out here? They were as big as a room. The expensive systems had headsets *and* interactive screens on every wall, for a better user experience. Somehow I couldn't imagine one of those out here in the woods, under open sky.

"I guess you could say they're like video games. Except we do everything on them. General Ed for school. Physical for exercise. Social for hanging out, catching up with friends. Gingle and Yooza for information. You know, simulators."

A flash of confusion crossed her face. "Your life is all simulated?" It was a look I had never seen before, in my A.I. world—a fleeting perplexity, passing so quickly it was as if it had never happened. But I knew it had, and it confirmed what I already knew—that she and I came from very different worlds.

My voice may have been slurred before, but now my tongue was an oozy, slimy slug blocking my throat. I tried to give her an answer, but after a moment of gargling and floundering, I doubled over and threw up all over my shoes.

As if that wasn't embarrassing enough, she reached into the puddle of green slime at my feet and began searching through the chunks. "Got it," she exclaimed, pulling something out between her fingers. She held it up to show the person behind me.

"What are you doing?" I protested.

"Want to see it?" She held her hand out.

"Uh, you mean what I ate for dinner? No, thanks. I'll pass." Curiosity got the better of my revulsion, however, and when she didn't move her hand away, I leaned in and peered at it. "I don't see anything."

She pushed back pieces of food and cleared a space for a tiny, black square in the center of her palm. I pursed my lips and looked a little closer. "What is it?"

"A microchip."

I frowned. "In my stomach?"

"They chip your medication to make sure you're taking it."

"How do you know I'm on medication?"

Another perplexed look. "You're all on medication."

If only my mind wasn't like a dryer on slow spin. Questions tumbled around and around, on top of one and then covering another. Before I had a chance to grab one and present it coherently, she had stood up and walked behind me.

Oddly, throwing up had made me feel better. The headache had gone from a ten to a nine-point-five, and the light didn't burn my retinas like before. With her out of my line of vision, I studied the environment around me as much as I could without disturbing my head.

We were in some sort of makeshift camp. A fire smoldered a few feet away, and the smell made my nose hairs curl up. I had never smelled a real fire before. Seven piles of branches topped with sleeping bags lay around the crackling logs like the spokes of a wheel, and six had been flattened as if they had been lain on. I wondered why the seventh was untouched.

The air had a chill-mixed-with-smell that I did not recognize. I was sure I had felt something similar in one of my exercise sims, but I couldn't put my finger on it. It meant something. Something about time.

A pile of branches lay next to me, their needles wiry as an old comb. I brushed one of them with the back of my hand, wincing at the sharp sensation that shot up to my elbow, every nerve recoiling in horror. In last night's "black-and-white movie," I had seen the same branches against my skin but not felt a single thing. Was this world of blazing light and overwhelming sensation better or worse?

The girl and her dad were talking in low voices behind me. I tried to tune in, but I only caught pieces of it here and there. "Could be a plant," was loud and clear (the words and the meaning); "…can't bring him back," should have been concerning (but wasn't); and "…dead man on our hands," didn't make any sense. Finally they seemed to come to an agreement, and the conversation stopped. Heavy footsteps made their way over to me.

"Autumn," I realized aloud. That was what the chill in the air meant—it was the season! Fall. Autumn. When the leaves came down off the trees, just in time for snow. I had seen it on sims, but the machines couldn't imitate that cold, crisp smell.

The footsteps turned to a desperate scramble, and suddenly my body was flipped around, face shoved in the ground, dirt in my mouth, and my hands were twisted in a vise grip at my back.

TWO

I wanted to cry out in pain, but I could only utter a weak moan.

"Who are you?" The voice in my ear was low and steady, but it simmered dangerously.

"I'm Oliver," I whispered through a mouthful of sand. "Oliver McNeil."

There was a pause. Then: "Who sent you?"

"Nobody!" Inhaling loose dirt sent me into a violent coughing spell, which was difficult, considering how tightly I was pinned to the ground. He was unsympathetic.

"How do you know my daughter?"

"Huh?" Convulsive cough. "I don't."

"You said her name out loud just now."

"Autumn? Her name is Autumn?" Cough. "I didn't know, I swear. I was remembering what season it is." Cough and gag. "I haven't been outside like this since I was a kid. I don't know anything about her, I swear!"

My voice was hoarse by now, but my lungs had cleared themselves and I let myself go, laying my head limply in the dirt and pine needles, trying to ignore the pain in my twisted shoulders and the throbbing in my head. It was back at a ten-point-five after the last coughing spell. The man relaxed his grip on my hands and let them fall on the ground.

I closed my eyes and pressed my cheek into the ground, strangely comforted by the cradling sensation of the earth. As circulation returned to my arms, the world spun around me, and if not for the firmness of the ground, I would have thought I was falling through space.

"Oliver." Light fingers on my back. It was as if she were calling to me through a long tunnel with really good acoustics.

"I didn't know your name, I swear." I kept my eyes closed, speaking to the abyss. "I have a bad habit of saying the wrong thing at the wrong time."

"I believe you."

I didn't answer. Instead, I contemplated falling asleep and never waking up.

"Oliver." Suddenly she was waking me.

"Hmm."

"You need to get up. It's time to go."

I opened one eye. She was squatting in front of me again, her hair pulled back in a ponytail, revealing a long, white neck. The sun had changed position and the air had a deeper chill to it. It was nearly nightfall.

"What happened?" I rubbed my face and sat up. My head still ached, but some of the edge was gone.

"You fell asleep a few hours ago. We already cleaned camp."

The fire pit was gone, and so were all the branches, footprints, and any trace of human activity.

"Everyone's started out already. We need to get going."

I still had so many questions (where were we going? Who had started out ahead of us? How long had I been sleeping? Why was I supposed to go with them?), but it was too much effort to ask, so I gave a brief nod and stood up.

I regretted it immediately. My legs became two useless sticks and I was engulfed by blackness.

When I came to, I was flat on my back and so disoriented, I couldn't tell up from down and right from left. It was her soft eyes and steady gaze that brought me back to reality, and the world came into focus around her. She handed me a small, leather bag.

"Wow, thanks." I took it slowly and admired it obligingly. It was soft and made a sloshing noise when I squeezed it.

The left corner of her mouth curled up in amusement. "Drink," she said, pointing to a leather thong at the top. "It's water."

I untied it to find a wooden cork, which I pulled out with great effort. I tilted the bag back cautiously and poured a few drops into my mouth.

She grinned. "You can just drink, you know. Like a cup." She opened her mouth and made a swigging motion.

"But I don't know where this came from. It could be infected."

Her smile vanished. "It is not *infected*. It's just water." She crossed her arms. "Anyway, you don't really have a choice. You can't survive without water."

I wouldn't survive an infection, either, but I kept my thoughts to myself. Deciding to take my chances, I held the flask up to my lips and drank thirstily.

"Why are you helping me?" I asked. "You could've just left me there, next to the road. Then you wouldn't have to go to all this trouble."

She tilted her head to the side and studied me with a soft expression. "'One touch of nature makes the whole world kin.'"

It didn't make any sense.

"Come on," she said, corking the flask and tying it hastily to a large, brown backpack she carried on her back. "We can't stay here any longer."

The sun had already gone down by the time I steadied myself on my feet and plodded forward, trailing along behind her, doing my best to keep up. Her backpack was so big it nearly blocked the back of her head, but I could still see her ponytail sticking out one side. Her strides were longer than mine, and she stepped with a confidence that I had never seen in a girl, one that stood out in striking contrast to my pathetic shuffle.

My headache had faded to a dull pulse, but that was the least of my worries. My shoulder throbbed from being twisted back, my lungs ached, and I had a jittery sensation in my muscles, as if someone had replaced my capillaries with low-voltage electrical wires. I shook my arms out, checking first to make sure Autumn wasn't looking back at me. The last thing I wanted was her thinking I was crazy. An invalid, sure. Sick—fine. But God help me if she ever mistook me for one of those homeless loonies who wandered around the city, their bodies trembling with every step, arms floating up like octopi, watching me with eyes that couldn't stay still for longer than ten seconds. The Forgotten, my mom had called them. An apt description, because anyone who's been around that kind of crazy knows that you do whatever it takes to stay away.

Just when I thought I had begun to get the hang of dragging my legs along through the brush, the ground suddenly disappeared beneath me and I lunged forward, so slow to bring my hands forward that my face caught the full brunt of my fall.

Dirt in my mouth, once again. This time I pushed it out with my tongue, feeling a dribble down my chin. I pulled myself up on my elbows and looked back at what had tripped me.

It was a hole. It was only about four feet wide and two feet deep, which is why I hadn't seen it (or so I told myself). The sides were smooth and there were no tree roots poking through, which confirmed my suspicion that this hole had not been created by erosion or wild animals, but rather, it was man-made.

"Dammit, Jesse!" Autumn muttered to herself. She ran over to help me up. Her brow was furrowed in two small triangles above her nose. "Are you okay?"

"Yeah." I wiped my chin, leaving a streak of blood on the back of my arm. I must've scraped it pretty badly. "Who's Jesse?"

She gave a frustrated sigh. "He's my little brother. For some reason he has this obsession with digging holes."

I did my best to raise an eyebrow. "How old is he?"

"Seven."

This time I winced as my eyebrow shot even higher. None of the seven-year-olds I knew would have ever been able to dig a hole that expertly. Not in real life, anyway.

"I didn't know it was legal to have a sibling." I immediately regretted saying it. She scowled at me and turned her back with an angry sigh. I had clearly stepped into dangerous territory, so I didn't pursue an answer. There were a lot of things I would never understand out here.

"I'm sorry you fell," she said, changing the subject. "I didn't think to look this far out. Usually he sticks a little closer to camp." She swung her pack off her back and set it on the ground. "I just have to get this thing covered up. We can't leave any trace that we were here."

She set to work pushing, kicking and tamping the soil back into the hole. She insisted that I sit against a tree and rest, and although I didn't argue, because the pain had grown increasingly worse, I did feel utterly useless as I watched her stomp around on the pile and throw leaves over the ground to make it look the same as every other place in the woods.

"What are you guys doing out here?" I asked, panting a little at the effort it took to speak.

She glanced at me warily from under her ponytail. "We live here."

"Out here in the woods? All on your own?"

She paused. She seemed uncertain if she should answer. "There are others," she said cautiously. She pushed her ponytail out of her face and stood. "Let's go."

I swallowed a groan as I stood, bracing myself against the tree. The world spun into a gyroscope of darkness and spots of color. When the near-blackout had passed, I was surprised to see the back of Autumn's backpack bobbing through the trees, several yards away.

"Wait," I whispered, hobbling after her. Why was she running away from me? Had I said something wrong? Or had she intended to leave me here in the first place? I looked around at the skeletal shapes made by the moonlight through the trees, and suddenly it all made sense. I had been brought to the woods to die. But not an easy death, like falling asleep in a bed of barbed wire, unable to feel a thing, drifting peacefully into nothingness. No, they wanted me to suffer. They wanted me to *feel* it—the pain, the loss, the confusion and terror. They wanted me to run shamelessly through the darkness after the most beautiful girl in the world, knowing I would never have her—I would never be anything but a slave to this pain—this searing, biting, unforgiving pain.

Crippled by it, my shoulders heavy under the impossible weight of it, I finally gave up and dove into a sea of the blackest night, grateful for the mercy of unconsciousness.

*

"Why is he breathing like that?" An unfamiliar voice. High-pitched.

"He's detoxing." It was her.

"What's that mean?"

"He's sick. From drugs. They're leaving his body, but it hurts."

A long, screeching moan. Sobbing. Exhausted gasps. Could those sounds be coming from me?

Delicate fingers on my shoulders, shaking me. "Oliver. You have to drink this."

More sobbing. Cries of, "Help me," over and over again. My voice. But it was so far away.

A fumbling sound. A man's hands pulling me upright. My body like a wet rag, head lolling over.

Something touching my lips. Wet. Hard. A bowl? A cup? When was the last time I'd eaten?

I was dying. I knew it. Why did it take so long?

Something warm and salty trickling over my tongue. An awkward swallow. More crying.

Again, the salty liquid. Less crying this time. Thirsty slurping.

Sleep.

*

"City man?"

Something tickled my nose. I scratched furiously.

Next to my right ear, someone gasped. I opened my eyes and turned my head, coming face to face with a pair of enormous, green eyes.

I yelped. He jumped. Then we stared at each other. He had a freckled nose, big ears and the unmistakable red hair of his older sister.

I said, "Hi, Jesse," and his eyes doubled in size (if that was possible).

"You know my name?"

Remembering the trouble I'd been in earlier for guessing Autumn's name, I said quickly, "Your sister told me about you. We've never met before."

His chest puffed out proudly, which was comical, considering his scrawny shoulders. "What did she tell you?"

"She said you're pretty strong."

He grinned. "Sure am."

Sunlight gleamed on rust-colored hair cut shaggily around his ears, the back coming down in a mullet against brown overalls. Based on the slant of the light, it must have been mid-afternoon.

"How long have I been asleep?" I asked, rubbing my face. Unshaven bristles scraped against my hand.

"Almost a day and a half. You been real sick."

Three nights. Three nights I had been gone. Was anyone even looking for me?

I winced at a twinge of pain running through my chest.

"You still got drugs in you?" He looked at me as if I were a scientific curiosity, a specimen in some kind of experimental sideshow.

"I don't know. Your sister seems to know more about that than I do."

"Did they stick you with a needle?"

"No." I frowned. Now that he was mentioning it, it had been days since I'd taken my medication. Maybe that was why I felt so sick.

"Wanna see my latest comic?"

My frown deepened. "I don't know what that is." I tried not to sound as irritated as I felt.

"You've never read a *comic*?" His mouth fell open.

I sighed, openly annoyed now. He was making me feel like an idiot. I turned my head away, pointedly ignoring him, and studied the trees overhead. They were still skeletons, but they didn't seem as terrifying as the last time I'd seen them. Now they were just *in my way*. What was their problem, anyway? Why so many of them? Didn't they know they were crowding the place? I felt like I couldn't breathe.

Suddenly that damn kid popped his head into my view. His ears stuck out almost as far as the branches. I sighed again. Couldn't he take a hint?

"I write comics," he piped up cheerily. "Wanna see one?"

Before I had a chance to say, "No," he had thrust his notebook in my face. It was covered in smudged, gray squares with two-dimensional characters in each square. Circles containing words floated above their heads.

"This is called *Edward the Entrail*. It's a comedy. See the part where his host eats too much?" He grinned and looked at me expectantly.

I blinked. "I don't get it."

He shrugged and flipped the page. "This one's *Cannibal Carrots*. It's a tragedy." A grimy finger directed me to the square on the bottom. "See? There were two carrots at the beginning… and now there's only one! The other one was hungry." He laughed.

"Jesse!" Autumn's voice hit us sharply. "Leave him alone!"

The boy ducked away sheepishly. I turned my head. She knelt over me with a mug in her hands, her hair blazing in the sunlight.

"Drink this," she urged, coaxing me to sit up. I propped my back up against a tree, squirming against it—why was the bark hard as a damn rock?—and took the warm mug in my hands. I remembered the salty liquid they'd given me the night before and my mouth began to water. I was surprised to find myself hungry.

After gulping it down ravenously, I wiped my mouth and leaned back. "I've never tasted anything so good," I said. "What is that?"

She tilted her head. "It's broth," she replied. "Chicken broth."

I smelled the cup. "That's not the kind of chicken broth we buy back home."

"Oh, we don't buy it. We make it ourselves."

I laughed. She didn't. She was totally serious. "What does that mean?"

"From our chickens."

I narrowed my eyes. "What, you kill them and eat them?"

That perplexed look again. "Yes." She leaned her head forward slightly. "Are there no chickens in your city?"

"Real chickens? No."

"What animals do you have?"

I tried to remember if I had ever seen a real animal. "We have animal sims," I said, trying to give her something. "I think I had a dog one time, when I played a soldier in Iraq. And I visited a zoo when I was a kid, but that was part of General Ed."

She looked at me quizzically. "You only have simulations of animals?"

I shrugged. "Sure. Pretty much everything is a simulation, isn't it? Other than eating and sleeping, what else is there?"

Autumn sat down in the dirt and crossed one leg over the other, propping her arms up on her knee. "Tell me about them."

I shifted forward, leaning so heavily under the weight of gravity that I could feel my shoulders pull my spine into a sharp "C." I looked up at her through droopy eyelids. "The sims? They're just computers."

"What kind of information do they give you?"

"Anything you want. How to fix a car, how to do algebra, recipes, that sort of thing."

She seemed intrigued. "You must know how to do a lot of different things, then."

"I guess." I tried to remember all the programs I had watched over the years. Had I ever actually done any of the things they showed me?

"Maybe you can help us. We have so much we want to learn." She blinked her eyes—those wide, vivid things, the color of a summer sky. If she had asked me to bring her the ocean in a bucket, I would've done it.

"Yeah, sure. Whatever you need."

Uncrossing her legs, she leaned over on her hands and knees and dragged her backpack towards her. "I have this machine," she said, unzipping the bag. "We just got back from a scavenge in one of the old abandoned cities. I found it in a store called 'Best Buy.'" She pulled out a bundle of brown cloth and unwrapped it carefully. In the center was a small, metal box with a circle of glass on the front and a variety of knobs and levers around the outside. It was just a bit bigger than her hand. She handed it to me.

It was heavier than I expected. Some of the knobs were loose, and they spun around with a dull, plastic click. It had the clunky appearance of something you'd see on an old Sci Fi movie, from back before they had CGI.

"What does it do?" she asked eagerly. A strand of hair fell over her shoulder and she tucked it behind her ear. It was such a feminine gesture, done innocently enough, but I swallowed nervously. She was so close I could smell her—some kind of strong soap mixed with the cool scent of the forest. She looked up at me and I realized I was staring like an idiot.

"Oh. Oh, this." I played with one of the levers. "Yeah, I saw a show on this once. It's a… uh… well, it looks like a camera."

Her eyes widened and the color drained from her face. "A *camera?*" She snatched it out of my hand. "This is a camera?"

I looked at it again, to be sure. I was certain I'd seen it on an old black and white film. A man had used it to take pictures of a woman walking along the streets of Paris. The woman had been throwing her head back in laughter, exposing her long, contoured neck, twirling a parasol behind her, and the man snapped a photo of her using a button on the top.

Sure enough, there was the button on top.

"Yes, it's one of those older models. Some people like all that vintage stuff, you know?"

She scrambled to her feet. With one long sweep of the arm, she sent the camera sailing through the air, throwing it a good sixty feet away.

"Why'd you do that?" I asked, aghast.

"Cameras are not allowed here," she said.

I opened my mouth in disbelief. "How do you make movies, then?"

There was a stubborn set to her jaw. "We don't have movies here," she said sternly. "No cameras. Period."

It felt like a blow to the chest. Movies were my life. I remembered all the times I had ended a day of sims, removing my headset and coming back to my dark bedroom feeling dazed, as if I couldn't quite locate myself, clutching at reality but feeling nothing but emptiness. My only salvation had been movies. I had to find them on the dark web, which was risky, but I'd always been smart with my money and I knew some pretty advanced encryption techniques. They were old, sure, and they only worked on one screen, not in my headset. They were grainy and tinny and the camera angles were strange and often way too slow. But the people were *real*, with raw emotions and human struggles. They didn't live in sterilized homes and guarded cities—they ate outside and drank from rivers and fought with each other and died for their friends. They were heroes and villains and they lived life the way I imagined it should be lived—not holed up in a dark room, listening to robots tell you everything you wanted to hear, but really *living*. Movies were the only things that had ever made me feel anything other than the Great Numbness that was my life.

"You guys are missing out," I mumbled helplessly.

Autumn crouched down in front of me again. She was closer than she had been before. Her expression had softened. "My dad told me about movies. He loved them, too." She shook her head sadly. "But we can't afford to be traced. Nothing we do can be digital. Our anonymity is our only protection."

She stood. I was too tired to raise my head, so I stared at her boots. She seemed to hesitate, although I didn't know why.

"I read plays," she said. "That's kind of like a movie."

I shrugged heavily. "Never heard of them."

She lingered for a moment, saying nothing. Then the boots turned and walked away, crunching across the leaves on the forest floor.

I looked around the clearing and realized this was a newly-made camp. The fire pit was bigger this time, and the logs crackled and spat more loudly, but the setup was the same—seven sleeping bags arranged like wheel spokes around the pit. Six were flattened as if someone had lain on them, and one was fresh and untouched. None were mine, though. My bed was here, on the outskirts of the camp.

"Hey, City Man!" That freckled face came down out of nowhere, ears and all, hanging upside down like a monkey.

At that point, something in me snapped. All the pent up pain, grief and anger that had been brewing for days suddenly erupted with volcanic ferocity. My hands shot out in front of me (were they even my hands? They looked like a stranger's) and grabbed that kid by his shoulders, yanking him out of the tree and flipping him over on the ground. His mouth opened in a wide O and he gaped like a fish.

I had knocked the wind out of him.

Just as it began to dawn on me what I had done, that I had physically harmed a kid half my size, I heard a loud, metal click at my ear. I knew the sound synthetically, from video games, but I had never heard it in real life.

My heart hammered in my throat as I shot my hands in the air and stood, turning carefully. Autumn's face stared at me from behind the barrel of a large revolver. My guess, based on the size, was a .357 Magnum.

"Get away from him," she snarled.

THREE

Jesse coughed. Out of the corner of my eye, I saw him stand and move slowly towards the camp.

"I'm so sorry," I whispered. I had a giant lump in my throat, like I was a toddler on the verge of tears or something. I blinked furiously. "I can't believe I just did that."

Autumn motioned towards my pile of branches. "Sit down," she ordered. Her mouth was set in a hard, thin line, and her voice was harsh. Too harsh. A "you can't be trusted" kind of harsh.

I sat down.

"What's going on?"

"Autumn?"

"Is everything all right?"

Three men and a girl entered the clearing. Two of the men carried branches, one held a pail of water, and the girl—she looked about eighteen or nineteen—had a basket of plants slung over her arm. Keeping the gun trained on me, Autumn spoke out of the side of her mouth. "You okay, Jess?"

"I'm fine."

I was relieved to hear from his voice that he was, in fact, fine.

Autumn's shoulders relaxed a little, but she didn't lower the gun. "You're lucky," she said to me through clenched teeth. "If he was more seriously hurt, you wouldn't be sitting there."

One of the men dropped the branches at his feet and walked over them, tripping slightly as he made his way over to Autumn. "What did he do?" I looked more closely at his face. He wasn't a man, he was a kid—maybe fourteen years old. He was built like a wrestler, his chest and shoulders sturdy as a tree trunk, but there was a boyish curve to his jaw and his eyes shone with naivety. He had chin-length blond hair that he tucked unsuccessfully behind his ear.

Autumn shook her head back and forth, back and forth, slowly, furiously. "You guys were right," she said. "I should never have brought him here."

The other man carrying branches set his down gently and came close. This one I recognized. Her dad. It was the first time I'd seen him up close, but he was exactly as I had pictured him when I first heard his voice—tall and lean, with a chestnut-colored beard and matching hair pulled back in a ponytail. He put one hand on her arm and held the other out to take the gun. She relaxed and handed it to him. He turned to face me with the gun pointed down towards the ground.

"What happened here, kid?"

There was something in his tone that wedged its way into my soul, cracking open emotions that I didn't even know were there. I had been expecting him to fly into a rage, give me a beating, or at least give me a scathing look. He did none of that. Instead, his voice was kind. It was so unexpected that I started to cry. Not the kind that you can blink back, either. This was the snotty-nosed, heavy-sob, river-of-tears kind of crying that was *way* more humiliating than throwing up in front of a pretty girl. This was rock bottom for me. I had turned into a giant baby.

"I don't know," I got out between sobs. "I haven't taken my meds in days. I never thought I was a violent person, but maybe I'm sicker than I thought." I wiped my nose on my sleeve. "Everything hurts. I'm hot and then I'm cold. I'm constantly fighting the urge to throw up. And I don't even know what's real or what's in my head. I just can't deal anymore, man. The pain is so bad. And it never ends." Long, heavy sobbing got in the way of my words. I pulled my knees up to my chest and buried my face in them, closing my eyes while the world spun. "Kill me," I whispered. "Please. Just do it. I'm useless. I'm a danger to you all. I don't even know why I'm still here."

A hand came down on my shoulder, and I jumped. Autumn's dad was pretty old when you looked at him up close. He had deep, sunbaked lines in his forehead and around his eyes, and his long hair had wisps of gray in it. But his eyes were a shocking shade of blue, his jaw was chiseled, and he reminded me of a movie star in those old-fashioned cowboy movies. He even wore blue jeans and a belt.

"You're gonna be okay, kid." He patted me. "This is the hardest part. It's warm sunshine on the other side. You just gotta get through this part."

I nodded, even though I had no idea what he was talking about.

"We're just gonna have to have someone on watch, twenty-four-seven. You're right, you are a danger to us. But that'll be over soon."

I still had no idea what he was talking about, but my head was just bobbing away like an idiot, while snot and tears poured down my cheeks and dripped onto my neck.

"You got that tea ready yet, Diana?" he called to the girl, who had brought her basket to the fire and was stirring a pot that hung over the flames.

"It's coming."

"You need to walk," he told me. "Get your blood flowing. You've been sleeping long enough." He stood and turned to the group. "Time to pack up," he said. "We're moving again."

Everyone got quietly to work. The man who had been carrying the water pail filled flasks using a wooden ladle. He, too, was younger than he had first appeared—he looked about sixteen or seventeen, closer to my age. Unlike the other men in the group, his hair was cut short, accentuating a large, aquiline nose. Branch piles were removed and scattered in the woods. Footprints were swept up. Jesse threw dirt on the fire to put it out. The girl with the basket—Diana—brought me a cup of tea in a wooden mug and although it tasted like dirt, it was soothing to my stomach, so I guzzled it back while she waited.

I darted a glance her way when I handed her the empty cup. She had smooth, blond hair and a long, blue dress, and boots sticking out from under the hem. She cradled the cup in her hands and studied me quizzically. Then she spun on her heel and walked quickly away.

Everyone set out through the trees, a line of backpacks bobbing in the scattered, golden light of the sunset. The two younger men, both a full head taller than I, flanked me as we walked. I knew they were on psycho duty, assigned to make sure I didn't flip out again and do more serious damage this time. I glanced at Autumn walking next to her father at the front of the convoy. Thank God they're all the way up there, I thought. They need to stay as far away from me as possible.

We hiked through the night. I kept my head down and tried to focus on keeping my feet an exact distance from the person in front of me. A pointless exercise, I guess, but it kept my mind off the acidic pain that pulsed through my veins. I tried not to think, but my mind was a noisy clatter of voices that tumbled over each other like hungry kittens. They started out as whispers, some full-fledged mumbles, but they grew louder as I walked on.

Loser.

Hater.

…violent… dangerous… killer…

Not worth an arm and a leg.

Or a brain.

I shook my head over and over again, trying to get rid of them, but they filled my mind with such a loud chorus that after a while, I couldn't separate delusion from reality. I looked up at the kid walking on my left, a strange sort of anchor to the real world. I studied his surfer-style hair, his massive arms that were all muscle and sinew, and the long, jagged scar that ran from his chin to his chest and disappeared under his shirt. I wondered what had happened to him.

He turned his head and gave me a weird look.

Embarrassed, I looked away. I tried counting my steps.

One.

Two.

Right.

Left.

They hate your guts.

They all want you dead.

I shook my head and turned to look at the big-nosed kid on my right. He was leaner than Scar Face, but I still would have thought twice before picking a fight with him. He wore jeans and a green jacket, like the other men, but he seemed tidier, somehow, as if his clothes knew that dirt and wrinkles were unacceptable, even out in the woods. With the rifle slung up next to his backpack, the cropped haircut, and the hard set of his jaw, he reminded me of a soldier from the video games I used to play on sim with my friends after school.

He shot me a suspicious look.

I looked down at my feet again and tried again to shake the voices out of my head.

"Guess you're not used to walking," Big Nose commented.

I watched my feet shuffle awkwardly over leaves and tree roots. "What do you mean?"

"I hear they only drive in the city. Nobody walks anywhere."

I remembered my mom's red sedan parked in the elevator at our apartment. On the rare occasion that we did go out of the house (for my bi-monthly physical or one of mom's meetings with Dr. Makoyiwa), it was simply a press of a button and the vehicle was there, ready to take us down eighteen stories and onto the street. I tried to imagine taking the elevator down on foot. Where would we even go?

"It's too dangerous," I explained. "The outside air carries disease."

"How d'you get any exercise?" Scar Face piped up from my left.

I looked at him strangely. "Workout sims."

"Oh right, I heard about this." Big Nose again. "They do everything on computers. Exercise, work, school, entertainment. They hardly ever leave the house."

"What? All on computers?" Scar Face flipped a strand of hair behind his ear and looked over my head at his bodyguard companion. "Even their shopping?"

Big Nose nodded soberly with his eyebrows raised.

"What, does the food just come out of the screen, then?" He looked down at me in awe. "Do you get many options, at least?"

"No, the sims don't make the food." I frowned, wondering if this guy was missing brain cells. "You just make your selection, and the store sends a courier."

They both looked at me expectantly.

"You know, a courier machine? It checks for contamination, delivers your stuff, that sort of thing."

A noise erupted from both of them, startling me out of my skin—a satisfied laugh from Big Nose, and a disappointed groan from Scar Face.

"See? Robots. Robots run the city. I told you, didn't I?"

Scar Face shook his head in disappointment. "Fine. I owe you *one* night of dishes."

We continued walking in silence. I studied the line of people lit by the moon in front of me. Autumn's dad led the front. Autumn and her brother followed, Jesse play-fighting with a stick while he walked. Diana, the girl in the blue dress, trailed along at least fifteen feet behind them. And then there was me, sandwiched in between Laurel and Hardy.

"Someone's missing," I said.

They studied the caravan and gave me a questioning look.

"There were seven beds around the fire. There are only six of you here."

They both rolled their eyes. "Oh, yeah. That's Emer. She likes to hide. Keeps to herself most of the time." Big Nose motioned toward a clump of trees on our left. "She's probably in there somewhere, waiting 'til we pass."

Scar Face laughed. "She's the best sister of them all, though, isn't she?"

"Why, because she doesn't make a sound?" Big Nose joined in, laughing heartily from his gut. "Don't you wish they were all like that?"

"Wait a second." I stopped. "Those girls up there are your sisters?"

Suddenly stern, they were both at my side in an instant with their arms under mine. "Gotta keep moving. We're not allowed to let you stop." They pulled me forward until I started walking again.

I examined the group through new eyes. "You're all *family*?"

"I sometimes wish we weren't, but yeah." Big Nose gave me a strange look. "So?"

"But… that means that man has *six* children."

"Well, technically Emer is adopted. But she's still family."

I rubbed my forehead. The headache was coming back. "Is that even legal? Birthing five children?"

The silence that followed was concerning. I glanced up to find them exchanging a look. All trace of joviality was gone, and they had both set their lips in a line as if to remind each other to *stop talking*.

The silence set in again, cutting to the bone. I shivered. The night air was just as strong as the quiet, and I wondered if anyone had ever been able to measure things like cold and loneliness and depict them on a screen. I decided to look that up when I got home.

When was I going home, anyway? I hadn't thought about that since I got here. I had been gone maybe four, five days. My mom had probably called the cops the first night I went missing. I tried to remember how I had ended up here. The last thing I could recall was running a basketball sim with my friends online. Everything after that was a big, black memory void until I woke up on the highway.

My guards both grabbed my arm at the same time, pulling me to an abrupt halt. I looked up to see the group standing still, staring back at me. I pulled myself up a little straighter, wondering if I had done something wrong.

"Time to cover you up," said Big Nose, pulling a scarf from his bag. "Can't let you see this part."

My churning mind had been turbulent enough without the blindfold, but with it on, I thought I would drown. Stumbling along in the darkness, relying on the guidance of two strangers, listening to the voices in my head swell like a demon chorus… I was a spinning top, a whirling dervish, both nowhere and everywhere at the same time. I think I tried to cry out, but it was hard to tell what was real—

and even when I did open my mouth, nothing came out. My feet came out from under me and the men at my side lifted me up by my arms, carrying me like a limp rag. My feet twisted and turned as they dragged along the ground, but for the life of me, I could not regain control of them. I was worthless, and I had the fleeting thought that these people were just as crazy as I, for bringing me along. Autumn was right, she should have left me there in that barbed wire to die. That would have been the merciful thing to do. For everyone's sake.

The air changed. The spice of wet leaves was replaced by a dank, earthy smell. The cold sharpened, setting in like an icy blanket. My feet no longer dragged through the dirt—instead, the ground became solid and unforgiving so that I had to lift my legs to stop hitting my ankles. It was so uneven that I couldn't confidently regain my footing, no matter how hard I tried.

...an arm and a leg... muttered the voice in my head. The mental cacophony began to die down.

The glow around my blindfold dimmed and flickered. I could hear the crackling of fire.

"He sure moves a lot more than he used to," whispered Scar Face over my head as we walked. His voice was subdued, the sibilance reverberating differently than it had a few minutes ago. "He won't stop wiggling around."

"Maybe he has tics," Big Nose whispered back. "I've heard all that medical stuff can cause seizures."

"How long does it take for that stuff to get out of him?"

"Don't know." Big Nose shifted, hoisting my arm up higher on his shoulder. "Emer was unconscious for two weeks after we found her. Funny, we found her around the same spot as this guy."

"He says he exercises, but I think his arms are pumped full of air." Scar Face laughed a loud, guttural snort. "Look at how light he is!"

"Right here, guys." I shook my head in disbelief. "I'm right here, listening to every word you're saying."

There was a long minute of silence. I blinked behind my blindfold. To break the awkwardness, I asked, "What are your names, anyway?"

"Little guy over there is Cecil," said Big Nose from my right. "And I'm Luca. The smart one."

Cecil snorted. "Your head's full of the same hot air as this guy's muscles."

"Says the man who believes the cave bats are secretly watching over us."

"They are. They're our guardian angels."

It was Luca's turn to snort. "They eat the bugs down here. End of story."

I stretched my feet out to feel the ground beneath me. It was hard rock and steeply inclined. We were descending. "We're in a cave?" That explained the change in acoustics.

There was silence again.

Then harsh whispering.

"You have *got* to stop talking so much!" hissed Luca over my head.

"You're the one who started talking about the bats. He's going to take the blindfold off at some point, anyway."

"Yeah, but Dad said not to tell him anything. That means nothing. Not our names, not our location, *nothing*."

I wanted to remind Luca that he had been the one to reveal their names, but I held my tongue.

"Look, we're pretty much there, anyway."

Cecil and Luca stopped walking and set me down on my feet. I put my hands out in front of myself to catch my balance and touched someone's shoulder just as the blindfold came off. I blinked. Autumn's dad stared back at me, holding the blindfold.

"Welcome to the Caves," he said. The name had a familiar ring to it, like an old acquaintance you meet online and struggle to place the face with the name. I blinked again, waiting for my eyes to adjust, catching glimpses of things around me. A torch on the wall, leaning out at an odd angle. A low-lying ceiling, like a room under the stairs I used to play in when I was a kid. A large boulder against the wall, reddish-gray in the dancing firelight of the torch. We were in a cave, all right. The air was cold and still, the shadows blacker than black, and the walls were so close it was like standing in an elevator full of people—Autumn, Jesse, Diana, Cecil and Luca, and their dad, the man with the electric blue eyes, staring at me with the blindfold in his hands, the torchlight creating eerie shadows on his face.

All of them were staring at me. Like I was a freak. Really they were just a bunch of freaks, living under the ground, probably about to cut me up into mini steaks and feed me to the bats.

Earth Parasites.

Every muscle in my body tensed up. The blood rushed through my head like a hurricane, drowning out the voices with its loud roar. I clenched my fists at my side, getting ready to fight back as soon as they tried to grab me.

That's when I saw the face in the shadows.

Off to the left, behind the group, she came forward into the torchlight. Her hair was shiny and black, like the darkest depths of a tidal pool. Her skin was the color of sand. She pushed her hair back over her right ear as she peered at me, and in that moment, she revealed three things: a long, beaded feather in her hair; a tattoo of a bird on her right hand; and a memory that had been buried in some kind of subconscious corner of my mind for days.

"It's you," I breathed.

Everyone turned to see who I was looking at.

"Emer!" Jesse exclaimed.

"Do you know this boy?" Autumn's dad sounded shocked.

The girl in the shadows—Emer—was still studying me, her head tilted to the side, her eyes narrowed quizzically. Clearly, she needed some help jogging her memory.

I clenched my fists again, harder this time. "You're the one who left me out there on the highway to die."

FOUR

You deserve it. The voice in my head was getting louder.

It was all coming back. Her black eyes, staring down at me from the back of a van. A syringe in her hand. The sound of the door slamming shut. The yellow strip down the middle of an empty highway.

"You drugged me," I said. "You took me from my house. Don't we know each other from somewhere online?"

Her eyes widened and her head snapped upright, and in that moment I knew she recognized me. Her jaw dropped open as if she were about to speak, but then she clamped her mouth shut and shrank back into the shadows.

"Wait!" I called, charging after her, pain shooting into my tailbone as I tried to run for the first time. My right leg dragged uselessly behind me and I hunched my shoulders over, shoving them forward in an attempt to compensate. I had to talk to her. She had been there. She knew things. I had to find out what had happened to me.

Running had never been so hard. The tunnel wasn't dark for long, as we turned a corner and another torch jutted out along the way, then another, and another. I could see her glistening black hair up ahead as she ran. Although I was still kicking rocks and grinding my leg over the ground, I was building up momentum and with it, speed. I trotted along behind her until the tunnel ended and the light changed.

I was not prepared for what came next.

At the end of the tunnel, the space opened up into a cavern the size of five football fields. The ceiling shot up at least fifty feet, an uneven collection of jagged stalactites and smooth stone, like an alien, upside-down mountain range. The cave floor was so green and rich in plant life that I assumed we had reached the mouth of the cave, but a quick scan of the chamber did not reveal any openings. How was it so well lit? A clear, white light filled the cave as if daylight had come into the mountain all on its own.

The issue of lighting was the least of the mystery, however. The strangest thing before my eyes was the cluster of tents that filled the valley. This was not a huddle of camping tents like the Boy Scout sim I joined once. These were vast, luxurious tents arranged in a grid-like pattern with walkways between them, like an Arabian bazaar. Rich draperies swathed broad, rectangular structures in crimson and gold. Lanterns of all shapes and sizes swung from tent poles and strung criss-crossed above the streets. These were shops, with hawkers selling their wares, and a sea of people making their way in and out with great interest.

As awe-struck as I was, I did not have time to stop and stare. Emer had scrambled down the cliff side and was making her way toward the market. Cursing my bad leg, which I had never noticed until I tried to run, I dragged myself along the path that had been cut from the tunnel down into the valley. Blood pulsed at my temples and I gasped for air, but I had to find out if this girl knew what had happened to me and why I was here.

Voices swelled like a warm rain around me as I made my way into the market. There wasn't a sim in the world that could have prepared me for the amount of color I would be surrounded with in that valley. Bolts of cloth in the brightest blues, richest reds and purest whites. Steeply-peaked mountains of powders and spices like turmeric, cinnamon and pepper. Baskets of food that covered the whole color spectrum, from mushrooms to some bright orange tuber

I didn't recognize. And dangling everywhere were those motley lanterns, their light speckled through tiny pieces of patchwork glass.

Emer's dark hair bobbed through the crowd. She was tall, which made her easy to spot. I hobbled down the street, dodging eager shopkeepers and ambling pedestrians. She walked quickly and looked back at me a few times, nudging people aside in an attempt to speed up. It was not easy to do in such an unmotivated throng.

When I finally reached the other side of the market, she had gained ground and was several yards ahead of me. We were in an open field containing long, straight rows of low-lying plants with people crouched down, tending to them. Although a path had been cut through the center, Emer had taken off through the field. I barreled after her.

"Get off the crops!" A man stood and gestured angrily at me.

"What are you doing?" a woman across the field cried out.

"Stop!" Another voice echoed from behind me.

I did not have time to stop and apologize. Emer was already clear across the field, making her way towards a clump of boulders against the back wall of the cave. There was another cave system over there, this one with multiple levels, like the floors of an apartment building. The tunnels ran along the front of the rock face before curving back into the mountain.

"Wait!" I called. "I just want to talk to you!"

She glanced over her shoulder at me before climbing onto the rocks. A set of rough-hewn stairs had been carved into the side, and she took two and three at a time. By the time I had reached the bottom, she was staring at me from the top. I hesitated, dreading the near-impossible climb, and leaned on the rock face as I panted.

"You shouldn't be here," she said, and although her voice was low, it sounded like she was right next to me.

"I didn't really have a choice," I called. "Why did you leave me out there on the highway?" It was a hazy memory, but I was sure it was her.

She cocked her head to the side and studied me for a minute. "You really don't remember, do you?"

"Remember what?"

She stared at me a little longer, bemused, as if I had disappointed some unspoken expectation. Then she shook her head. "We went to school together."

I blinked. "We did?"

"You were on my basketball sim."

I clutched at a distant memory. It seemed too far away to grasp.

"Internet crawlers found you cheating in algebra. The school took you off the sim team. You kept playing incognito, anyway."

I shrugged. "Sounds about right."

She put her hands on her hips, arms akimbo, that bird tattoo staring down at me. "You were a patient of my dad's."

Something clicked and suddenly the memory of that day on the highway changed. Still in the back of a van, yes—still a syringe dangling from a pair of fingers—but they belonged to someone else, not Emer. A man. He had the same black eyes as hers, the same bone structure, the same sleek, black hair. He even had a feather in his hair. But his stern expression was not hers. It was his hands, not hers, that shoved me onto the pavement. It was he who stared at me as they drove away and left me there, in the middle of nowhere.

"Dr. Makoyiwa," I remembered.

Emer nodded. "That's not my life any more. I've lived here for three years. This is my home now." She crossed her arms and glared down at me. "I wish you hadn't come. You're going to ruin it all."

Something in her tone set a heaviness in the pit of my stomach. Her dad, Dr. Makoyiwa, had been treating me for fifteen years. We had had a therapy session at least once a week since I was a baby. He had watched me play, studied my behavior, put me under hypnosis. He had uncovered things about my mind that I would probably never know. He had told me numerous times that I was a danger to myself and others. And based on the way Emer was looking at me, she must have thought so, too.

"Do you know why I'm here?" I asked in one last burst of desperation.

She shook her head and her eyes filled with tears. "You shouldn't be here," she repeated. Then she spun on her heel and disappeared into the tunnel.

"City Man!" Jesse's voice echoed through the cavern behind me, and I cringed. I turned to find him walking across the field with his dad.

"That was quite a sprint," the old man said. "Guess you're on the mend?"

I was still wheezing, and my head and shoulders ached as if I had carried one of the boulders over here myself. But I shrugged and said, "I guess so."

"Good. I've got a job for you."

"Oh, no... Mr...."

"It's Tom. Tom Montgomery. Just call me Tom."

"...Tom, I really think you should put me away somewhere. Otherwise someone else might get hurt. I'm off my medication." I pointed up to the caves above the stairs. "Do you have any holding cells up there?"

"Holding cells?" Jesse looked horrified. "Like jail?"

I glared at him. *Don't you remember?* I wanted to say. *I beat you up, kid.*

Suddenly I remembered something Autumn had said the day she found me. "I can't believe they did this to you." What did she know about me that I didn't?

Tom laughed heartily and swung a friendly arm around his son. That was when I noticed that his fingers and the back of his hands were mottled with black and blue ink. "That's foolish talk. Those are living spaces. No one's going to jail."

My heart sank. "But what if..."

This time Tom swung his arm over my shoulders. He smelled like peppermint and some kind of chemical I didn't recognize. "We're just gonna put you to work, kid. Trust me. That's all you need."

Jesse, not to be left out, came over and wrapped a scrawny arm around my waist.

As quickly and carefully as I could, I peeled his arm off and turned away. The kid was a new level of crazy. He was a mouse settling down for a nap in the jaws of a lion; he was a goose dining with a fox. He didn't seem to remember what I had done. I would have to be extra alert whenever he was around.

As we crossed the field, I asked, "Where does the light come from?"

Tom pointed to an area on the other side of the field, against the back wall of the cave. "There's an opening down there," he said. "The ceiling caved in before we got here."

"But this whole place is lit up like it's the middle of the day."

"We use mirrors to point the daylight where we want it." He pointed to the ceiling. "And at night, we use grow lights."

It was true. I looked up and realized that as I changed position, spots appeared and glowed like tiny suns.

I scratched my head. "Where do you get grow lights?"

But he wasn't listening. He had his head craned, looking toward the market. I followed his line of vision to a woman standing outside one of the tents, smiling and waving at him.

It was strange, this place. An entire town beneath the earth. Loud, laughing people. The smell of damp. Echoey sounds and too many bright colors. But the strangest part of it all was this family. Tom and his wife embraced, and he introduced her to me as Margaret. She was elegant and smiley, with soft, blue eyes and auburn hair. Her children clustered around her in excitement, genuinely excited to see her, their voices overlapping as they told her highlights of their journey.

I tried to remember the last time I had seen a family like this in real life. There were sims, for sure, but the parents were dull and stiff and repeated the same things—"Of course, dear," "Whatever you say, dear," and they were always offering you donuts and cookies and offering to take you to Disney World. Those sims were so fake. In real life, family was just me and my mom. We hardly spoke to each other except for logistical reasons like when groceries would be arriving or what time our weekly doctor appointment was. She had her sim room and I had mine, and that was how we lived our lives. But at least she didn't feign happiness and pretend to be something she wasn't.

This family, though. They were definitely not fake. They were loud. And they did not practice social distancing. In fact, with all the hugging and hand holding and kissing, these people must have been breeding grounds for germs. It was a good thing I didn't care whether I lived or died.

Or did I?

I looked at Autumn. She was laughing, and it was the first time I'd ever seen her smile with her teeth. She laughed with every part of her face—her eyes squinted a little, her nose bunched up at the bridge, and her mouth opened wide in unfettered joy. I'd never seen anyone so free.

A seed of purpose began to plant itself in my mind. Someday I was going to make her laugh that way.

FIVE

"You're letting him work in the *shop*?"

Two people spoke in harsh whispers outside my sleep chamber. I had woken with my heart pounding, forgetting for a moment why I had been swallowed in darkness, wondering if I had gone blind or had died after all. It was the sibilance that drew me back to reality as their voices bounced off the cave walls, drawing out the room in sonar. I was not in my pristine room at home. I was buried deep within the earth, in a chamber probably swimming with bacteria and fungi and certainly a lot of bat guano.

"Dad, the guy's a live wire. You saw how he body slammed Jesse. You'll put everyone in that shop at risk." Even though she was whispering, I knew it was Autumn.

"He's been off his medication for at least a week. He's healing. Haven't you seen his eyes?"

"They're still bloodshot."

"But not as doped. Not crazed. Just tired."

It was true. I did feel different. The headaches were milder, and my muscles weren't as jumpy. I actually felt rested when I slept.

"But the meds stay in the system for years," Autumn said. "You told me that yourself. Things might be quiet right now, but he could flip at any moment."

Tom paused. "It's true that the medication makes them

unpredictable. Especially when they're coming off it. I'm sure he's on a mental roller coaster ride right now, even if he feels better physically. I just have a feeling about this kid. He's tough—tougher than the drugs."

I nearly laughed. Tough? Me, the Big Baby?

Loser.

Yeah. That was me. Always losing. Losing grades, losing friends, losing respect. I was the kid who cheated on every test I could because I couldn't care less about the quadratic equation and the dates of every battle in the European Civil War; and then I got caught and got locked out of every social website online for a whole month. I was the guy who started a fight with the most popular kid in high school because he wouldn't stop picking on the nerdy kid with the 4.0 GPA and the awkward social skills—a choice of social suicide that got me a smear campaign online and started the "Own Oliver" trend, which went viral for its humiliating pranks on me before I figured out what was going on. The truth was, after everything I'd done, everyone back home was probably glad I was gone.

No one was looking for me. Not online, not in the city, not in the woods. Their lives were all better because I was gone.

"Oliver?"

Light splashed against the rock formations above me. "Uh huh?"

Tom carried a candle over and set it on a small, wooden table next to my bed. "I know you can't tell, but it's morning."

I sat up and rubbed my eyes, nodding.

"You hungry?"

My nod deepened.

"I've got a change of clothes for you down by the river. Margaret has breakfast for us after we wash up."

I dragged myself out of bed—a strange, lumpy thing with a coarse, woolen blanket—and followed him out of the chamber. Autumn was nowhere to be seen. The candlelight made eerie shadows on the wall as we made our way through the tunnel.

"The air is different down here," I remarked. "It doesn't move."

"That's right. It also stays the same temperature year-round."

"How do you sanitize it?" I asked.

He glanced back at me. "The air?" He shrugged. "We don't."

The tunnel dropped into a steep incline. I had to lean back to keep myself from falling into Tom. Rocks tumbled in front of me.

Klutz.

Idiot.

I gave my head a shake. What were these voices in my head, anyway? I had never experienced them in the city.

"The river was what led us here," said Tom, his voice echoing off the rocks. "It's fed by glacier water coming from higher up the mountain." As if reading my mind, he continued, "The water is clean. There's a separate spring we use for drinking water."

I remembered the crystal-clear water that flowed from the taps in our apartment in the city. Hospital-grade metal. Decontamination sites in multiple locations. Even with the water reports available in an instant, showing us every single particle detected in the system, mom still made me filter it again before drinking.

I decided not to ask how they checked the content of their water.

The sound of laughter greeted us as we reached level ground. Tom set his candle on a rock ledge. He had no need for it now. At least a dozen torches blazed along the cave wall.

The river was wide and low. It did not rush madly, as I had expected, but rather it drifted along lazily from one dark side of the cave to the other. While the torchlight brought a warm glow to the cave, its angle left the river in darkness, making the water look black. I shuddered. There was no way to tell how dirty, how deep, or how unoccupied it was.

"You gonna wash up?" Tom called from the water's edge. He was on his knees, splashing water on his face.

"Yeah." I knelt down next to him on the bank and dipped my hands into the water. It was icy. I threw it on my face and smothered a gasp.

"Awake now?" Tom chuckled as he rubbed a white lather on his forearms. "Get scrubbing, kid. Margaret will never let you eat with all that dirt under those fingernails." He handed me a small bar of soap.

Someone laughed again. I heard the sound of gargling. I looked up to see a group of six or seven kids swimming in the shadows—some floating lazily on their backs, others treading water like an eerie game of apple bobbing. One of them looked like he was about my age.

"Those are the Charleston kids," said Tom. "They don't take kindly to strangers."

I put my head down and washed my hands, but I looked up periodically to see what they were up to. Splashing, floating, pushing. Watching me.

"They're related?" I asked.

"Siblings."

I counted more carefully. Seven. *Seven* brothers and sisters. "All from the same parents?" I asked.

"Yep." Tom wrapped the bar of soap in a handkerchief and put it in his pocket. "Their father passed, though. Killed by a cougar last year when he went out on his own for supplies." He rinsed his hands and stood. "It's been hard on them. The oldest, especially. Ben."

The swimmers had stopped their splashing and were all staring at us now. Tom waved. "Hello, kids."

They didn't answer. They just kept staring.

Tom handed me a pile of clothes that sat in a neat pile on the rock ledge. They were made of rough wool, even the pants, but they smelled fresh and were a welcome relief from my week-old city clothes. After I had changed in the shadows, Tom grabbed the candle and led me back up the path. "Ben's about your age," he said. "He grew up with my Autumn. They were attached at the hip when they were younger."

You'd think that it would've been easier to climb up the incline, but not for me. I grabbed at the tunnel wall as my feet scraped unsteadily along the gravel. A dim light came from up ahead.

Tom continued. "Ben tried to take on a fatherly role in the family, but that's nearly impossible for a sibling. His struggle to gain the respect of his brothers and sisters and the pain of losing his father hardened him. He lost his temper one day and beat up his younger brother, and at that point Autumn distanced herself completely." He sighed regretfully. "Autumn's always been a bit of a lone wolf, though. She spends most of her free time in the shop on her own. Especially when we get a new shipment in from the scavengers who bring artifacts back from the old cities. She's fascinated by you city folk and all your technology." He shook his head. "That girl is still trying to find her place in the world."

"Why are you doing this?" I blurted. "Why are you so nice to me?"

He stopped. "What do you mean, son?" He turned to look at me, his figure silhouetted in the tunnel.

"I'm not your son. And I'm not a good person. Why would you take someone like me into this place, into your home?"

Tom came toward me and placed his hand on my shoulder. His face was shadowed, but I could still see the sober look in his eyes. "Everyone deserves a chance to put their old life behind them and start again. Son." Then he turned and continued up the incline.

The tunnel forked, and Tom took a left turn into the darkness. The light at the top of the other path must have been the way to the main cavern. We were in the living spaces, the ones Emer had disappeared into when I tried to follow her the day before, and we passed chamber after chamber as we climbed, the light of our candle illuminating the outline of open doorways. This place was like an anthill. Weren't the inhabitants of these chambers worried about their privacy, having no doors? Not to mention their security?

"Our dining chamber is just up here." Tom had picked up speed, walking with long, brisk strides toward the food. I understood the urgency. I was hungry, too.

I heard them before we reached the chamber. Loud chatter and sporadic laughter. A swell of voices that, had it been anywhere else, I might have mistaken for a loud row. As it was, I knew by now that this was normal. This family said things like, "Pass the rolls!" at decibels that were physically unreachable back home. My mom spoke in monotones and we hardly spoke at all, anyway.

This cave was larger than the sleep chambers. It had no

stalactites, but the terrain was uneven and littered with boulders. An old wooden table stood in the middle of the room, long enough to seat eight people—which it did. They talked and argued and laughed and ate and hardly noticed that we had come to join the feast. Tom took his place at the head of the table and I sat down in an empty seat between Luca and Cecil, directly across from Autumn.

"Mornin', sunshine," Luca said through a spoonful of gruel.

"Did you meet Agnes yet?" Cecil reached across the table for a roll.

Luca pointedly rolled his eyes. "Will you shut up about that stupid ghost?"

Cecil shoved the entire roll in his mouth and shrugged.

"Ghost?" I asked.

Cecil nodded, his eyes shining. "Ahrolaravesaight."

"Chew your food, moron!" Luca reached behind me and swatted him on the back of the head. "We can't understand a word you're saying."

Cecil swallowed loudly. "She roams the caves at night. Sometimes you can hear her crying, but sometimes she just stands quietly next to your bed, watching you sleep. She loves newcomers, especially."

I rubbed the back of my neck.

"Any temperature changes? Sudden gusts of cold air?"

I tried to remember the night before. I'd fallen asleep almost instantly and had slept deeply.

"Or maybe you got the feeling that someone was watching you?" Cecil grabbed another roll, breaking it in half this time.

"I don't think so."

Cecil shook his head fondly. "Yep. Good ol' Agnes. She's a tough broad. A real survivor. She died with her husband down here in the caves, and she's not giving up until she finds him again." He took a bite of his roll and gestured with the other piece in his hand. "Don't you wish you had that kind of love?"

"City Man!" Jesse popped his head up over the table, taking a seat next to Autumn. "Did you see the stick I whittled for you?"

I frowned and shook my head.

"I left it outside your room. It's so you can protect yourself."

"From ghosts?" Luca flashed a sarcastic grin.

Cecil shook his head. "Agnes won't hurt you. Plus, a stick won't—"

Luca smacked him again. Cecil glared at his brother.

"Everybody should have a way to protect themselves," Jesse urged, resting his elbows on the table. He'd brought his notebook; it sat next to his empty plate with the pencil tucked in the side. "You should get it."

Autumn spoke the words that were in my head. "I don't think that's a very good idea."

"I worked really hard on it." Jesse's freckled nose scrunched up in a pout. "You always say we need everyone to take care of themselves."

Your stick won't save me from myself, kid.

"Eat something, Oliver." Margaret, the matriarch who sat at the other end of the table from Tom, gestured to the array of food. "Will you get him something, honey?" she asked Autumn. Her voice carried over the din of voices and clattering plates with unexpected volume for a woman as calm and collected as she was.

Autumn sighed and passed me a bowl frostily. She had hardly looked at me since the incident with Jesse in the woods the day before.

"Where do you get all this food?" I asked, spooning gruel into my bowl. A pitcher of milk sat on the table in front of me, along with a plate of butter, rolls, some kind of yellow mash, and a vegetable-mushroom stir fry of some kind. The smells made my mouth water.

"My friend Bill," Jesse said proudly.

"A sheep farmer," Luca explained. "He and his wife live near the plains a few hundred miles from here. He lets us use half his herd in exchange for mushrooms and bat guano for his garden."

"And labor," said Autumn.

"Yeah. A lot of our boys help him with shearing and butchering and the milking in the warmer months."

I tried not to grimace. I'd never tried sheep milk. In the end, my growling stomach got the best of me, and I splashed the white liquid over the gruel and dug in.

"We also hunt," Cecil piped up. "Some of us." From the proud tone of his voice, I gathered that he was one of the elite.

I tried to imagine shooting, killing and butchering an animal in real life. I got a flash of real blood dripping off my fingers.

You could try human blood.

An arm and a leg. Maybe a brain.

I shut my eyes and gave my head a shake. When would these intrusive thoughts stop?

"City Man?"

I opened my eyes. Everyone was staring at me.

"Sorry," I said. "I think I got something in my eye. This food is delicious, by the way, thanks. What's next on the agenda today? You say you need work done?"

Tom put his fingers together, steeple-like, and looked pensively at me.

"I'll do whatever you need," I said nervously. "Go ahead and put me to work." Anything to keep my mind occupied.

"Yes," Tom said. "I think I'll put you on the press."

"What?" Autumn, Diana, Cecil and Luca spoke in unison.

"You're putting him on machine duty, right on day one?" Autumn put her fork down with a clatter.

"He has no experience," Luca protested.

Tom put his hands down firmly on the table. "I don't have to explain myself," he said. "I want him on the press. He can apprentice with you, Autumn. You're our best technician."

Her mouth fell open. She looked at me like I had leprosy. She looked back at her dad. I thought she might protest, but instead she clamped her lips together in a long, angry line, pushed her chair back and stood. "I have a lot of work to do," she said, her voice on low boil.

"I'll join you," I said, jumping to my feet. Call me an opportunist, but hey, when fate opens a door like that, only an idiot wouldn't walk through.

She shot me a glare and grabbed one of the torches from the wall. I followed her into the tunnel, willing my bad leg to stop dragging so noisily along the ground. I had to jog to keep up.

"What's the press?" I asked, trying not to sound too out of breath.

She gave an irritated sigh. "The printing press? It's how we run the news."

"You guys have *news*?"

She plodded forward with a loud *harrumph*. "You don't have to be so condescending. We're not a bunch of simpletons, you know."

"I didn't mean it like that," I said, my voice echoing in the tunnel amid an embarrassing stream of panting. "I just didn't expect—"

"It's not like yours, you know." We had reached the mouth of the tunnel and she turned to confront me. "It's not a propaganda machine. We just have to have a way to share information with the other cave-cities. What the sentries are seeing, instructions to prepare for winter, that sort of thing."

I had so many questions. There were other cave-cities? Where were they? How many people were over there? How long had they been down here? Were there caves like this all over the world? Curiosity consumed me like a swarm of bees, clamoring for answers, overwhelming and scattering my thoughts.

In the end, what came out was the least important question of all. "What do you mean, propaganda machine?"

Her face turned crimson. She spun on her heel, exasperated, and marched down the stairs.

My mom liked to watch the news. When I was younger and still wanted to be held, I'd sit with her in her sim room and listen to the buzz in her earpiece. I didn't understand what they were saying, but I did notice the helpless way she'd crumple in her chair, the way she'd check the blinds in the apartment afterwards to make sure they were sealed tight, the calls to security to verify that the alarm system was engaged. I hadn't noticed anything different about the world around us, but apparently the news knew something I didn't.

"I'm not messing with you," I said, hurrying after her. "I genuinely don't know what you're talking about. Can you explain it to me?"

We reached the bottom of the stairs and she turned to face me.

"I don't want to talk to you anymore," she said. She turned again and walked across the field. Her angry ranting didn't stop, not even for a breath. "This is just some ploy to get me out of my comfort zone. My dad is always saying I need to be 'challenged.' I've got enough challenge! There are at least three backlogged shipments to sort through, two machines that need fixing, the shop needs cleaning, and Mrs. Beth needs help with her stall at the market. I've got plenty to do without having to babysit you."

I tried to suppress a grin. "I thought you weren't going to talk to me anymore."

She turned again, scowled at me, *harrumphed*, and continued hurrying across the field.

"Who's Mrs. Beth?" I asked after a minute.

She didn't answer at first. When she did, her tone was still icy, but softer. "She's my godmother. She makes candles and sells them here at the market."

We cut through the streets of the bazaar. It was not as busy as the night before, and some of the tent flaps were closed, but the lanterns still twinkled brightly, sending millions of rainbows across the path. Autumn's hair was a waterfall of color. It was all I could do not to reach out and touch it.

That would have gone over really well.

We left the market and made our way to the far wall of the cavern, an area I had not seen yet. Another set of tunnels and caves were cut into the rock face, as well, but one of them was very different. This one had a door. A tall, wide, wooden door with a large key hole. Autumn took a key from her pocket and unlocked it with a noisy *clunk*. She set her torch in the stand outside the door. Pulling a candle out of her pocket, she lit the wick with the torch and made her way inside.

As my eyes adjusted and she lit candles throughout the room, I began to make out the arrangement of things. Wet rags hung limply overhead, long rows of dejected flags hanging on an invisible string. Rolls of paper spilled from trunks and boxes lining the walls. Four enormous tables stood in a "U" shape around the center of the room, surrounding a machine that was nearly as tall as I. It had a crank wheel on the side, a flat, metal platform in the center, and all kinds of gears and pulleys. I put my hand on the wheel and it turned with a creak.

"Don't touch that," she said sharply.

I pulled my hand away. "Is that the press?"

"Yes." She was still lighting candles. "I've already repaired it a dozen times, and parts are really hard to come by, so just wait until I show you before you try to work it."

"No problem."

A large vat stood next to the machine. It was half full of some kind of dark liquid. The smell was familiar, so I leaned over to get a deeper whiff, trying to remember where I had smelled it before.

"Linseed oil," she explained. "It makes the ink stick better, but it's a bit strong."

I remembered now. "Your dad smells like that."

She looked up in surprise. "Yes."

"What's over there?" I pointed behind her, into the shadows. Objects were piled up in some kind of storage area.

"That's where we keep most of the stuff when shipments come in." She picked up a candle and motioned for me to follow her.

"Shipments?"

"From the surface. We send scavengers to find things from up there, things that might be useful to us."

"You send your people to steal things from the *city*? Isn't that risky?"

"No! Absolutely not. That's forbidden." She looked back at me with wide eyes. The candlelight danced on her face, creating eerie shadows under her eyebrows and in the hollows of her cheeks. "But half the planet is made up of abandoned cities, Oliver. From the Old World."

I frowned. Abandoned cities? Old World?

"Surely you've learned about this in school. They were the kind of cities that spread out, like fingers reaching for each other. The cities today reach toward the sky, each one trying to out-build the other. There are only fifteen cities left now. The Old World had thousands."

I tried to envision it. "They never taught us that in school."

She shook her head. "Of course not. They only teach you what *they* want you to know." She turned back towards the alcove and held her candle high. "This is from the latest shipment."

Objects were piled on top of one another in a jumbled mass of metal, plastic and wood. I knew a lot of them from movies. Furniture, clocks, old-fashioned telephones. A typewriter. Many of them I did not recognize, however. Strange boxes with gears, nozzles and levers. A metal balloon. Tubes and buttons and keys.

"We use most of the machines for parts," she explained. "Our books lack explanations for many of them, although we are continually searching to learn what they are used for." She looked at me hopefully. "Do you know what any of these are for?"

Taking the weight off my bad leg, I crouched down in front of the pile and rummaged through it. A rusty, claw-toothed machine could have been farming equipment, but I wasn't sure. A hand-held instrument with a circular blade could have been for building things, but I didn't want to guess. Finally I found a rectangular box with a metal cover, just the size to fit in my lap. I lifted the top. Inside was a large, black disc next to a wooden lever. The lever had a needle on the end of it.

"I remember this," I said distantly, clutching after the memory. Whether it was from an old movie or a sim, I wasn't sure, but somehow I knew that the lever lifted to bring the needle onto the disc. I turned the rusty, metal crank on the front of it. "It plays music."

Sure enough, there was a scratching sound, the disc began to spin, and a song emerged from the machine. A guitar, rough and ragged, just three chords and a few fast strums. Then a man's voice.

'Twas in another lifetime, one of toil and blood
When blackness was a virtue and the road was full of mud
I came in from the wilderness, a creature void of form
"Come in," she said, "I'll give you shelter from the storm."

Autumn seemed mesmerized by it. She set her candle on the

ground and sat cross-legged next to me. I was keenly aware of how close our knees were.

> *And if I pass this way again, you can rest assured*
> *I'll always do my best for her, on that I give my word*
> *In a world of steel-eyed death, and men who are fighting to be warm*
> *"Come in," she said, "I'll give you shelter from the storm."*

> *Not a word was spoke between us, there was little risk involved*
> *Everything up to that point had been left unresolved*
> *Try imagining a place where it's always safe and warm*
> *"Come in," she said, "I'll give you shelter from the storm.*

I continued to turn the hand crank, but I couldn't take my eyes off her. I didn't care if she caught me staring. She had her elbow on her knees and her chin in her palm, head down, listening. As tough as she was, in that moment she seemed so soft. I watched the auburn crown of her head while I listened to the rest of the song.

> *Suddenly I turned around and she was standin' there*
> *With silver bracelets on her wrists and flowers in her hair*
> *She walked up to me so gracefully and took my crown of thorns*
> *"Come in," she said, "I'll give you shelter from the storm."*

When the song was finished, she looked up and caught my gaze. Her cheeks were flushed and her eyes shone. "That was beautiful," she breathed.

I didn't even think—the words just poured out of my mouth like water from a broken dam. "You're beautiful," I said.

Her face fell. She looked shocked. Then her cheeks blazed and her eyes snapped like a raging brushfire. "Don't say that," she said, standing. The next song was already playing.

If you're traveling to the North Country fair...

"Turn that off," she demanded.

I snapped my fingers. "Aha! I remember now. It's a *record* player.

That black thing is a vinyl record. It was in a movie I saw once."

...remember me to one who lives there...

"I said turn it off, Oliver."

I had hoisted myself to my feet, and I stood in front of her. "Listen," I said. "I didn't mean anything by it. I told you I have a bad habit of saying the wrong thing at the wrong time."

...a true love of mine...

"Autumn! City Man! What are you doing?" A loud whisper cut through the music. We turned to see Jesse standing behind us. "The alarm!"

Autumn gasped and pulled the needle off the record with a screech. I stopped turning the crank. A dull ticking filled the newfound silence. I followed the sound with my eye to the far wall, where a string of wooden blocks clattered against each other. That was an alarm?

The candles were quickly extinguished. Autumn grabbed my arm and guided me to the back wall, where we sat on the floor behind the pile of goods. "No noise," she said under her breath.

I listened to the sound of three people breathing. The darkness was as thick as my fear. We had a pretty good hiding place, but we were also cornered, so I wondered how formidable the enemy was and what they intended to do. As if reading my mind, Autumn pulled her gun out and cocked it with a slow click.

Then the door banged open and light streamed in around the tall silhouette of a man holding a rifle.

SIX

It took me a second to realize that the man was Tom. He had to stoop to get in the doorway. He set his gun in the corner of the room and set to work lighting the room again with his starter candle.

"All clear," he said. "It was a bear."

Jesse jumped to his feet. "Can I see it?"

"We chased it out. Must've been looking for a place to hibernate."

Autumn stood and gave me a hand. "But how did it get in? Where's the sentry?"

"Exactly." Tom gave her a somber look. "That is the question of the day."

"Who was on duty?" Autumn pulled me to my feet and left me leaning against the wall to catch my breath. She un-cocked her gun and returned it to its holster, pulling her shirt over it firmly, and set to work helping her dad light the candles again.

"It was supposed to be Edgar. He's stationed at the north entrance. His wife said he left their chamber at the usual time last night. He wasn't sick, nothing unusual to report."

"Except that he's missing."

Tom set his candle down, spread his long arms across the width of the table, and looked up at her with a sigh. "Right."

The door banged open again and Cecil lumbered in, hitting his head on the lintel along the way. "Ow," he cried, rubbing his skull and pushing his long hair out of his eyes.

Luca ducked in behind him and shook his head in disgust. "I don't know why you won't let mom cut your dang hair."

Cecil tried to glare at him through a face contorted with pain. "It is a reflection of my *personality*."

"What personality?"

The door opened again. A head of shiny, black hair ducked under the door frame and Emer stood just inside the entryway. She cupped her hand lightly on the doorknob, waiting, as if she needed permission to speak, or even to be there.

"You have news?" Tom prompted her gently.

"Yes." She tucked her hair behind her ear. The feathers hung loosely against her neck. "A search party is being sent. To find Edgar. To find out what happened." She rubbed the back of her arm. "I want to go with them."

Tom frowned. He seemed uncertain.

"I'm the best tracker here," she continued. "And I'm quiet. No one will even know I'm with them."

Cecil and Luca nodded. It was true. She was the quietest of them all.

Tom bent his head in consent. "You can take Cecil with you."

"No." Her dark eyes glistened in the candlelight. "I want to go alone."

"Why?"

"Cecil's a sentry and a scavenger, not a tracker. He'll slow us down." She gave Cecil an apologetic half-smile, as if to say, *nothing personal*. He shrugged in response. "I want to get to the bottom of this," she continued. "Edgar was a friend."

Tom had been leaning over the table, as if he carried an enormous weight between his shoulders and he needed a moment of relief. He pushed himself up with a sigh. It dawned on me that in spite of his seemingly cheerful outlook on things, he was more troubled than he let on.

"I promised to take care of you," he said. "You're only sixteen, yet."

"You have," she replied. "Because of you, I know exactly how to take care of myself."

He studied her for a moment. Then he nodded. "All right. But if you're not back in two weeks, I'll come after you myself."

Her face lit up. "Okay." She rubbed the back of her arm again, this time in excitement. "Okay." She gave everyone a half-wave. "Well, see you, then."

Jesse ran across the room and hit her like a missile, wrapping his tiny arms around one of her legs. "Be safe," he cried. "Come back soon."

Patting his head gingerly, she peeled his arms off of her and stepped away. "I will," she said softly. And then she was gone.

Everyone set to work quietly. I tried to understand the silence, which seemed to mean something different to each person. Tom was worried. He pulled out fresh sheets of paper and laid them on the table, checking the sides to make sure the stack lined up evenly. I could practically hear his thoughts as he wondered if he had made the right choice in allowing a sixteen-year-old girl to join a search party in the woods by herself. Jesse was sad, blinking fat tears into the vat of ink as he stirred. Luca and Cecil trod carefully through the shop, eyeing their father as they organized the artifacts from their scavenges, taking care not to bother him as he mused. And Autumn... well, Autumn was fuming. She shifted around levers and turned gears on the machine, getting the press ready for printing, and at first glance appeared to be focused intensely on each part. But I knew her expressions well enough to know that she was angry. The whole family seemed to love Emer as their own—but not Autumn. She clearly despised her family's affection for this adopted sister.

A search party was a big deal, I gathered. Out here, it could mean that people might not come back. I wondered if Margaret had been this worried when her family left to scavenge, before they found me. That's the hard part about loving people—you're so afraid to lose them.

"Why don't you guys find some old solar-powered security cameras from those cities you loot?" I asked. "I could help you set them up. Then you would have footage if anyone went missing again."

Everyone stopped what they were doing and gaped at me. It was as if I had suggested we all get up and move into a live volcano.

"Are you nuts?" asked Luca.

"We *don't* have cameras here," Autumn admonished. I remembered the day she had thrown that vintage camera into the woods, like it burned her hand.

"Why are you guys so afraid of technology?" I asked. "Things are so inconvenient without it. Not to mention dangerous."

Tom put down the wooden paddle he had been using to pull the flags down from where they were strung up around the room. I realized, as he pulled one off the paddle and laid it on the table, that these were not flags, they were printed words on some kind of soft paper. They had been draped around the room to dry.

"I'll tell you what's inconvenient," he said, his lips tight and his voice husky. "Government surveillance. People invading your privacy, telling you what to feed your kids, what kind of medication they should be on, banning them from school or social activities until you do what they want. People spying on you in your own home, telling you how to run your water, when you're allowed to go outside, threatening to arrest you if you let your kids run free or hug each other or try to breathe fresh air." His hands shook with emotion as he crossed his arms. "We left that world for good, Oliver. I'd rather die than live behind your technology bars. What kind of a life is that?" He shook his head vehemently. "Cameras, phones, recording devices… they create a weak link; they bare us open to the outside world. Even the most amateur hacker could find us. Under no circumstances are they permitted here."

I nodded slowly. "I think I understand."

These people are crazy. The voices in my head dripped with hate. *Mad in the brain.*

Like moles hiding from the sun, burrowing blindly through their purposeless existence.

I gave my head a shake.

"Hey." Autumn stood at the machine, staring at me. "I can show you how this works now."

Everyone in the room was trying to pretend they weren't looking at me. I wondered how long I had been standing there while Autumn tried to get my attention. The back of my ears burned as I lolloped over to her.

"Here's some ink for you." Jesse set a small jar on the table next to the press and smiled up at me. The pity practically oozed out of his eyes and tumbled down to his mouth with his freckles. I scowled. The last thing I wanted was sympathy. These people had no idea how much wickedness lived within me.

Autumn pulled a paintbrush out of the jar. "You only need a little bit," she explained, dabbing black ink on the flat, metal disc that lay at the top of the machine. "The rollers will spread it across the whole plate." With surprising adroitness, she pulled the crank wheel down, pumped a pedal with her foot, yanked on a lever, and suddenly the machine was a whirlwind of motion. "You have to be really alert," she said, raising her voice above the whir of the machine. "Once you get going, the paper tray comes up every few seconds. You have to be ready to feed the paper on the exact right spot on that tray, even while you're pumping the foot pedal and moving the lever."

Sure enough, she was doing all those things as she described them. I watched in awe while she fed sheet after sheet to the machine and it stamped a solid block of type on each. After a few minutes, she stopped the foot pedal, pushed the lever back, and brought the crank wheel to a halt. She turned to look at me.

"I can barely get my legs to sync up with my brain," I said. "You actually think I can do all those things at once?"

The corner of her mouth twitched. "Of course not. Not yet." She cocked her head to the side. "My dad thinks you can, though."

"Yeah. Well. You did say he's obsessed with challenge." I crossed my arms and glared at the machine. "That is not a challenge. That's impossible."

She shrugged. "You won't ever know that unless you try."

I looked over at Tom. He was busy arranging metal letters on a tray. Cecil had begun singing loudly into the handle of a broom while he swept the floor. Jesse and Luca were sorting through the pile of objects at the back of the room. No one had any idea that I was about to put my idiocy on full display.

"Fine." I shuffled over and took her place in front of the machine. The burnt, oily smell of the ink was stronger over here.

"That's the inking plate," she explained, pointing at the large disc in front of me. "The rollers come up with each cycle, suck up the ink, and pull it down onto the type." She pointed to a space below the disc where a tray of letters like the ones Tom was using faced out towards us. "You just pull the crank wheel like this—" she yanked the wheel forward, "—and pump the pedal with your foot."

I waited.

The crank wheel rocked back and forth and came to a standstill.

"Why didn't you pump the pedal?"

I shrugged. "I have no idea."

"Okay." She seemed amused. "Try again."

This time when she pulled the crank wheel, her foot shot out and covered mine, pressing down. Both our feet pumped the foot pedal together, and the crank wheel began turning on its own.

"Now the lever!" she commanded over the din of the machine.

Lever, lever, chicken denner.

Better step to it, soldier.

Listen to your master.

"Pull it!" she yelled. "Oliver!"

I put my hand on the lever, but I felt myself begin to snap, like a rubber band inside me had been wound too tight and the sides were fraying.

She was too close.

We were too close.

I was dangerous.

She was unsafe.

I dropped the lever, wrenched my foot out from under hers, and tumbled backwards onto the floor. My feet scraped noisily on the gravel as I scrambled away from her.

The whirring stopped and voices tumbled over each other.

"What happened?"

"Is he having another seizure?"

I shoved my hands under my armpits, clamped my arms down, and huddled against the wall.

She owns you.

I squeezed my eyes shut and pulled my knees toward my forehead. When would the damn voices go away? What did these phrases even mean?

Someone put their hand on my shoulder. I yelped. I tried to fold in on myself even more tightly than I was. The hand didn't go away.

"It's not safe," I cried, shuddering. "Stay away from me! You're not safe!"

This time it was not a voice I heard, but music. Four notes in slow succession.

Do

Re

Mi

Fa

Not those words, of course, but the tones. Almost like a beeping. Oh.

I remembered that sound.

Every time a sim was booting up or shutting down, it went through that simple progression of notes. It was my signal that entertainment was coming, of some form or another. I had heard that sound every single day of my life, morning and night, until I had come to the caves.

Do, Re, Mi, Fa.

Good morning, Oliver. What do you want to do today?

The voice of my sim was female. She spoke slowly and soothingly, with a slightly British accent. She said her name was Sia.

"I'll go for a jog through Central Park."

Of course. Time of year?

"Fall."

Very well.

I'd slip on my headset—designed to help create the three dimensional experience—and all four walls would shimmer, going from black to high definition color until the leaves on the trees and all the sidewalk curbs were crisp and clear. Holograms emerged from the floor. The staggered buildings of Central Park West stood at my left. To my right, a couple sat on a blanket on the grass, their voices a low murmur. I began to run, and the sim moved the floor beneath me to create the illusion of movement.

"Sia," I said. "Music, please."

Would you like the usual?

My jogging soundtrack was almost always electronic. I had to have that heavy bass and synthesizer when my feet were hitting the pavement. Today was different, though, and this is what made the memory distinct from the blur of other jogging days.

"No. Play Chopin," I commanded.

Playing Chopin.

A soft progression of piano notes filled the room. As if the computer knew what classical music did to the mood, sunlight poured out from behind a cloud, bringing a soft glow to the crimson and gold landscape of the park.

I followed the path around a bend and took a set of stairs down a hill. A small bridge arched over the walkway up ahead, and as I neared the tunnel, I noticed a familiar silhouette in its shadows. My heart lurched.

"Emer," I whispered.

This had been a buried memory, but now I knew why. It all came back to me when I saw her there, leaning back against the wall of the tunnel with one leg bent, foot pressed against the brick.

"Oliver." She turned to face me, her eyes big and brown, hair shiny and black. "I'm so glad you came."

My jog did not slow. Instead I sped up, running towards her at top speed, watching the curious way her eyes doubled in size when she realized what was happening. For a split second she winced, and then I was on top of her, my hands at her throat, shoving her backwards into the pavement.

"I hate you," I said, gritting my teeth while I squeezed the soft flesh of her neck. Her head lolled sideways on the concrete.

Her eyes rolled forward and seemed to focus on me. "Wait—" her voice gargled, "Please. I'm sorry."

"You're sorry?" I pressed her head between my hands. "You're sorry, huh? Sorry for what, ruining my life? Humiliating me? Alienating me from literally everyone I know?"

"It was just a joke." Her hands clutched at my forearms, trying to pull them away from her neck. "Please. Let me explain."

"Oh." I laughed bitterly. "You already did. You explained it very clearly, all over social. Now the whole world knows that Emer Makoyiwa went out with me *on a dare*, convinced me she was in love with me, and laughed right in my face when I told her how I felt."

She didn't have a response. Her hands locked around my wrists, held for a moment, and slid softly to the ground. Her eyes went blank.

My breath caught in my throat and I yanked my hands away. Her head fell limply to the side, the feather across her neck. The music of Chopin crescendoed around me, an eerie soundtrack to the murder that had just taken place.

"Sia! Cancel!"

Simulation canceled.

Emer's body shimmered and disappeared. I ripped my headpiece off while the screens faded to black. My hands were shaking.

"It's just a sim," I murmured, getting up off my knees. "It wasn't real. It's just a sim." But it had felt real. Horrifyingly real. And the scariest part was how good it felt for me to choke Emer to death.

"Oliver?"

I jolted out of the memory. The hand was still on my back, soft and warm. I opened my eyes and lifted my head. Autumn's gaze grabbed mine, her eyebrows drawn in concern.

"I'm a monster," I whispered. "Get away from me." I snarled and pushed her. "Get away! Do you hear me? I'm a monster!"

Autumn recoiled in alarm. Everyone in the room froze, staring at me. *They think you belong in a zoo.* Tom was the only one who didn't seem afraid. He approached me calmly. "You're okay," he said. "It's been a big morning. Let's get you to your room for a rest. You're okay." He said it again, a mantra, as if it would come true if he said it enough. But he was wrong. I was not okay.

I was evil.

SEVEN

The work days were long, but they were a welcome distraction to the madness going on in my head. Tom was right, I did feel better after getting more sleep. But there was a darkness within, as if there were two of me—the Oliver on the surface, who was interested in this new world and all the people in it; and the vicious, wild animal that lived inside me and could not be tamed. I was terrified of it and the possibility that it might take over.

Weeks passed, and I eventually got the hang of the machine. It became my new obsession. Staying busy meant my mind was busy, and the voices and thoughts would fade to a dull pulse while I focused on printing. Sometimes I would read the headlines—"*Wildcats spotted at Crystal Falls,*" or "*Frost sets in early in Blue Ridge region,*"—place names I did not recognize—but mostly I just paid attention to the even click of the cogs and the steady whir as I pumped the pedal with my foot and placed the paper on the platform. I grew to love the smell of the ink, and when my hands became more stained than Tom's, I was somewhat proud, suddenly considering myself a printer when I had been nothing before.

Even though I understood the machine after a few days, I played dumb for a while so that Autumn wouldn't go anywhere. It was a strange push-pull—I couldn't trust myself to get too close to her, but I couldn't bear the thought of being apart. I found my happy medium, keeping a set distance and putting myself on guard when we got too close. She was the most patient person I had ever known. She had probably repeated, "Pump the foot pedal," about fifty times, but each time she said it, it sounded like she'd never said it before.

When it became impossible to hide the fact that I knew what I was doing, she let me run the machine and she took over the typesetting from her dad. It was one of the hardest jobs in the shop. The letters had to go in the tray backwards and upside down. She sat with her back to me on a stool at the table, a candle at her side, poring over the letters with painstaking care. We never talked—the machine was too loud—but I felt calmer with her working nearby.

"Is it easier now, City Man?" Jesse asked me one day on our way back to the living quarters. It was the custom to leave the shop together, because Tom had a hard rule about family eating together every day. I knew that didn't include me, but they couldn't leave me alone at the shop. Every day, it was locked securely after the shelf clock pealed for the end of the work day.

"Is what easier?" I asked through gritted teeth. I usually tried to trail behind them, but Jesse walked with me.

"Your life."

I frowned. What a strange question. How could my life be *easier* now? It had gone from fully automatic to the most mechanical you could get. I was literally washing my clothes in a stream with a bar of soap. I had to carry candles and matches in my pocket so I didn't get stuck somewhere without light. I slept in a cold, dark room with no door, and all I had to protect myself was a sharp stick. On the other hand, I didn't feel sick anymore. My body was getting stronger.

"I don't know if I'd say it's *easier*," I said. "It's more interesting, though."

"Interesting how? We pretty much do the same thing every day."

Autumn was walking a few yards ahead of us, so I lowered my voice. I didn't want to be caught confiding in a seven-year-old. "I *feel* more down here. Back home, everything was electronic." I tapped the side of my head. "All the action was in here."

"Are you still crazy in there?"

I scowled at him. How did he know what was going on in my head?

"Hey, Jesse." Autumn had fallen back in step with us. "Why don't you go tell Dad what you heard from that kid at the market today?"

Jesse's eyes got big. "Oh, yeah!" He trotted up to walk next to Tom.

I glanced over at her. She had her hair pulled back and her sleeves rolled up, and she crossed her arms while she walked, as if we were taking a casual stroll by the river.

"Sorry about that," she said. "Jesse's at that age where he doesn't seem to have any filter."

I shrugged. "No big deal."

"He admires you a lot."

"He should keep his distance from me," I said, angrily scuffing the ground. "He's too naïve."

"Love all, trust a few, do wrong to none," she said.

I cocked my head to the side. "What's that?"

"Shakespeare," she said. "It's from *All's Well that Ends Well*. Jesse's good at the 'love all, do wrong to none,' part, but not so good at 'trust a few.'"

I gave her a blank look.

"Wait a second," she said, stopping. "Don't tell me you've never heard of Shakespeare."

I racked my brain. "I'm into old-fashioned movies," I said, trying to explain my ignorance. "If that show is from 2050 onwards, I probably haven't seen it."

Her mouth fell open. "Shakespeare is *not* a show," she said. "He's a playwright from the sixteenth century."

"Oh." I kept clutching at memories. "I must have missed that in history class."

"He's not just a history lesson," she said. "He singled-handedly changed the English language and started a movement that brought art and literature out of the Dark Ages." She started walking again, but she continued to shake her head in disbelief. "You've never heard of *Hamlet*? *The Tempest*? *Romeo and Juliet*?"

I shook my head.

"It's a tragedy," she murmured. "They say you live in the information age."

We had reached the entrance to the dining chamber. We must have fallen far behind the group, because dinner preparations had already begun, with the usual loud chatter as everyone cooked and set the table together. Without thinking, I put my hand on Autumn's wrist and pulled her back into the tunnel, away from the light and the noise. She looked up at me in surprise.

"Can I just ask you something?" I said.

"Okay." The muscles in her forearm tightened warily.

"I know you don't trust me. And I don't blame you."

Her eyes wavered slightly, just enough to confirm what I already knew.

"I'm trouble. Always have been. But you said something when I first met you, and it's been bugging me ever since. You said, 'I can't believe they did this to you.'" I looked at her earnestly. "What did you mean by that?"

This time her eyes hit the floor with nervous sweep of her lashes. It surprised me. Until this point, I had thought of her as invincible.

"I don't know how to explain that to you," she said hesitantly. "You won't believe me. You won't understand."

"Why?"

She looked up at me. The candlelight danced in her eyes. She seemed to be mustering up the courage to say the next words. "How do you explain to someone that their entire life is a lie?"

I cocked my head to the side. "What do you mean?"

"Your air and water are sterile, and yet you city people are always sick. You have endless knowledge available at the push of a button, but you do not think or imagine or create. You visit a psychiatrist once a week, and yet you believe you are mentally ill. You have infinite forms of entertainment at your fingertips, yet you are unhappy. Do you not question any of this?" She shook her head vehemently. "I've seen too many of you suffer, and all because of the cloud of lies that you live beneath. How long does it take to see through that?" She lowered her eyes again. "Will you ever see through it?"

There was something unfamiliar in her voice—an emotion with sharp edges.

"I've never known anything different," I said.

"I know." She shook her head, still looking down. I was close enough to smell the woodsy musk of her hair, and it was all I could do not to lean down and put my lips on it. "Your prison walls have always been invisible, but oh, so comfortable. And *that* is what I meant." She looked up at me and her eyes were brimming with tears. "I hate the people who did this to you. Doctors. Politicians. Media. Businessmen. I *hate* them."

"How do you know all this?" I asked.

She hesitated.

It hit me. "Have you been to the city?"

She blinked, and the line of tears that had been teetering on her bottom eyelid disappeared. "I lived in the Fifth City until I was ten," she explained haltingly. "My parents worked for the government. They both had degrees in computer science, and they managed A.I. systems for some of the highest agencies."

"Are you serious?" Blood rushed to my head at the thought of her living in my city. "How come I never saw you online?" I had studied nearly every one of the thousands of student accounts at my school, the only one in City 5. I would have remembered her.

"We weren't allowed on the Internet," she said. "We had nothing digital in our house, actually, other than in my parents' office, which we weren't allowed to enter. I'd never heard of a sim until you described it to me."

I frowned. "How is that possible? What about truancy laws?"

She shrugged. "Mom and dad homeschooled us. I'm sure with their computer skills and high government clearance levels, they figured out how to keep us out of the system." Her face darkened. "We couldn't miss our weekly psych appointments, though. It's the only way our parents got enough rations approved to feed us all. But they used false identities and A.I. to cover up the illegal pregnancies.

According to government records, Diana is the only child of Tom and Margaret Montgomery."

Dishes clattered noisily in the dining chamber. It sounded like dinner was about to begin. I had to get to the bottom of something before this moment ended, when I had her undivided attention and unexpected willingness to open up to me.

"If you've never been on the Internet, then how do you know all this about us?"

"I've always been fascinated with your technology," she said. "Even when we moved here, to the caves, I longed to know more about your world. I read every book I could get my hands on about computers, the Internet, robots, and modern machinery. I got to know all the engineers who had moved here from the city, and I picked their brains every chance I got. I saw all the machines the scavengers brought in from their trips, and I signed up to become one myself just so I could get my hands on all those old artifacts." The candle in her right hand sputtered, nearing the bottom of the wick. "I don't even know what half of them are, but to me, they're the embodiment of genius. I wanted to meet the people who had created them. I wanted to know who had the brilliance to invent such amazing things."

I read between the lines, hearing the longing in her voice. "You went back to the city."

She nodded. "It was not long after Emer came to us. The things she was describing to us… they seemed like magic. I envied her her life, her apparent freedom. A world where you didn't have to work all day? Where you could sit in your room and learn things, all day long? It sounded like a dream. I left in the night, using a map I had found in my father's library. I followed the river down the mountain, walked for three days, and finally, I came to it. Those towers of glass were so tall they really did seem to scrape the sky. I felt like Dorothy visiting the Emerald City for the first time."

I wondered if this was another reference to that play writer she was so into. Shakespeare. I had to remember that.

Her eyes welled up with tears again. "I don't know why I'm telling you all this," she said, her voice catching. "But let's just say that it wasn't what I expected. The streets were clean and beautiful, the buildings engineered perfection. But the *people*." The tears spilled over onto her cheeks. "They wander around like hopeless, empty shells. They barely have enough to eat. The children are illiterate. They are so lost."

"The Forgotten," I explained. "They're homeless, and crazy, released from the mental institution when they couldn't hold them anymore." I smiled at her, trying to cheer her up. "They aren't really *people*."

She looked at me like I had just slapped her in the face. "Of course they are. How can you say that?"

I didn't know how to answer her. How could I say that? That's just what my mom had taught me. They had always just been part of the landscape.

"I talked to them. They told me their stories. Their parents came from the Old World, from farms and towns that were once brimming with life. They were told their homes were contaminated. They were promised a better life in the city, where they would be safe and cared for. Many of them had it, for a time. They were coddled and sheltered and hidden away." She wiped her cheeks, but it was pointless. The tears tumbled down and soaked into her shirt. "They were just like you, once."

You're nothing. Lower than The Forgotten.

Her words hit me like a slap in the face. I stepped back, dropping her hand, which I had been holding this whole time. She had compared me to the Forgotten, which was humiliating. But she was wrong. The Forgotten were mere nuisances—I was a liability. I could have murdered her right where we stood.

"What am I doing?" I mumbled.

She looked at me curiously. "What do you mean?"

I rubbed the back of my neck, which was hot. "We should go. We're late for dinner."

She pressed her hands on either side of her nose and swept the tears away. Then she nodded. The ponytail came down and she spread her hair around her face to hide the signs of her weeping. She glanced at me again, and I gave her an encouraging smile and an "after you" motion through the doorway.

What a mess. It was dangerous for me to be alone with her like that, and I wanted to kick myself for allowing it. But I didn't know how to stay away from her. The voice in my head was right, though. I was worse than the Forgotten. They had never tried to kill anyone.

"Those Charleston kids are up to no good again," Margaret was saying as I sat down to dinner. "Mrs. Beth found a bag of burning guano in front of her stall again."

"How do you know it was them?" asked Diana.

Margaret gave her a knowing look. "Really? Who else could it be?"

Diana shrugged. "Maybe one of the younger kids."

"Those boys are trouble with a capital T. They know they're not supposed to burn anything down here without permission."

"Bet it was funny, though," Cecil chuckled. "Probably still stinks down there."

Autumn threw a chestnut at him. It bounced off his head and he cried out in pain. He looked up at her fuming face and swallowed a retort.

"I'll check on Mrs. Beth in the morning," said Autumn.

Margaret smiled. "She's fine, darling, but that would be nice. She would probably love a visit from you."

"One of the news boys said they had a wildcat in their cave," Jesse announced. "One of their sentries went missing, too. They had to take the cat out with a rifle before it pounced on one of the kids."

Tom set his fork down and exchanged a glance with Margaret. "Another sentry missing?"

The soft creases between her eyebrows deepened. "Is this verified, Jesse?"

"I promise." He nodded emphatically. "It was Owen Stevens who told me, and he would never lie."

"Winter must be coming early this year if the animals are in the cave already." Tom stood. "I have to revise tomorrow morning's paper."

Margaret's face fell. "Can't it wait until the morning?"

"I'm sorry. People need to know."

The room was unusually quiet when he left. The worry was tangible. Even Jesse put down his notebook and pencil and just chewed quietly, staring down at the table.

"Lessons start early tonight," Margaret announced, her tone cheery but strained. "I have a surprise for you all."

Possibly the strangest thing about this family was how hard they worked. They were like a bunch of batteries without expiration dates. I had never met anyone who had labored at such physically exhausting work from morning to night, only to go home and *study* for hours before bed. But I guess there was no other time for school. Margaret was the schoolmarm, gathering them together on a bunch of old couches and chairs at the back of the chamber, passing out books and putting them to work. Those kids read more books than I had ever read online in my entire life. They read aloud to each other or silently, depending on their mood. They curled up on the couch or sat on the floor, depending on the day. And believe it or not, they actually seemed to enjoy themselves.

I, on the other hand, struggled to stay awake, and often found myself slumped over on the couch, book sliding off my lap, drool oozing down my chin. I was not used to reading paper books. I didn't even like e-books.

We quickly cleaned up from dinner and made our way to the living room chamber next door. Candles were set on all the tables and around the floor, casting a warm glow over the furniture. Bookshelves of different heights lined the cave wall. A tattered, purple love-seat sat in the corner. Three couches formed a triangle in front of the books. A wooden rocking chair sat in the middle of it all, presiding over the furniture like a matriarch, making it clear whose spot that was.

Jesse bounced into the love-seat right away, draping his legs over one of the arms. Luca settled on the floor in front of him, leaning his back against the other arm. Cecil and Diana sat at opposite ends of the floral-print couch. I waited, as I always did, to see what Autumn would do. When she sat on the red-and-black checkered loveseat, I opted to sit alone on the black leather couch in the middle.

"The scavengers found some things that were very special," said Margaret, crossing the room and leaning down to open a cabinet. "The town they visited had a music shop in it."

I looked sideways at Autumn, remembering the night with the record player. She leaned forward with her elbows on her knees, suddenly very interested in what her mother had to say.

"Music is a gift," she continued, "but it is not always easy. It is a singular language that takes time to learn." Her voice was muffled inside the cabinet. "Not only that, it takes physical stamina to learn an instrument of any kind. You will find yourself with bleeding fingers and numb lips, all in the name of art." She emerged from the cabinet with a smile. "The great ones persist."

In her arms were five different instruments, which I recognized from an old movie I'd seen about a group of kids in a band. I tried to remember their names. Violin. Guitar. Banjo. All with strings. Then there was a flute, long and silver, shimmering in the candlelight. Then a brass one. Trompet? No, trumpet. That was it. Trumpet.

"They brought back music books, as well." She beamed. "Your father and I found someone in the caves who used to teach music. He will come once a week, and you must practice every day."

I looked at all of them. From Jesse to Autumn, everyone sat forward eagerly like kids at Christmas, getting ready to dive on their shiny new toys.

Pathetic.

"Can I have the gold one?" Jesse asked.

Margaret nodded and handed him the trumpet.

Diana reached for the violin. Cecil and Luca wanted to share the banjo. Autumn took the guitar.

"And you?" Margaret held the flute out to me.

"Nah." I shrugged. "I'm good."

The others were talking and poring over the instruments, so Margaret was the only one who heard me. "You don't have to play this one," she said. "You can use any of them you like."

I shook my head. "It's just not my thing."

She sat down next to me, setting the flute across her lap and folding her slender hands. "What is 'your thing,' Oliver?"

Her scrutiny made me uncomfortable. "What do you mean?"

"You must have something that interests you. An activity you'd like to try, for fun." She smiled encouragingly. "It would be good for you."

I stuck my finger in a rip in the couch and thought about it for a minute. Interest? I couldn't fathom it. These days were a constant battle just to keep my mind quiet. Besides, I'd never really had any hobbies, other than watching old movies.

She was right, though. It would be good to take my mind off… well, off my mind.

Suddenly I had a flicker of an idea.

An "interest."

It was probably crazy. But for me, that ship had sailed *long* ago.

"There is one thing." I stopped picking at the couch and looked up at her. "Can you get me a book by Shakespeare?"

EIGHT

"Bats are the only creatures that can fly without stopping." Jesse sat next to me on my bed, whittling and talking my ear off.

"Huh."

"Other birds have to take a break once in a while. That's why you see them gliding. But bats can fly forever."

"Interesting."

"They sleep during the day and hunt at night. Did you know that they see things by listening to their own echo? Wouldn't it be awesome if we could do that?"

I sat forward with a sigh. "Listen, kid. As fascinating as this conversation is, I'm really trying to read." I held up the book I had splayed between my fingers. "And this isn't exactly 'light' reading. This guy must've gotten paid in gold bars for every letter he used, or something, because it takes him like two pages to say one thing." The book was weathered and dog-eared, but the words *William Shakespeare* and *The Comedy of Errors* were scrawled clearly across the cover.

Jesse scrunched up his nose in disgust. "My sister likes that stuff."

I shrugged. "It's kind of good. I mean, it's a funny idea. This guy named Aegeon has two twin boys and buys them another pair of twins to be their servants, but then one son and his servant get separated from the family during a shipwreck. Thirty years later, they find them again in a nearby city, but no one knows who's who, and they keep getting everyone mixed up." I chuckled. "Even the wife thinks the other brother is her husband. Who does that? I mean, even if they were twins, wouldn't you think that a wife would know the difference?"

"Maybe she did know," he said. "Girls are good at hiding secrets."

I raised an eyebrow. He had a point.

"Anyway," I said, "I can't read with you talking to me like that. You shouldn't even be in here without supervision—your sister will kill us both. Isn't it past your bedtime?"

Jesse gave his head a quick shake and bent over his whittling again. "I'll be quiet," he assured me.

I frowned and considered being hard-nosed. It had been weeks since my violent outburst with him, but what if Autumn was right, that I could flip at any moment? I watched his tousled hair bob over his work and decided it would be okay. I wasn't going to hurt him.

I went back to my book. Just as I was gut-laughing at the hilarious mix-up of characters in Epheus, Jesse laid another stick next to me, its tip sharp as a needle.

My blood boiled. I snapped the book shut and threw the stick back at him. "Stop doing that," I said angrily.

He looked hurt. "Doing what?"

"Trying to give me weapons! Why do you insist on putting yourself in danger like that? Are you stupid or something?"

Jesse looked like I'd just slapped him in the face. He even got red from his neck to his hairline. I'd never seen him so mad. He flung all the wood shavings off his lap and onto my bed. Then he punched me in the shoulder.

"Ow!" I rubbed my bicep. I hadn't expected him to be that strong.

"You say you're sorry, you big oaf!"

I snickered. "Oaf? Do we live in the nineteenth century?"

Believe it or not, his face got redder. His fists clenched so hard that the veins popped out of his skinny, white arms. With a cry of rage, he hurled himself on top of me, pummeling my head and my back with windmill blows. I tried to reach up and pry him off, but he had clamped his knees around my arms, pinning them down, and I didn't want to accidentally throw him to the ground. "Jesse!" I cried between blows. "Okay! I'm sorry! Jesse! I'm sorry, okay?"

The storm subsided and he slid down off my back. We both bent over, huffing and puffing. I couldn't believe that I was actually sore from fighting with a little kid. I looked up and he stood there, arms akimbo, a proud grin on his face. "I made you cry uncle."

I coughed a sputtering laugh. "Yeah, I guess you did."

He sobered. "I know how to take care of myself."

I nodded.

"I'm not afraid of you. And I'm not stupid."

I sat down on the bed again. "Okay, kid. Fine." I caught my breath. "Just promise me you'll run away—fast—if I start acting weird."

"You mean like Jekyll and Hyde?" He looked intrigued. "Is that what happens when your eyes get all glassy and you stare off into nothing for a long time? Is that the danger you keep talking about?"

I shrugged. "I guess so. I don't really know how it works. Just that I don't trust myself. There's some kind of crazy in there, and I don't know if it'll ever go away."

Jesse sat down next to me again. "Emer had that when she first came here. She was louder than you, though. She used to cry and scream all night. You just talk and mumble sometimes."

An arm and a leg.

I closed my eyes and shook my head. *Change the subject, Oliver.* The sound of Emer's name brought a memory I did not want to look at—that feather across her long throat, flushed with the imprint of my hands choking her.

Your interest, Oliver. Remember your interest.

I shoved the memory aside. "Listen, kid."

Jesse leaned forward eagerly.

"I have this plan. I'm doing something big. It's kinda cheesy. But it'll be fun." I picked the book up off the bed and clapped it between my two hands, smothering the scrawling name of *William Shakespeare*. "I'm going to need your help."

*

"Hand me that piece of lumber!"

"Shhh!"

Cecil, Luca, Jesse and I were in the shop. It was the middle of the night, and we all knew we weren't supposed to be there. A lone candle danced on the table, a co-conspirator in our crime, casting just enough light for us to rummage through the pile of artifacts at the back of the cave. We were building props.

"Luca, will you stop trying to shut me up? That's just how I talk." Cecil stood at the edge of the pile. "Jesse, pass me that round, wood thing."

Jesse was in the middle of the pile, rummaging. He pulled a wheel out from under some blankets and handed it to his brother. "What're you going to use that for?"

A soft knock at the door made us freeze. "It's Diana," said a voice through the keyhole. We all sighed. I held the candle behind the door while I opened it and ushered her inside.

"What're you doing here?" asked Luca.

"I want to help." She held up a basket full of yarn and cloth. "I can sew."

"How did you know we were here?"

"I overheard Cecil and Luca talking about it after dinner tonight."

I glowered at them.

"Mom didn't hear, but if you guys want to keep it a secret, you'd better not talk about it. Cecil is *so loud*."

Luca's hand came up and whopped his brother on the back of the head.

"Ow!" Cecil scowled at his brother and rubbed his head.

"Does Autumn know?" I asked.

Diana shook her head. "She wasn't there. She went to visit Mrs. Beth."

I breathed a sigh of relief. "The whole point is to surprise her, okay? You've got to keep it quiet."

Everyone nodded soberly.

"Okay, Diana. You're in charge of all the costumes." She beamed. "Cecil and Luca, you can make the sets, but we need a place to hide them every night when we leave."

"There's an empty chamber full of stalagmites about eighty yards from the shop," said Luca. "No one really goes there."

I nodded. "Perfect. And Jesse, I want you to help me write the storyboard."

He gave me a blank look. "Storyboard?"

"They used to use them to make movies. I saw a documentary on it. Each scene needs to be sketched out, from start to finish, like your comics."

He grinned and pulled his pencil out from behind his ear. "Oh yeah, I can definitely do that."

"Um, Oliver?" Diana seemed hesitant. "Don't you need actors for your play?"

I grinned. "Of course we do. That's us."

Cecil and Luca beamed. Jesse looked confused. Diana seemed to fold up into herself.

"We'll have to play multiple parts, of course. We don't have enough for a full cast."

"I'm not playing a girl," Cecil and Luca both said in unison.

"All female roles were played by men back then," said Diana. "Women weren't allowed to act."

"Yeah, well, we don't live in Shakespearean England," said Luca.

"But as you can see, we don't have enough girls." Diana motioned to herself.

"She's right," I said. "We need everyone to do their part. We either do this right, or we don't do it at all."

We all looked at each other. My candle began to sputter. It was nearly time to go home. I wondered what I would do if they didn't go for it. I supposed I could try a one-man show, but it would take me weeks to build the sets on my own, and I'd look pretty stupid up there playing all those parts by myself. Autumn wouldn't laugh at the humor of the play—she'd be laughing at me.

"You two must really be meant for each other," said Cecil, as if he read my mind. "I've done a lot of dumb stuff in my life, but this one takes the cake. All in the name of *love*." He pushed his hair back, batted his eyelashes, and pushed his nose into Luca's face. "C'mon, Brother, let's help the star-crossed lovers."

Luca tried to box his ears, but Cecil dodged him and laughed.

"I'll do it," said Jesse, stepping forward. "I'll play a girl. I'll do whatever you need me to do."

Diana came closer, as well. Her cheeks were flushed and the candlelight danced in her eyes. "I'll do it, too." She smiled softly at me. "I've never seen anyone do something so nice for my sister."

Cecil marched over and hung his arm over my shoulders. He smelled like sweat and dirt. "You know I'm on board," he said.

We all looked at Luca. He crossed his arms skeptically. "How do you know she's going to like it?"

Cecil rolled his eyes. "Do you even know who we're talking about? This is *Autumn*, for God's sake. Miss Shakespeare herself." He grinned down at me.

"How do you know how to put on a play?" Luca asked.

I shrugged. "I don't know. I figure it's just like making a movie, only without the camera."

Luca studied me for a minute. Then he unfolded his arms and nodded begrudgingly. "Fine," he said. "I'm in."

*

Over the weeks that followed, we tried not to interact with each other at the shop too much, for fear we'd give something away in front of Autumn. I wondered if everyone else was lying awake at night, buzzing with excitement, like I was. I kept the machine busy as long as I could during the day to avoid conversation. With the idea of the play on everyone's mind, I didn't want someone slipping up.

One day, after I had been up all night working on sets, I fell asleep at the press.

"Oliver." Tom's voice startled me awake. "You've been printing blanks for the last two minutes."

I stopped the pedal and pushed the lever aside. "Ah! Sorry!" I started rifling through the pile, trying to find the last printed page.

"The ink's all wrong, too." He ran his finger along the edge of the plate and pulled it up to his nose to examine it. "Jesse, I think you got red mixed up with blue."

Jesse cringed guiltily.

"Did you guys eat enough breakfast this morning?"

"Yes sir," I said absentmindedly. I had found a page with print on it, and I was surprised by the headline. *Sentries Go Mysteriously Missing in Caves 10 and 11.* "You're publishing the story about the missing people?"

Autumn looked up from her typesetting. "What?" She pushed her chair back and came over to take a look. "Dad?"

Tom frowned. "Yes. People need to know."

Luca came over with his eyebrows drawn. "Dad, you never print stuff like that."

"It's verified. I wouldn't print it if it wasn't true." He ran his fingers across his scalp. "Maybe it will help them be found."

"But won't it alarm everyone?" Autumn asked.

"You always say we need to avoid the stampede effect." Even Cecil looked concerned. "Making people afraid turns them into animals."

"I tried not to write it that way. I tried to empower people with the facts, not scare them. I asked for help bringing us information they might have." He sighed. "It was a hard call, but I think I made the right choice."

By the looks on everyone's faces, this was serious.

Suddenly the door banged open and a man came in. He was dressed in the camo uniform that all the sentries, hunters and scavengers wore. "Mayor Montgomery," he said, saluting Tom.

Mayor? I looked at Cecil in surprise. He shrugged and nodded.

"The search party has returned," he went on hurriedly. "Your daughter did a fine job. I tried to keep an eye on her like I promised, but..."

"It's okay, Trent," said Tom. "She's not easy to keep track of. She's back safely?"

"Yes, sir."

"What of the missing sentries?"

"They were found." The man looked washed-out, like he hadn't slept in weeks. He crossed his arms to keep his hands from shaking.

A dark-skinned woman wearing a long dress, a brightly-colored hair wrap, and jangly jewelry entered the room and stood quietly next to the hunter.

"And?" Tom prompted Trent to continue.

Trent shook his head. "Dead, sir. Both of them."

Tom leaned against the table as if he had just been knocked backwards. "Was it an animal?"

The man shook his head again. He seemed unable to speak.

Tom's voice was hoarse when he asked the next question. It was only one word, but it hit my chest like a swinging anvil.

"Murder?"

The man nodded.

Another woman entered the room, this one elderly, her hair like tufts of cotton. She shuffled in with the aid of a walking cane. She smiled at Autumn and squeezed her hand as she walked past, then she sobered as she took her place next to Trent and the young gypsy-woman.

"How?" Tom asked breathlessly.

"One, choking. The other, some kind of blow to the head."

Tom wiped his forehead with the back of his sleeve. He seemed bowled over by an invisible weight. "We've tried so hard," he murmured. "Yet even in our nonexistence, our fool-proof secrecy, our subterranean sanctuary, they have reached us with their violence."

The gypsy-woman stepped forward, her bracelets tinkling as she moved. "Mayor?" she asked, her voice urgent. "We, as your council, have come to speak to you on this matter. The farming community I represent is growing increasingly frightened."

"The merchants, as well." The old woman leaned on her walking stick as she spoke. "It's all they ever talk about down at the market now."

Trent was nodding. "The hunters and scavengers, too. Some of them are preparing their families for the very real possibility that they may not return from the next trip."

Pushing back from the table, Tom paced across the room. I had never seen him like this. He was supposed to be unwavering as iron, immovable as stone. He had always had an unabating certainty that everything was going to turn out all right. His worry was unsettling.

Trent took a step forward, and when he spoke, this time it was more hushed than before. "Some are saying this is your fault, sir."

Everyone looked at him in shock. There were murmurs of protest throughout the room. "My fault?" Tom stopped pacing and stared at Trent.

"They say it was started by your bringing that boy to the caves."

An arm and a leg. And a brain.

I blinked.

Me?

Everyone looked at me and back at Tom.

"How could that boy be responsible for the murder of two people?" he asked.

Trent lifted his hands palm-up toward the ceiling. "Word has it that he's wrong in the head."

Tom looked at me. I felt like telling him what I thought—*I didn't kill them, but I very well could have*—but I didn't.

"Oliver hasn't left the caves since he got here," said Luca. "There's no way he could have murdered those sentries."

Tom looked at him in surprise. "How do you know?"

"We've had him on watch since he got here." Luca shot me a guilty look. "Cecil and I switch off every night. Autumn watches him during the day. No one leaves him alone, even for a second."

I frowned. They had all been monitoring me?

Of course they don't trust you.

You'll always be an outsider.

I shook my head and realized that the room looked different.

Everyone was looking at me, and Emer was standing in the doorway. I must have blacked out for a minute. I wondered how long it had been.

"You get out of here!" Jesse was at my side, his skinny arms clamped around my forearm. He screamed at the man in uniform. "You don't know what you're talking about, Trent! You better stop spreading lies about him!" He was breathing funny—some kind of gasping sob.

Autumn came over to soothe her little brother. "He's right, Trent. You can't assume someone is guilty without proof, you know that."

"I'm just telling you what people are saying."

Tom frowned. "What are you doing to stop them, Trent? Lies spread faster than viruses. They turn people against each other. They make people go mad. We can't allow that to happen in the caves." He sighed. "We came here to get away from that."

"Did you do it?" Emer's voice filled the room as if she were making an announcement, but when I looked over at her it was clear her question was directed at me.

Did I do what? Kill them? I looked down at my hands. For a second, they appeared to be dripping with blood. I shuddered. Had I *murdered*? If I did, was it real life, or a dream? Or a sim, from long ago?

I looked up at the people in the cave and envied them their sanity. They all had memories that they knew were theirs. They could probably remember what they'd had for breakfast three months ago. I had been practically numb my entire life. How was I supposed to know what was real and what wasn't? I was a threat to these people, and I needed to be locked up.

Then I remembered the day I had sat with Autumn on the cave floor, listening to the old record player, watching candlelight dance on her cheeks. That had been real.

I remembered pulling her close to me outside the dining chamber, watching her eyes brim with tears as she told me about the Forgotten. That was real.

As vague as it was, I even remembered the day she had climbed up on that barbed wire and cut me loose.

Pools of someone else's blood? That wasn't real.

I looked at Emer across the room. My gaze was steady. "No," I said. "I did not."

The conviction in my voice was also real, and everyone seemed to breathe a sigh of relief. Trent nodded, saluted, and left the room. Tom announced it was time for lunch. Cecil hit his head on the door frame as we all left the room. Things seemed to go back to normal.

Emer brushed past me on our way into the dining chamber, and using that uncanny ability she had to send her voice to my ears only, she spoke five of the most terrifying words I had ever heard.

"Simulated murder is still murder."

NINE

So she knew.

We were all up late again, building sets for the play, but my mind was a bottomless, churning vortex of uncertainty.

Emer had been there that day, on the other end of the sim, when I choked her to death in Central Park. And unlike me, she hadn't forgotten it. I wondered what she intended to do with that information. True, it was just a simulation. I hadn't *really* killed her. But I had wanted to.

She seemed to have settled in here in the caves. This family loved her. But the Emer I remembered had two faces. The first was kind and beautiful, with espresso eyes full of warmth, staring at you with interest while you told her everything about yourself. It had satiny skin and soft lips that bewitched you over candlelight dinner, and a mesmerizing laugh that made you feel like the funniest guy in the world. The second face was smug and derisive, with laughing eyes and a triumphant mouth that revealed all your secrets to the world. *He's obsessed with me,* she had posted in the school group chat called *Buzz,* the one we all went on after class. *Look at those puppy dog eyes.* The undercover video of our date, which was really a dare, had over a thousand comments within the first fifteen minutes. I read about ten of them before I tore my headpiece off and cracked it in half.

It was after that that my online restriction level hit juvenile delinquent status. I had told her about the old movies I watched on the dark web, and once the video was uploaded, it was public domain. It would remain on my criminal record for the rest of my life. Worst of all, because of my restricted status, I would never watch another movie again.

"Oliver?"

I looked up from the board I had been hammering. Jesse had his pencil in his mouth and his notebook open in his hands.

"You done, bud?" I flipped my hammer around and hung it on my belt. "I can't wait to see what you came up with."

Jesse pulled his notebook away from my outstretched arms and cringed sheepishly. "I have to tell you something first."

"Okay."

"I kind of... changed it."

I cocked my head to the side. "What do you mean?"

His words tumbled out nervously. "I didn't change the story or anything, I just made it easier to understand. I made it fit... the caves."

I pursed my lips and nodded pensively. "Okay. Okay. Let's check it out."

Gingerly, he passed me the notebook. I sat down on a nearby boulder and began reading. He had clearly read the book, which blew me away—a seven-year-old kid, reading Shakespeare? The strange part, however, was in the presentation. *A Comedy of Errors* was supposed to take place in ancient Greece. I had expected to see Greek columns, tunics and billowing ladies' dresses. Jesse's story board showed characters in cave chambers, dressed in modern clothes, with the women wearing pants. He had probably struggled with the task I had given him, wanting to make the story board perfect, but he was only able to write what he knew. All he had ever known was the caves.

When I finished, I looked up at him with newfound respect. "I've seen a lot of good movies, kid." I remembered all the relics I had found on the dark web—*Indiana Jones*, *Star Wars*, *Back to the Future*, spaghetti Westerns, even black-and-whites like *Citizen Kane* and *It's a Wonderful Life*. Each one was its own adventure, with heroes who led me through hell and back again, drowning me in their losses but anchoring me with their victories. "I've spent most of my life watching movies. You're a natural."

Jesse beamed. "It's good?"

I raised my eyebrows and nodded. "Real good."

"Oliver?" Diana stood in front of us with her knitting basket in the crook of her arm. "We're going home a little early tonight." Her eyes were half-open and she looked exhausted.

I jumped up off the rock and looked at Cecil and Luca. They, too, looked like they wanted to sleep standing up. "Absolutely," I said. "Go home, get some rest."

"Sets are all done," said Luca. "Just one more bench to build."

"We can start learning lines tomorrow, then," I said. I beamed at all of them. "Thank you guys for everything. I'll clean everything up."

Diana patted my shoulder softly and left. Luca motioned to Jesse to follow them, but he shook his head. "I wanna help Oliver." He looked over at me and crossed his arms.

"No, Jesse." Luca gave him a stern look.

I looked down at that kid trying so hard to be a man and swallowed a smile. "I think it's okay," I said. "I'll make sure he gets home safely."

Jesse puffed his chest out. "More like *I'll* make sure *you* get home."

Luca contemplated us for a second, his head bent to the side, and I wondered what was going through his head. "Fine," he conceded. "You better be home in an hour, though."

Jesse grinned. "Yep."

Cecil slapped my back when he walked past. "If something happens to my brother, we'll kill you."

I nodded.

"People said mean things about Emer, too, you know. When she first came to us." Jesse kept up his usual chatter while we cleaned up the tools that everyone had left on a makeshift workbench Cecil had made. "Most people down here don't want anything to do with outsiders."

"Why did you take her in?"

Jesse looked at me gravely. His eyes were sea-green in the candlelight. "I fell in the river and almost drowned. She pulled me out." He shrugged. "Dad said he would give her anything he owned, in gratitude. Said he owed her his own life."

"So she weaseled her way in." I said it without thinking and immediately wished I hadn't.

Jesse stopped what he was doing and scowled at me. "She's not a weasel. She's an eagle. She even wears their feathers."

I remembered that feather in her hair. She said her father had given it to her. Some kind of family heirloom. I wondered what story she had told Jesse to glorify it.

"You don't like her," he said accusatively.

"It's more like… I don't trust her." I shrugged. "But then, I don't even trust myself. So I'm not really one to talk."

Jesse shook his head sadly. Candlelight danced on yam-colored hair. "You city people are so strange," he said. "So… separate." He gazed at me with a wisdom beyond his years. "Don't you know that we can only survive together? We need each other."

I shrugged and nodded. Down here, I guessed that was true.

When the tools had been boxed up and put away, Jesse and I carried the workbench and remaining lumber into the nearby chamber and hid them behind a thick, dark stalagmite. My eyes were heavy from lack of sleep, but I had more vitality than I had in years. My muscles were stronger, I no longer walked with a limp, and I seemed to breathe better. I felt… normal. Better than normal.

Just as we were locking up, murmuring voices tumbled from a cluster of boulders a few yards away. Jesse and I both frowned at each other, bewildered. Who would be out at this time of night? We made our way over to the rocks and peered around them.

Three figures faced each other in an uneven triangle behind the boulder. Light scattered erratically around the cave as the man holding the only candle darted back and forth. He was lanky and had an anxious way about him, as if he could not hold still. The other man was also tall, but stocky, and his stance was more firmly grounded, giving him the appearance of a confrontational bulldog. A few feet in front of them was Autumn, her jaw set in a stubborn line and her arms crossed defiantly.

"The Charleston boys," whispered Jesse.

"Where's your boyfriend?" the stocky one asked.

Autumn scoffed. "Are you jealous, Ben?"

"Aw, shut your mouth." He ground down on the "r" so that it sounded like a dog's growl. "I got no interest in that cripple."

She shrugged. "Dad's been letting him use the equipment. He's a bona fide printer by now." She knew she was digging into him. "Maybe he should give you lessons. I know you always wanted in on my family's print shop."

Ben clenched his hands into tight fists. "So he is your boyfriend, then?"

"That's none of your business."

He had a frustrated way of rubbing his head, which was shaved so closely that his skin shone like a bowling ball in the candlelight. It reminded me of the way my mom used to run her hands through her hair when she was irritated—the movements were fast and clipped. "It is my business when a nut job brings problems into my caves. We never had no dead people until that guy came along."

Autumn raised an eyebrow.

"Other than by natural causes, I mean." He mumbled the last part. "Besides, I thought we had a good thing going." He sidled up to her and put his hands on her hips. "I had my eye on you way before he showed up."

Autumn shoved his hands away and looked at him in disgust. "Don't touch me."

The guy holding the candle snickered.

Ben made a smacking sound with his lips. "So feisty," he said. "I always liked that about you." He moved closer and put his hands back on her hips.

I had heard the term "seeing red," before. They used it all the time in the old black-and-whites. I had never understood it until now. Except that I didn't just see it, I *felt* it—like a thousand tiny fire-ants swarming through my veins. Hot, jagged rage compelled me forward, and I smacked my hands on that bulldog's shoulders, flipped him around, and started pummeling him before he even knew what hit him. By the time he started hitting back, I already had the advantage, throwing him to the ground and pinning him with my knees while I continued to deliver blow after blow.

"Oliver," someone said in a distant voice. My ears were a rush of adrenaline and a mumbling of voices.

An arm and a leg. Not much of a brain, though.

Do, Re, Mi, Fa.

"Oliver."

Blood sprayed from my knuckles and now I was really seeing red. I hardly felt the blows, but I saw Ben's face crumple under my fists, and I soon realized that he had stopped fighting back. The violent impetus faded and I sat back on my haunches, breathing hard.

He's done.

Ben the bulldog (looking more like a mangy coyote) flung his arms up to cover his face, which had already begun to swell.

I remembered all the sim fights I'd gotten into over the years. I wasn't one for slinging words around the Internet, but a good brawl was something I could get behind. It normally happened at school, when some kid called me a simp or tried to take credit for something I'd done. The worst one was when I saw a bunch of bullies picking on a nerdy kid in the library. He was just sitting there, minding his own business, trying to study, and these jerks with nothing better to do decided to push his books to the floor and start hitting him on the back of the head. I didn't care that they were just holographic images—I couldn't let them get away with it. Holographic fights were crazy, though—somehow the sims made them feel real, like I was hitting real flesh and bone. Something to do with the neurological connection in the headset. The only problem was, as soon as fists were swinging, I blacked out. Every. Single. Time.

This was the first time I'd ever made it through a fight totally awake.

"What's your flipping problem?" Ben demanded, pushing me

off. I'd split the skin open above his eye, and I knew the crimson waterfall on his face made it look worse than it was.

"She said not to touch her." I tipped my chin forward. "So don't touch her."

"Whatever, psycho." He wiped his mouth with the back of his hand and walked away, gesturing for his brother to follow. "I'll remember this."

I watched their candlelight recede and wondered what Autumn had ever seen in him. Maybe he had been different before his father died. I wondered if he had always had that hunched look, like a boxer holding the weight of every fight he had ever lost.

Something rammed into my side, and I looked down to see Jesse with his arms wrapped around me. "You saved my sister," he cried.

I turned to Autumn, who stood behind him, looking at me with wide eyes. "What were you doing out here this time of night?" I demanded angrily.

"I couldn't sleep," she said softly. "I thought I'd get some work done, take my mind off it."

"This is not the time of night to be out alone!"

She didn't say anything. Instead, she stepped toward me, put out her hand, and touched my cheek. It was a gesture of gratitude, but it had a tenderness that I had never felt in my life. My adrenaline slowed and I leaned into her palm, craving every bit of skin on her body.

Don't get too close.

"You're bleeding," she said softly. "Let's get you cleaned up."

We went back into the shop, where she put ointment on a laceration on my face and wrapped my bloody knuckles with cotton. Jesse fell asleep on a bench near the door. She worked slowly, pressing her fingers gently on my wounds and taking care not to wind the cloth too tightly.

"I think I'm healing," I said.

She nodded. She knew I wasn't talking about tonight's injuries.

"I was sicker than I thought."

She nodded again.

"I always thought I was a strong guy. I worked out every day. I was good at sports." I sighed. "I had no idea I could feel this way. I didn't even… feel. At all."

"I know." She looked up at me. "You're not the only one."

I frowned, not understanding.

"It starts in the womb, you know. They raise the dose for pregnant women, so enough of it gets to the child." She shook her head sadly. "My brother is the first generation to be born without a single drop of medication in his body."

I looked at her in shock. "Wait, you too?"

She laughed bitterly. "Yeah. It makes you feel like a block of wood, doesn't it? Only you don't know it until it's gone."

I blew air out of my mouth in a loud whoosh. "Yeah! Yeah, that's it. That's exactly it."

She nodded in understanding. "I remember the moment I realized it had left my body. I was ten. I was standing outside the hen house on Bill's farm. All of a sudden, I could feel how smooth the eggs were between my fingers. How heavy the basket was on my arm." She smiled and shook her head, remembering. "I could even feel the temperature of the wind against my cheeks."

"So you had to detox, too? You went through everything I went through? The sweats, the pain, pins and needles in your limbs?" I shuddered at the memory. "Wanting to die?"

She shook her head. "I wasn't medicated as long as you were, or in such high doses. My parents left early enough. They took us away when mom got pregnant with Jesse. She told dad she'd sooner die than abort her own baby."

"How did they know about this place?"

"My dad first heard about it in college. He came from old money, and he was educated. Thoroughly. He could gain access to information in places on the Internet that most people don't even know exists. And you know how people talk in college."

I shook my head. "I'm not really the college type. And I definitely don't come from money."

"Well, someone told him about a place off the grid, where people live underground, and things are set up like the Old World. I was ten, but I remember bits and pieces of it. Worried conversations between my parents; leaving in the night; living in the woods for what seemed like months. Then we were here." She secured the last bandage around my hand and looked up at me. Her expression was raw and unfiltered, one of those rare moments when she decided to give me her most vulnerable, innermost self. "But I don't belong here," she whispered.

The wind came out of my lungs like a torn sail. She didn't belong here? What was she saying? That she belonged in the city? I tried to imagine her there, confined to a prison of steel and glass, just another nameless person in a sea of meaningless buildings. No one there would care to feel the softness of her hair; no one would know the rhythm of her breathing; the light in her eyes would fade into a final, irreversible sunset and she would disappear. I could have written the script. The thought of her in the city terrified me.

"Where do you belong, then?" I asked.

She shook her head and looked at the ground. Her voice caught in her throat. "I'm having a really hard time figuring that out." Then she laughed diffidently, standing suddenly, as if she realized she had gone too far.

I stood quickly, grasping her hand and pulling her so close that our noses nearly touched. "I know what you mean." I had startled her, but I didn't care. I didn't want to lose the unfiltered her. "Maybe we can figure it out together."

For the second time since I'd met her, I watched her eyes flood with tears. She nodded quickly. I smiled. She smiled. Then we closed up the shop and I carried Jesse home, we put him to bed, and I said a gentleman's good night. I didn't sleep for hours, thinking only of the way her eyes lit up when she smiled, the smell of her skin when she touched me, and the fact that she had never corrected Ben when he accused me of being her boyfriend.

TEN

It took another month, but we finally got the play together. We used nearly all the lumber in the shop. The sets were indestructible. We made paint out of soot and rock dust from various places in the cave where the deposits were yellow, red and blue-green. Diana did costume fittings and we drilled lines until our throats were dry, and I spent so much time on blocking that I found myself dreaming nightly about the positions of the actors on stage. We started slipping during the day, and we got many a strange look from Tom when one of us said something like, "But, soft!" under our breath.

I had no idea that so many people would show up. Jesse had started a whispering campaign about it by giving a mysterious tip to one of the other newspaper boys. Apparently word spreads like wildfire in the caves, because it was standing room only. We knew because we couldn't stop peeking around the curtains from back stage.

"I think I'm going to throw up," groaned Cecil.

"You can just swallow it back down, you candy-ass drip. Nobody wants to deal with that mess right now." Luca fumbled nervously with the collar of his costume. He was opening the play as Aegeon of Syracuse, and Diana had made him a thick, brown jacket for the role.

"I can't wait," said Jesse, peering at the audience as inconspicuously as he could. "Mom and dad are in the front row!"

Cecil poked his head out over the top of Jesse's. "Oh, no. I think that's my whole platoon." He hung his head in his hands. "I'm going to flub all my lines and they'll never let me live it down."

Their nervous chatter faded into a low hum. Angling my head back to be sure I was in the shadows, I gazed over Jesse's head and scoured the audience, looking for the only person who mattered. Tom and Margaret sat in the front row, near the aisle. They were talking to an elderly woman in a purple tunic who sat next to them, her hands clasped over tightly crossed knees. I didn't recognize anyone else.

"Where is she?" I murmured.

Then I saw her. Her unmistakable red hair stuck out out around a bewildered face as she made her way down the aisle, gazing at the rowdy crowd. The purple-garbed woman next to Margaret stood and called her name, motioning for her to join them. Autumn's face lit up when she saw her.

"It's time," said Diana in a trembling voice.

Everyone looked at me. They wanted me to call it off, I could feel it. They were hoping I would get stage fright, too—or maybe have one of my episodes (which were becoming less and less frequent). Anything to get them out of this. I could see from their wide eyes and the beads of moisture on their foreheads that they were wishing they had never agreed to this crazy idea. Even Jesse.

"We have to do this," I blurted. "They're all here because we promised them a show. I know you guys wouldn't break a promise."

Diana and Cecil gave me obligatory nods. *Yes, of course, we won't break a promise,* they conveyed begrudgingly.

Jesse began to cry. "This is scary," he said.

What a predicament. We couldn't go on stage like this. Jesse had tears streaming down his face in rivulets of orange and black makeup. Diana looked as if she might faint. Cecil really did look like he was going to throw up. And Luca just looked mad. We were not theater actors, we were impostors—kids, playing some stupid game of pretend. And now every single person in the caves was going to see us at our most vulnerable.

I remembered all the movies I had watched in my room back

home. Did those actors ever feel this way? They had been so convincing, I hardly noticed I was watching a movie—they locked arms with my mind and yanked me into the story. But that was just it! It was not about them. It was about the story.

I pulled Jesse under my arm and patted him on the head. "Why do you guys do the news?" I asked.

Diana cocked her head to the side and frowned. Cecil looked at me quizzically. Jesse wiped his eyes and sniffled.

"I mean it. What is it that drives you guys to spend all that time in that shop, printing newspapers?"

"It's just what we've always done," said Diana.

"But there's still something about it that makes it worth doing every day. Otherwise you'd find something else to do. Go work in the fields or something. There's plenty of work."

"People need to know what's happening," said Luca. "It's what keeps us all… together. I think everyone would go crazy down here if they didn't have my father's sensible words to guide us every day."

"And my comics," piped Jesse, wiping his nose. "For entertainment."

"Yes, that's true," Diana said. "I've received quite a few letters thanking me for the advice I give in my column for girls."

"So what you're saying," I pointed out, "is that people need your help."

They all nodded slowly, trying to understand what I was getting at.

"These people—" I gestured toward the milling crowd, "—they need your help. Whether you know it or not, they need to laugh the way you're going to make them laugh; they need a good story to revive rusty imaginations; they need to see the world differently, the way they will when they leave this place after we're done. I *know* what it feels like to be carried away by a story — whether it's a movie, a book or a play. It's food for the soul." I ran my fingers through my hair. "Don't you get it? This is not about us—this is about them! They need you. They need what you can give them." I shrugged diffidently, not sure if I was making my point. "We need to do this—for them."

A loud shouting came from the crowd. People were getting restless.

"Oliver's right," Luca blurted. "We need to get out of our heads and do what needs to be done. We started this whole thing. Let's finish it."

Five nods and we all held ourselves a little straighter. Diana wiped Jesse's tear-stained cheeks. Cecil straightened Luca's collar. I double-checked that Autumn was still in the front row. All was in order.

"LADIES AND GENTLEMEN!" Cecil bounded on stage. We saw one raised arm before the curtains swished closed behind him. A hush fell over the house. "It is my pleasure to welcome you to the first-ever theatrical performance to ever take place in the caves."

I grinned to myself. So far, so good. Cecil was made for the stage.

"Folks, do we have a treat for you tonight. The talent is off the charts. This is like nothing you've ever seen before. You'll laugh, you'll cry, you'll beg to see more."

I peeked around the curtain again. Autumn was smiling bemusedly while she listened to her brother.

"Now, I'm not one to leave out credit when credit's due. And this production would be nothing without our good friend, Oliver McNeil. He's an odd one, for sure, but he knows not to pass up a good story—or an opportunity to win over a girl."

I cringed. I had forgotten to drill him on this part. I should have told him not to mention me.

"So if you find yourself entertained this evening, you can thank Oliver, yours truly (of course), and the whole crew for a *lot* of hard work. And if you hate it, well… then it's all his fault."

The audience laughed. I rolled my eyes.

His voice swelled. "Without further ado, I give you William Shakespeare's *Comedy of Errors*."

We had instructed four of the newspaper boys to snuff the house torches after Cecil's introduction, and they were right on cue. The house went dark just as the curtains opened. The stage was lit from behind.

"Proceed, Solinus, to procure my fall!" Luca's voice boomed from center stage. He held his hands together in supplication. "And by the doom of death end woes and all."

Jesse held his head high, looking stately and majestic as Duke Solinas. His small stature was inconsequential, and he seemed two decades older when he began to speak. I couldn't believe this kid. Twenty-three lines and he didn't miss a beat.

To be honest, everyone blew me away. Hardly anyone forgot their lines, and when they did, they glided around it so gracefully that the audience didn't notice. Diana was the only one who had a hard time speaking up, but she remembered all her blocking and smiled so endearingly that no one seemed to mind having to lean in to hear her. The audience was in stitches over the mix-ups between twin brothers Antipholus of Syracuse and Antipholus of Ephesus, and their twin servants Dromio of Syracuse and Dromio of Antipholus. We switched roles frequently, being limited in number, and the costume changes were a frantic struggle back stage to get arms through jackets and belts on in time, but somehow we kept the audience entertained all along the way and the play ended with a standing ovation that went on for five minutes.

Hoards of people approached us afterwards, wondering when the next one was and could they participate? I ducked out to find Autumn.

She was waiting for me at the exit. Her eyes were like two full moons in the darkness, watching me make my way through the crowd toward her. She grabbed my hand and pulled me into the tunnel, and soon we were jogging, weaving through the throng until we broke through to the main cavern. Then we were sprinting, and even though I had no idea where we were going or what we were doing, I laughed, and it was guttural and raw. *This is heaven,* I thought.

As if hearing my thoughts and agreeing, she laughed, too.

"Do you want to see something amazing?" she asked.

"Yes."

She pulled me down into the valley of the cave, past the market and through the crop fields. No one was working—they must have all been at the play—and the air seemed more still than usual, without any activity or life out there. I imagined this must have been what it was like when the first settlers arrived at the caves. Except that it would have been much, much darker.

She brought me to the far corner of the cavern, on the other side of the fields, where Tom had said the ceiling had caved in and brought in the daylight. It was dark now, but I caught a gust of fresh air and inhaled sharply. It was my first taste of the outside world in months.

"It's cold," I remarked.

"It's winter."

The cave ceiling gave way to darkness and I found myself looking up at the night sky. It was soft and gray and devoid of stars. Even under cloud cover, I was struck by the overwhelming vastness of it all. I felt like a child looking up from the ankles of the world. Tiny, cottony specks drifted down from the darkness and landed on my nose, my forehead, my arms.

"Is that snow?" I asked incredulously.

She nodded.

"I've never seen snow in real life," I said slowly, holding my arms out and watching little feathers of white melt into my skin. "I didn't even like using it in sims, because it seemed so unrealistic. You couldn't feel it."

"Can you feel it now?" she asked.

"I feel everything now. Really vividly."

She was studying me. Looking for something. "And me?" she asked. "What do you feel about me?"

I turned sharply to look at her. There it was again—that soft, vulnerable side of her that I had glimpsed that day in the tunnel when she told me about the Forgotten. Her guard was down, and what she wanted was written all over her face. Me. She wanted me.

I needed no further prompting. I couldn't have held myself back if I tried. In two strides, I closed the gap between us, slipped my hands around her neck, and kissed her. She sighed and leaned into me, her lips soft and pliable under mine. Her skin was wet with melting snowflakes.

"I've been wanting you to do that for the longest time," she said. She threw her head back and laughed. "What *do* you think of me, anyway? I've been horrid."

"I fell in love with you the moment I saw you, that day you cut me out of that barbed wire," I said matter-of-factly. "You were some kind of guardian angel." I looked at her curiously. "You've been wanting me to do that? For how long?"

She blushed. "It doesn't matter. A long time. I just didn't know if I could trust you."

I kissed her again—longer this time.

"Are you sure you can trust me now?"

She looked at me softly. "*I'm* sure. Are you?"

I paused, remembering that day in the woods with Jesse, when rage had boiled out of me and I flipped him to the ground like a wild bear. I remembered the hatred I felt for Emer when I choked her to death in the sim. I remembered the satisfaction I felt when I beat up Ben Charleston. There was no doubt about it. I was wicked to the core.

Don't forget it.

"No." I closed my eyes in disgust and shook my head. "I can't trust myself with anyone. But I can't seem to stay away from you, no matter what I do. You magnetize me. You're the craving I always had but never knew what it was for. The only thing I can trust is your ability to protect yourself from me."

A shadow of sadness darkened her face. She reached up and touched the small beard that had begun to grow along my jaw after weeks without a razor. "I hope you will change your mind someday. 'For the eye sees not itself, but by reflection, by some other things.' I wish you would see yourself as you really are."

I didn't know what it meant, but it sounded nice. I pulled her out of the clearing, realizing she was cold, and wrapped my arms around her. We stood on the rock and watched the snow fall.

"I ran away from home once, too," I said, resting my chin on her head. Her hair was damp from the snow. "I was six. It was the first time I'd ever been outside."

"Your mom must've been terrified."

"She didn't notice at first. Our family's a little different than yours. She stays in her room, and I stay in mine. She probably realized I was gone when she went to make sure I was in bed. That was the only time she checked on me."

"But you were six!"

"Like I said, our families are different." I shrugged. "Anyway, I still remember the smell of the air when I got out. It was fall. It had this crisp, fresh edge to it." I breathed deeply, taking in the scent of winter that clung to her hair. "I had *almost* forgotten that smell. Almost. It stayed in the back of my mind from that day on—this gnawing hunger for something I couldn't quite put my finger on. And now that I have it, I don't ever want to let it go." I touched her cheek lightly with the palm of my hand. "That's how I feel about you."

She sighed and looked up at me. "I wish we could stay here for hours," she said, "but I think we have to head back. I have a feeling everyone is getting worried."

I nodded regretfully and kissed her one last time, this time longer than all the rest.

"Didn't you ever get sick of the sims?" she asked as we crossed the field. "Of never doing anything else?"

I shrugged. "I don't remember. I think I did at the beginning. That's why I ran away. I just needed to see the sun, you know?"

She nodded. "I do know."

"But the outside environment was made to feel... dangerous. My mom put special locks on the doors when I came back. She showed me videos of scientists and doctors talking about how toxic the air and water were. She cried and told me she didn't want me to die, she just wanted me safe in there with her forever." I shrugged. "I never knew any other world existed."

Autumn slipped her hand in mine. It was soft and warm. "I don't know why you were on the highway that day," she said, "but I'm really glad you were."

I started to tell her that I was, too, but my words were cut off by a rumbling growl at my back.

Without thinking, I pulled Autumn behind me and turned to face the noise. The growling had erupted into a full-fledged roar coming from the wide-open mouth of a very angry black bear.

ELEVEN

"Get back!" cried Autumn, pushing me aside while she fumbled for her gun. The bear towered over both of us on hind legs, lips vibrating in the midst of its thundering outcry. It seemed to shout, "OUT!" and I wondered at this strange dichotomy—a civilization in the wild; human beings attempting to live in an animal habitat.

The bear landed on all fours just as Autumn cocked her gun. It was a .357 with a black barrel, just like the ones used in my favorite old westerns—movies like *Unforgiven* and *3:10 to Yuma*. I'd always loved the gritty suspense, but this was a lot different than a movie. I could taste death on my tongue. For the first time in my life, it frightened me.

She fired a bullet through its shoulder. Stunned, it sat back on its haunches. One bullet was not enough. Autumn knew this, and she was already pulling the hammer back, but it wouldn't go. The bear stood, angrier than ever, as Autumn struggled with the jammed gun. It roared again, spittle flying from its teeth, claws pointing like black daggers.

My mind quieted. Thoughts were useless at this point. The brute force of nature was on full display, and the only chance of survival was action. I reached into my pocket and grabbed one of the sharp sticks that Jesse had always insisted I carry with me for self defense.

My fist flew hard against the bear's chest, sinking the stick into fur and flesh. This was not virtual reality—this was *real*. Brutally real. And so was the searing pain as the bear bit down on my shoulder.

The world became a cacophony of sounds. My screaming, high-pitched and primal. The bear's growling, deep and guttural. The scraping of our feet on the ground and the shuffling of our bodies against each other. And then a gunshot, sharp and final.

The bear collapsed.

Panting, I looked up to find Emer standing five yards away, pistol in hand. Her eyes were dark and unreadable.

"Thank you," Autumn gasped, rushing to my side. "My gun… I couldn't…"

"Better get him to Medical," said Emer. She holstered her gun and walked away.

It's not your time yet, said the old, familiar voice in my head. *We still need you.*

Autumn pulled off her sweatshirt. "We have to get that off of you," she said hurriedly, pointing to my t-shirt. I was shocked to find it soaked in blood.

I couldn't lift my arm without searing pain, but she found a way to peel the shirt over my head and roll it down my arm. "Is she always so secluded?" I asked, watching Emer get swallowed up by the shadows.

"Yes."

I shot Autumn a sideways glance. "You don't like her."

She looked at my shoulder and winced. "We have to stop this bleeding," she murmured. "I just can't let it get infected." She turned her sweater inside out and pressed it into my shoulder. I gritted my teeth as pain shot down my arm.

"You didn't answer me," I said.

She sighed. "We can talk on the way. She's right, I have to get you to Medical."

I hobbled alongside her, holding her sweater to my wound. I could feel the blood throbbing in my shoulder, hammering against the cloth as we jogged.

"I tended to her during her withdrawal," Autumn began. "She had rescued my brother from drowning, and for that, I would have done anything. I was also overwhelmingly curious, because she was from the city. I had so many questions. I waited eagerly for her to get through it." She looked over at me. "People say a lot when they're going through withdrawals. Most of it makes no sense at all. But her sleep-talking was more than delusional mumbo-jumbo. It was dark, vicious and full of hate."

"What did she say?"

"She talked to her father a lot, as if he were in the room. Although she called him 'dad' once in a while, it was mostly 'Dr. Makoyiwa.' She talked about us, comparing us to rats, hiding in the dark and living off the earth in secret. She called us *earth parasites*."

I frowned. "Parasites?" I had heard that term before.

"She said we take but do not give back. We use earth's valuable resources—food, water, air—and do nothing in return. And we hide like cowards while the rest of the world suffers."

As much as I disliked Emer, it sounded very far-fetched. I remembered the conversation by the cliffs, when I first arrived. She seemed to want nothing but to protect these people and this place.

"Maybe it was just the drugs talking," I said. I remembered the voices in my head. *An arm and a leg.*

"Perhaps." She sounded unconvinced. "I thought so at first, too. She's so quiet, and kind of shy. I felt sorry for her. I tried talking to her, making her feel at home. I asked her about the city. She didn't ever seem to want to talk." She sighed. "But I watched her. I saw the way she looked at us. Even Jesse. I've learned never to discredit what I know." She looked at me soberly. "She's disgusted by us."

The throbbing in my arm had increased. I began to shiver uncontrollably. My body was going into shock. I needed to keep Autumn talking to keep my mind off of it. We were still a long way from the other side of the cavern.

"Why would she save my life, then?" I asked. "And Jesse's? Why would she even be here?"

Autumn shrugged. "I've been trying to figure that out. It's been three years since she came here, and she's been nothing but helpful. She works in the fields, she works in the shop, she keeps her head down and does her work. But I've learned to trust my instinct—it's never been wrong. And my instinct tells me there's more to her than meets the eye."

My fingers were numb. I glanced down at Autumn's sweater, which I had been holding against the wounded shoulder, and realized it was soaked in blood. My heart sank to my stomach. Is this it? I wondered. Is this how my life ends? Just when it was getting good?

"Oliver." Autumn's voice was soft and distant. "Stay with me. Oliver."

I slid to my knees, but someone caught me from behind, holding me up by my armpits. A cloud of voices surrounded me, their words unrecognizable. I felt so tired all of a sudden. Two people hoisted me up and carried me somewhere. I fell in and out of consciousness, then deep into sleep. When I came to, I lay on a table, wet with sweat. A dark-haired man leaned over me, examining my shoulder.

"It's on fire, Doc," I said. "My whole body hurts."

"It's infected," he replied. "I've cleaned and dressed the wound multiple times, but it's been two days and you're feverish now. You're going to need antibiotics."

"Okay, I'll take whatever you give me."

He looked up at me with somber eyes. "We don't have those down here."

Once again, my heart sank. "Oh."

So I *was* going to die. I had never cared until now. I wondered what would happen to me. Would I turn into dust, like my body? Or would I get to hang around, like Cecil's cave ghost, Agnes? I'd rather do that than go to heaven, if there was one. There was no Autumn in heaven.

"I'm taking him to Bill's farm." She was there, on the other side of me. I turned my head to find her standing against the wall, her arms crossed, staring at me with a furrowed brow.

"You can't," said Tom, who leaned against the door casing in the same stance as his daughter. "It isn't safe."

Autumn set her jaw stubbornly. "I don't care. Bill knows how to make penicillin."

Tom stood straighter. "No, *I* don't care. You are not going out there until we figure this out. Three of our sentries have been murdered, for God's sake!"

"So what, you're just going to let him die?"

The silence was thick. Even the doctor seemed to stop breathing. I knew what was going through Tom's head, because I was in the same quandary. Protect Autumn at all costs, or let her save my life? Could one even say no to her, when she had that stubborn look in her eye?

Tom's face sank. "Of course not," he said.

Autumn's shoulders softened.

"Your brothers will go with you," he ordered. "I can't leave the caves in this state. We have to figure out what is killing our sentries."

"Bill may know something," she said. "I will ask him."

Tom nodded. He had that tired look about him again. His eyes drooped and he seemed so heavy, so inexplicably burdened. I began to worry about leaving him here.

"Maybe it's a bad idea," I said. The caves had become such a cocoon, I could hardly bear the thought of leaving. The outside world was cold and lifeless compared to the joy that this place had given me these past few months. "Maybe it's not worth it."

Tom patted my foot and smiled. "Life is always worth it," he said. "Even when it's hard." He looked at Autumn, then back at me. "Just like love."

*

In order to make the three-day journey to Bill's farm, I had to be strapped down on a gurney made from canvas cloth stretched between two wooden poles. It was much more sophisticated (and comfortable) than the stretcher Autumn had fashioned from branches that day she cut me from the barbed wire. Yet I knew this trip would be a lot more difficult.

"The only downside to feeling everything again," I said, "is pain."

Tom, Margaret and Diana had come to say goodbye. Cecil and Luca were ready to carry the gurney. Autumn had her hair in a ponytail over a well stocked backpack. Even Emer was there, hovering behind everyone, her face quiet and unreadable. The only one missing was Jesse.

"He's mad at me, isn't he?" I guessed. "For leaving without him?"

Margaret nodded softly. "He asked me to give you this, though." She stepped forward and handed me a small notebook and a well-sharpened stick. She tucked both items carefully in the crook of my arm, cradled in my blankets.

I tried to find the energy to smile. "Tell him I say thanks."

"You take care of yourself, now." She patted my leg. "And don't let anything happen to my children." She said it gently, but I knew from her tone that she would follow me into the afterlife if I didn't make good on my promise.

Diana grabbed my hand in a spurt of desperation. "That play was the most fun I've ever had," she said. Her gray eyes brimmed with tears. "Please come back so we can put on another show."

"Get it ready for me," I said. "Pick one you like. Start making the costumes. We can start practicing lines as soon as I get back."

She nodded quietly and released my hand. Cecil and Luca grabbed hold of the gurney and lifted it in unison. Autumn adjusted her backpack. I lay my head back, shutting my eyes in shame as I realized what a burden I was to these people. I was grateful, of course. But what had I ever done to deserve their help?

TWELVE

We arrived three days later, at nightfall. I was delirious with fever, but I caught snippets of things as I fell in and out of consciousness. The smell of hay. Cold, winter air. A large, metal star against a wood wall. A bitter liquid coaxed down my throat.

"Guess he's someone important, if you made that journey on your own in these conditions," said a deep voice I didn't recognize.

"He is important to me," Autumn replied.

A blanket was placed over my shoulders. *I've never been important to anyone*, I thought, before drifting into a deep sleep.

When I woke up, the sun was seeping through brown curtains, bringing a warm glow to the room I lay in. A rich, savory smell touched my nose—something I didn't recognize, although my body seemed to. My mouth watered.

"Well, well, well. Look who finished his beauty sleep."

I turned my head to find Cecil reclining in a wooden chair he had tipped back against the wall. He grinned at me. "Longest beauty sleep ever."

The bedroom door crashed open. Cecil's chair clattered to the floor and he went with it. Autumn rushed into the room, her boots clomping loudly on the wood floors. "How do you feel?" she demanded, putting her hand on my forehead.

I grabbed her wrist and pulled her towards me. Her lips smiled under my kiss.

"I take it he's feeling just fine!" Cecil bellowed. He righted his chair and rubbed his hip unhappily.

An unfamiliar figure appeared in the doorway. "What's all this ruckus?" She was an older woman, her skin creased like old leather, her silver hair tied up in a bun. She was wiping her hands on her apron. "Oh, look!" She said to me. "You've gotten some color back in your cheeks."

"Guess the penicillin did the trick." The man with the deep voice slipped his arm around her waist and stood behind her, smiling at me from the doorway. I gathered that this was Bill. He had the same leathery skin, with lines that were so deep, they didn't change even when his expression did. "You had quite the infection," he said. "I thought we were gonna have to take the arm."

His wife clucked her tongue at him and came over to the bedside. "You're going to be just fine," she assured me, pulling back the bandages to check on the wound. "It's just a little redness around the edges, is all. I'll put some more salve on there and you'll be healed up in a few days." She hurried away.

Bill entered the room, and it was the first time I had been able to get a good look at him. He was so tall he had to stoop under the doorway. Although the weathering on his face gave away his old age, his demeanor did not. Wide-shouldered and bow-legged, he walked with a swagger reserved only for those who had lived so much life, they had nothing left to fear — not even death itself. His poise coupled with the dirty jeans, leather belt and thick, gray beard made me certain of one indisputable fact. This man was a cowboy.

"Now, just what were you doing that close to a bear, kid?" Bill pulled a wooden chair from the corner of the room and flipped it around to sit on it backwards. "Don't you know to stay away from them predators?"

"We didn't know it was there until it was too late."

"Where was your weapon?"

"My gun jammed," Autumn interjected.

"What about yours?" He looked at me steadily. "Don't you have a gun?"

"Oh. I can't have anything like that."

His eyebrows shrank over his eyes and he blew air forcefully through his teeth. "Why in the devil not?"

I fidgeted with the blanket. "I don't know how to use one," I mumbled. *I'd probably end up killing someone,* I thought.

Bill turned to Autumn. "Fresh from the city, I gather."

"He's been with us for about five months."

"A man can't survive out here without a way to protect himself," he said to me. "We'll teach you how to use one when you're all healed up."

I was struck by the image of my hands around Emer's neck. Could I really trust myself with a gun?

But he was right. A sharp stick had been useless against the colossal strength of a bear. If Emer hadn't been there... I shuddered at the thought of what might have happened.

"It wasn't the first wild animal in the caves, either," said Autumn. "Three of our sentries have been killed."

"Killed!" The old woman had come back with a tray in her hands. She set it down on the dresser and brought the plate over to my lap. Eggs, bacon, sausage and a pile of toast. A cup of coffee on the nightstand. "Did you hear that, Bill?"

He nodded soberly. "I heard it, Donna."

"How did they die?"

"Edgar was choked to death. The others had fatal blows to the back of their heads." Autumn leaned forward. "We were wondering if you've seen anything suspicious."

Bill and Donna looked at each other with concerned frowns. They shook their heads. "Nothing much has changed 'round here," Bill said. "Just the three of us and the wildlife."

"Three of you?" I asked with a mouth full of bacon.

They smiled affectionately. "Our daughter, Julia. She just turned seventeen."

Cecil stood at the window. "Why do you think we haven't seen Luca all morning?"

I followed his gaze across the pasture to a small, rust-colored barn tucked under a stand of pine trees. A small figure stood next to a brown horse, her hand wound casually around the reins, and Luca stood next to her with his hand on the horse's belly.

"There's been talk of an uprising in the cities," said Donna. "One of the scavengers from the Crystal Falls cave stopped by to drop off a few supplies, and he told us his cousin from City Five was involved in a small rebellion. Some of the Forgotten breached the security systems and made their way into some of the buildings. Those people are severely underestimated."

"Starvation will drive any man to desperate measures," said Bill.

"Hacking into the federal security system is not an act of desperation. It's calculated."

He raised his eyebrows at his wife. "That's true."

"Do you think that has anything to do with the murders?" Cecil asked, still looking out the window. The girl had mounted her horse, and Luca was leading a pinto out of the barn. Cecil rubbed his chin thoughtfully.

"I'm sure the cities are barricaded," said Donna. "Anyway, hardly anyone comes around here anymore." She smiled. "Heavens, we're more forgotten than the Forgotten."

Autumn sighed. "So our worst fears are true, then." She stood, looking out the window with Cecil. "The murderer is someone from within the caves. He's one of us."

I shivered. All this talk of murder made me feel sick. I pushed my food away and lay my head back.

"You need your rest," said Donna, gathering the dishes and picking up the tray. "Everyone out. Come on. Leave him be."

Autumn came over to kiss me on the forehead and I grabbed her hand. "Stay with me," I begged.

"Absolutely not," clucked Donna. "No distractions." She ushered Autumn out the door and wagged her finger at me. "To sleep, now, you hear?" The door clicked behind them, and suddenly I was alone.

"I'm not tired," I mumbled. I looked around the room. My sneakers, ragged and black with cave dust, sat next to the door. My clothes had been neatly folded and placed on the dresser. Next to them lay a sharp stick and a small notebook. Jesse's notebook.

I pulled the covers back and stepped out of bed, wincing at a deep pain in my shoulder. Tiptoeing across the room so I wouldn't be heard, I grabbed the book and got back under the covers. Page one contained a message from Jesse.

"*Dear City Man,*

"*Dad says that when the Bad Men changed our world, they rewrote our history. So it's our duty to write our own stories for the people in the future who might need to know the truth. Dad says that history is made up of real stories belonging to real people. Since you're a real person, you need to write your story.*"

I flipped through the rest of the book, which was blank. The smell of leather filled the room. A small pencil was tucked in between the pages, so I pulled it out and began to write.

"*Dear Jesse,*

"*We are at the cabin now. Bill and Donna are nice. The medicine helped a lot. I'm healing.*"

I put the pencil between my teeth for a minute, thinking. Jesse would want to hear more of the details.

"*Bill reminds me of a character out of an old western movie. Do you know how old he is? I'm afraid to ask. I didn't know people lived that long out here, away from the city. Maybe the air and the water aren't so dirty, after all.*

"*Luca has a girlfriend. Julia. I don't know how he can stay away from her for so long. Maybe that's why he's so angry all the time. I haven't met her yet, but I wonder if she's as serious as he is about everything.*

"*I don't understand how this farm supplies our cave with so much food. Do the other caves have farmers who support them, too? How can three people get so much work done? And why would they work so hard just to give all their food away?*

"It feels good to see the sun again."

It was the most I had ever written at one time. My eyes drooped. It seemed I was tired after all.

THIRTEEN

After a week in bed, watching snow fall outside, counting knots in the pine boards on the ceiling and listening to the bubble of laughter outside my door, I no longer cared about the pain in my shoulder or any remaining infection. I knew I would go mad if I didn't get up.

Donna helped me dress. Autumn fashioned a sling out of an old towel, and we placed my arm in it as if it were a loaf of bread. Donna explained that my nerves had been severed, which is why it had so little sensation. I stared at the ceiling in humiliation while Autumn tied my shoes.

"Have patience," she said softly, seeing my frustration. "'What wound did ever heal but by degrees?'"

"That sounds like that writer you told me about," Donna said while helping me don my jacket. "I tried reading the play you brought me, but I didn't understand hardly a word. Why does he talk so strange?"

"It's from the Old Time," Autumn explained. "Sure, the language takes some getting used to, but stories were told with such grace. Even tragedies never left you feeling empty." She sighed wistfully. "I've never met Shakespeare, but doesn't it strike you with awe that we can read the words of a man who has been dead more than eight hundred years? Wouldn't we all love to be so immortal?"

I looked at her in wonder.

She finished tying my shoes and we both stood. "Oliver knows how important stories are," she said, smiling at me. "In one's darkest moments, they remind you of who you are, wouldn't you agree? Stories give you back pieces of yourself."

I remembered all the times I had spent watching movies in my room. They were simpler than the sims—some might say primitive. They didn't have the same "immersive experience." But to me, the stories were a reminder of an earlier time and place, when people had adventures and fought for loyalty and fell in love. They satisfied a craving for a world in which I would much rather live than my four-walled prison in the city.

"I think you're right," I said. "Stories are a reflection of one's soul."

"You coming?" Cecil barged in the front door, his hair sticking out like straw under a brown felt hat. "Luca's got your horse ready."

"Horse?" Donna and Autumn said in unison.

Bill appeared on the porch behind Cecil.

"Don't you dare put him on a horse, Bill. He's never ridden before. And he's injured!" Donna put her hand on my elbow as if she intended to wrestle me from their greedy fingers.

To be honest, it sounded a lot more fun than lying in bed all week. But Bill grinned and rolled his eyes. "He's only kidding. We're putting him on fences. He can paint them one-handed."

Cecil ducked out sheepishly before Autumn could swat him. "Wishful thinking!" he called. I followed Bill outside. The air smelled like ice. I pulled my jacket up to my chin and squinted in the sunlight gleaming off the snow.

"Now, these here fences are old. Almost as old as I am. And that's ancient." Bill chuckled as he led me down the hill towards the barn. "We just keep whitewashing them every year, and they keep holding up. I swear they're nailed together with spit and a prayer."

"How long have you lived out here?" I asked.

"Eighty-seven years. I was born on this farm, and this is where I'll die."

Around the side of the barn was a man-door with a metal star above the lintel. "This here's the tack room," said Bill, leading me inside. It was small, warm and smelled like leather. Halters and saddles lined the walls. Blankets hung over bales of hay. An enormous, wood table took up much of the space. The room was full of equipment and the floor was covered in dirt and straw, but it was as neat and tidy as Tom's print shop.

"Grab me that bucket, son." Bill pulled a jar of white powder off one of the shelves and placed it on the table. "We use lime on all our fences," he explained, measuring powder into the pail I brought him. "It keeps the wood from rotting. That's why they've stayed good so long."

"So if you've lived here all your life, and you're eighty-seven, then you were born in 1998. You lived through the Great Change."

He lifted the bucket into a plastic mop sink tucked in the corner of the room. "I didn't pay mind to what they called it, but yeah, I remember it." He turned on the tap. "My mama used to take me to town for supplies, and to visit the library. That all disappeared when they moved everyone to the cities."

"How did you avoid going with them?"

"Well, they tried. They sent a few soldiers out here. Scared the neighbors pretty good with stories about sickness in the air and the water. They damn near sprinted to those trucks." He sighed. "But like I said, I was born on this farm, and this is where I'm gonna die. Whether it's a virus, a bullet, or old age—my last living steps gonna be on this soil."

The pail was full. He pulled it out of the sink and we went outside to the fence behind the barn. "Stir it first," he said, handing me a stick and a paintbrush. "Try to get the north fence done before lunch." Then he was gone, striding up over the hill with his bowed legs silhouetted against the snow.

I shifted the sling and leaned over the bucket, using the stick to stir with my one good arm. The snow crunched under my feet as I moved. The air was crisp and still as I dipped the paintbrush in the white liquid and began spreading it on the fence. As I worked, I imagined what I would write to Jamie in my notebook later that night.

It's a lot quieter up here, believe it or not. Even though the air is different from the caves and it carries the sound of the birds, there's so much space I don't know how to take it all in. I don't think I've ever seen such vastness in my life.

The fence carried on over the hill, so I followed it with my paintbrush and bucket, feeling awkward as I tried to do everything one-handed. Dip, paint, carry, hobble. Dip, paint, carry, hobble. I continued this sequence over the crest of the hill, stopped to wipe the sweat off my forehead, and froze. Acres of white fields stretched across the valley with an expanse that made me dizzy. The land rolled, as if someone had shaken an enormous blanket under the earth and left it that way. Herds of hump-backed animals roamed the valley, their auburn coats a stark contrast against the snow-covered ground. It was more majestic than anything I had ever seen in the movies.

Suddenly something warm touched the back of my neck.

With a cry of surprise, I jumped and fell sideways into the fence. My accoster snorted. I looked up into the soft, brown muzzle of a horse.

"Oh, man." I laughed and stood. "You can't creep up behind me like that."

The creature nudged me again, and her strength surprised me. Movies and sims had not prepared me for the massive size of this animal.

"What do you want?" I asked.

She lowered her nose to my height and held it in front of me. A long, white star stretched from her nostrils to the space between her ears. Without thinking, I reached up to touch it. She didn't move.

"You're such a good girl," I murmured.

A set of footsteps thudded softly behind her. She swished her tail. I looked up at a girl with white-blond hair sitting comfortably atop a chestnut horse. She was short and stocky, and she wore a fur coat and leather chaps. She glared at me.

I tipped my head as respectfully as I could. "You must be Julia."

She didn't answer. Her horse blinked.

"I'm Oliver," I said. "Your dad asked me to whitewash these fences. This horse came out of nowhere. Do you know her name?"

The girl just stared at me, saying nothing. Her horse shifted his stance.

What was her problem?

A second set of hooves crunched across the snow behind her. Luca sat casually in the saddle of a brown-and-white spotted horse, his arms crossed over the saddle horn. "She can't hear you," he said. "She's deaf."

I looked at her in surprise. "I'm sorry," I said, hoping she could read my lips.

She rolled her eyes. Apparently she could decipher that.

"How do you talk to her?" I asked.

"Sign language."

"Can you ask her the name of this horse?"

Luca reached over and put his hand on her back. She turned to look at him. Folding his thumbs into his palms and forming various shapes and gestures, he quickly asked the question. She signed something in return.

"Ginger," he told me.

I rubbed the star-shaped patch of white on her nose again. "Can you ask her what the horse wants?"

More signing.

"She says she likes you."

I frowned. "Why?"

Luca chuckled and asked Julia the question. She rolled her eyes again and responded.

"The horse has claimed you," he translated. "Horses need us as much as we need them."

"I don't know anything about horses."

More signing.

"She says you're going to have to learn quick. You're useless around here if you can't ride a horse."

I sighed. I was useless everywhere I went.

"Julia wants to ask you something."

I shrugged. "Go ahead."

This time her signing took a while longer. She leaned over her saddle with more eagerness. Luca nodded in understanding before translating.

"She wants to know if it's true, that city people live inside computers."

I raised my eyebrows. "I guess you could say that."

"She asks how they fit inside them."

It was a perspective I had never considered before, but one I suddenly saw in stark contrast to my life now. Tiny people stuck inside computers, living in miniature universes. That had been my world just five months ago. I never imagined the real world was as big as this.

"The computers are built around them," I explained. "They don't need to go anywhere. Everything is brought to them."

Julia stared at me and signed something slowly.

"A comfortable prison."

I nodded.

Then she turned her horse and rode away, with Luca at her side.

Ginger nuzzled me again. I rubbed her nose thoughtfully, then dipped my brush in the whitewash and got back to work.

FOURTEEN

A blizzard struck the farm that night. The wind shook the walls and whistled through the rafters. By morning, snowdrifts had reached the windowsills.

"Seeing as how you'll be here a while, we oughta teach you to handle a horse for real," said Bill at breakfast. He signed with his hands while he spoke, for Julia's sake.

I poured myself a cup of coffee from the pot on the wood stove. "Why are we going to be here a while?"

"Why, you're snowed in, son. Winter won't let you leave now."

Autumn passed me the molasses I liked in my coffee. "The roads are too dangerous to travel now," she explained. "The snow is going to keep coming. We won't be journeying back until winter's over."

I looked out the window at the whitewashed world. Evergreens stood strong under a heavy dusting of snow. Those bearded, humpbacked animals grazed contentedly, somehow finding food in a frozen pasture. A few remaining storm clouds clung to the mountain as an actor would linger after a show. This was nature as I had never experienced it—raw, rugged and dramatic. It was exhilarating.

"Fine by me," I said. "Can I use Ginger?"

Bill raised an eyebrow. "You've been making friends, I see."

I glanced across the table at Julia, who was eating scrambled eggs and studying me.

Donna brought more pancakes to the table and set the plate down sharply. "I thought I told you not to put him on a horse."

"He can start with groundwork. It's a good way to bond with her, anyway. His arm should be healed up by the time he's ready to ride."

Before she could respond, there was a loud crash from the front porch. Bill was on his feet in an instant, crossing the room in five strides to grab the shotgun leaning up against the doorframe. Chairs scraped back and Luca, Cecil, Autumn, Julia and Donna all stood in doorways and behind furniture with their pistols cocked and ready. I stood against the wall near the stove.

Several minutes passed. Bill eased an eyeball around the window casing and peered behind the curtain. "There's a girl lying on the front porch," he whispered. "I can't tell if she's living or dead. Or playing possum."

We waited several more minutes, hearing nothing but the sound of our breathing. Finally Bill called out, "Who's there?"

There was no response.

"You're trespassing on private land," he said. "Best be on your way, or you'll be shot."

There was a sound of stirring, and then a feeble voice cried, "Help."

Bill looked across the room at Donna. She nodded as if she had read his mind. While he unlocked the door, she crossed the room with the pistol pointed at the floor, her finger next to the trigger. She covered him while he stepped onto the front porch.

When he came back inside, his pace was more urgent. "It's hypothermia," he said. "We need to get her to the barn." He uncocked the shotgun and leaned it in the corner of the room. "Boys, help me get her there."

Luca and Cecil uncocked their pistols and pocketed them. They knew not to question Bill. They followed him out onto the porch while Donna ordered the girls to work gathering cloths, warm water and blankets.

I stared out the window at the body being carried across the yard.

"They might need your help, Oliver." Autumn motioned from the kitchen sink, where she was filling the kettle. "You should go with them."

"Where do you think she came from?" I asked suspiciously. "Have they ever had someone just show up on their front porch like that?"

"I don't think so. It's pretty solitary out here."

"What if she's from the city?" I whispered the last part, resisting the sound of the word. *City.* It had been such a distant memory. Like a bad movie.

She shrugged. "You were from the city. I helped you."

I nodded pensively. "True." Something about it still didn't sit right, though. I threw my jacket on and headed outside toward the barn, trudging through the path everyone's footsteps had made in the knee-high snow.

Bill was covering a couple of hay bales with a horse blanket. Cecil and Luca lay the stranger on top and started removing her jacket, which was thin and wet. Her teeth began to chatter loudly.

"Add some more firewood to the stove, Oliver." Bill's voice was low and steady.

An old cast-iron wood stove crouched in the corner of the barn, probably installed ages ago to keep the animals warm during winters such as this. The door opened with a loud creak and I put two more logs in. The stranger's teeth were still clattering like a typewriter behind me.

"How's she doing?" Donna entered the barn holding a basket of towels and the teakettle. Autumn and Julia followed her, their arms loaded with blankets.

"She's stirring a bit," said Bill. "Might break her teeth, though."

"That's an improvement." She pulled some cloth from her basket. "Put this in her mouth. I'll get the towels warmed up." Wincing, she looked over at the girl on the hay bale. "First order of business when she wakes up will be a *bath*."

We all nodded in agreement. The stench was horrific. Like onions, sewage and dirt all mixed together.

The women set to work on the fine details, warming towels on the stove and heating a brick to put at the girl's feet. Autumn piled on more blankets, laying them on thick and heavy so that all we could see was her pale, unconscious face sticking out of the top. If it weren't for the chattering teeth, I would've sworn she was dead.

"Where did she come from, though?" I questioned. "I thought you said no one ever comes out here."

Donna was pouring hot water into a cup. "We don't know, sweetheart. We'll have to ask her when she wakes up."

"But what if she's dangerous?"

She gave me a sideways glance. "That's why we brought her out to the barn."

Cecil slung his arm over my shoulders. His coat smelled like dirt and wet hay. "Come help me feed the horses," he said. "This is gonna be a while."

I followed him to the other side of the barn, where the stalls were not empty. Soft muzzles reached over the stall doors, nostrils pulsing. Small, wooden signs hung on nails over each stall, labeling the name of each resident. George. Sandy. Honda. Chloe. Ginger.

"Hey, girl," I said, approaching the stall to visit my old friend. The white star on her nose nodded up and down. "Why is she moving like that?" I asked Cecil.

"She's excited to see you." He pulled a bale of hay down off a stack and cut the twine that held it together. "Give her some of this."

I pulled a few fistfuls out of the bale and brought it over to her. She grabbed it with her lips and began eating, the crunching sound strangely satisfying.

"Bill would never put us in danger," said Cecil. He opened a cabinet against the wall and pulled out a jar labeled *Grain*. "You know that, right?"

I shrugged. "If you say so."

He poured the grain into a metal pail that hung on the wall. "I don't know how you do things in the city," he said, "but out here, we don't leave people to freeze out in the cold. Whether strangers or friends, we help those in need."

"Even if they kill you?"

Cecil raised an eyebrow at me. I remembered my first day with them in the forest, when I snapped and knocked the wind out of Jesse. I shuddered. I was one to talk.

"You have to put into the world the things you want back." He opened the stall door and put the bucket of grain inside. "Like a tree. It puts out oxygen so it can take it back as carbon dioxide. Or this grain, which feeds the horse, which in turn feeds the land, so that grain will grow again. We put out pieces of ourselves because someday, they come back to us better than they were before. That's how kindness works." He latched the door again. "If you ever hope to have a stranger save your life when you need it, then you have to be willing to risk everything to do that for someone else."

It was the most profound thing I had ever heard Cecil say.

"Anyway, aren't you curious?" He grinned. "I want to know who she is and where she came from. Maybe she'll bring news from the city."

I sighed. That's what I was afraid of.

*

It took her nearly five hours to wake up. Her teeth stopped chattering in the first hour, and she seemed to relax somewhat, but her face was a sheet of white oblivion. We took turns watching her in pairs—Autumn and I for the first hour and a half, Julia and Luca for the next, Cecil and Donna after that. Autumn and I were out feeding the pigs when Cecil called us back to the barn.

The girl was sitting up with a mound of blankets on her shoulders.

"Drink up, now." Donna was helping her hold a mug of steaming liquid. "We've got to warm your insides."

Her hands trembled but she took several gulps. She looked over at us as we entered the barn, her eyes a shocking shade of blue under raven-colored hair. Her cheekbones were sharp and her skin rubbed red by the wind, but she had a quiet expression and a steady gaze.

"Thank you," she said as she handed the cup back to Donna. "I thought I was a goner for sure."

"What are you doing out here?" Cecil asked. "Where did you come from?"

"I'm from the Fifth City. All hell's breaking loose. I'm one to pass a good time, all right, but I ain't no match for a Reeve. I been on the street all my life and I don't know nothing about computers."

We all exchanged confused looks. She must have had a stroke.

"Now, slow down, sweetheart." Donna put her hand on the girl's arm soothingly. "We don't know what you're talking about. What's happening in the city?"

She didn't answer. Instead, she looked curiously at each one of us, studying us as if we were animals at a zoo. "You all are not what I expected."

So she had been sent for us. She knew who we were.

The rest of the group tensed, too.

"How do you know us?" Autumn asked gravely.

"It's just a street legend," she explained, "that folks still live out here on their own. We thought most of you all had died. I thought I might get shot by the ones who are left. But it's gotten so bitter, I can't live on the street no more. Food stamps stopped working. Ain't no more doctors that will see us. Our tents don't even keep the rain out no more. My little sister caught pneumonia and died last week. She was the last of my family living." Her voice caught in her throat. "It's bitter. Real bitter."

"What are Reeves?" Cecil asked.

She frowned. "They're police. Soldiers, really. They work for the men who live at the tops of those buildings."

"Oh," I cried out in realization. "My mom called mine Mr. Reeve. Do they visit you once in a while, take your blood, follow you around?"

Her eyes widened. "Some of them do, when they want to spy on you. You from the city?"

I nodded. "I'm not one of the Forgotten, though."

"Yeah." Her face fell. "Yeah. That we are. Forgotten."

"Did you get kicked out or something?" Cecil was clearly burning with curiosity. "Why did you come all the way out here? We're five hundred miles from the nearest city."

"Like I said, I couldn't stay there. It's a hot mess. Even my fam joined the rebellion—the smart ones, anyway—hacking into the system and shutting whole buildings down. They only go down for a few minutes before the Reeves get everything online again, but it's enough to boil their blood. I don't know nothing about computers. I'm useless to them. And plus, I don't want no trouble. They killed my parents. Like I mentioned, my sister died of sickness. I decided to survive. I just been trying to find food."

I wondered how much of her story was true. She did look pretty scrawny, with narrow shoulders and a skinny neck. But Donna had said that the cities were barricaded. Could she really have walked five hundred miles in a blizzard? How did she know to make her way out here, to us? Was she really that lucky?

"I'll go make some lunch," said Donna, patting the girl's arm as she stood. "What's your name, sweetheart?"

"Lizabeth."

"Elizabeth?"

She shook her head. "Lizabeth."

Donna and Autumn trudged up the hill towards the house, the open door of the barn framing their slim figures as snowflakes fell softly on a head of silver and a head of fire. Cecil made himself comfortable on a wooden chair against the wall, clearly settled on being the caretaker—or warden, depending on how you looked at it. I preferred the latter.

Julia signed something to Luca, who turned to me. "We need to exercise the horses," he said.

I glanced down at my useless arm, dangling in its sling. Then I heard Ginger whinny from her stall, as if sensing my uncertainty and wanting to kick me for it. I put my head down and followed the two of them out of the barn.

On the other side of the building from the tack room was a large paddock covered in untouched snow. It was empty except for a large, round water trough in the corner. It had been built up against the side of the barn, where there was a row of closed doors. Julia climbed over the fence, pulled a rope halter from a hook on the wall, and went in the first door. When she came out, she was leading Ginger.

Luca opened the gate and Julia motioned with her chin. I entered the paddock and stood awkwardly against the fence, waiting for instructions. Julia beckoned to me again, and that's when I realized this was going to be a silent lesson. I walked cautiously across the ring and stood next to Ginger.

Julia handed me a small bag of apple slices and pointed at my pocket, which is where I put them. With her hands held out in front of her, she showed me how to hold the lead—one hand clasped close to Ginger's chin, the other holding the slack, wound around in a figure 8. I took the lead, holding it loosely with my bad arm. I hoped the horse couldn't smell my uncertainty.

Julia stood in front of me and pointed at her mouth. I looked down at her, suddenly aware of how short she was. She made a clucking noise with her tongue. Then she pointed at me. I had seen cowboys make that sound in movies—it seemed to mean, "Go." I nodded, telling her I understood. She stepped aside and swept her arm forward, urging me to walk.

"Help me out, girl," I murmured to Ginger. Clucking my tongue the way Julia had shown me, I began to march forward through the snow—but she did not move. Instead, I felt something nuzzling my side. I looked down to find her nose in my pocket, rummaging through the bag of apple slices.

"Hey!" I exclaimed, dropping the rope. The bag fell to the ground and I made a lunge for it. Startled, Ginger pranced backwards, her front hooves coming down inches from my fingers in the snow.

Someone grabbed me by the collar, yanking me away. I landed on my butt and looked up at Julia, who stood over me with her hands on her hips. Her eyes shot daggers.

"Do you have any idea how heavy that animal is?" Luca stood next to her, translating her furious sign language. "Do you want to lose your other hand? What were you thinking?"

My heart pounding, I looked over at Ginger. She stood against the fence, her ears swiveling and nostrils flaring. "I'm sorry," I said, chagrined. "I really messed things up, didn't I?" I shook my head in disgust. "Why do I always mess everything up?"

Julia seemed to soften. Her signing became less intense. "Horses are prey animals," Luca translated. "They rely on you to tell them everything is safe. When you act strange, they get spooked."

I nodded, understanding. "I'm sorry," I said again.

"Don't tell me that. Tell her."

I stood and crossed the paddock to stand next to Ginger. She turned her face away and became very still. She was ignoring me. It reminded me of Autumn when she was angry.

Girls, I thought. *They sure do know how to make a guy suffer.*

It was as if she heard me. Her head came around and she showed me both her eyes.

"I'm sorry, girl," I murmured as I rubbed her neck. "I have a lot of learning to do."

And suddenly, all was forgiven. It was that easy. She nuzzled me and we got back to work. Julia taught me to use the apples as a reward. I got good at walking her, learning to keep my eyes forward and guide her with direction. Then I loosened the lead and she walked around me in a circle, eventually working up to a trot. After about twenty minutes of exercise, it was time to put her back in the stall.

Julia was smiling at me when I came out. I grinned back at her. "Thanks for the lesson," I said. "Sorry about the rough start."

She approached me and put her hands over my heart. "Horse whisperer," she said aloud, her speech slurred. "Natural."

I looked over at Luca in shock. He seemed just as surprised as I. It was the first time I had ever heard her speak.

"Am I?" I asked, dumbfounded.

But she had already turned and left the paddock.

FIFTEEN

Three weeks went by. My arm began to heal, and I was able to remove the sling. Bill taught me some exercises—holding a hammer out to the side, straight in front, and up over my head, the goal being to touch it to my nose without dropping it. I could only use a lightweight hammer, and I could barely lift it above my shoulder, but it gave me something proactive to do and it did seem to be helping. I was able to ride Ginger carefully, with my left arm held tightly to my side. I rode her as often as I could.

Lizbeth was healing, too, although she was still unnaturally skinny and pale. She still lived in the barn, but she came in the house for meals now. She seemed harmless enough. In fact, she seemed incredibly naive. Her favorite word was, "Wow."

"Wow, your house is so warm!"

"Wow, is that a real, live chicken?"

"Are you going to throw that crust away? Wow! I can save it for later."

Wherever she went, Cecil went, too. He was full of questions about her, her family, and her life on the streets of the Fifth City. I listened quietly to her stories, fascinated by the life she described—a life very different from what I had read on the Internet.

We had been taught that the Forgotten were crazy. They had been released from overflowing mental hospitals. They were so unhinged that they couldn't live inside any building, because of claustrophobia. They could not be trusted with tools or weapons, because they might become violent. They were mentally inferior. And the worst crime of all was that they carried disease.

On social, we made fun of them. In history class, we were taught that they were more like animals than humans. My mom looked at them with disgust whenever we had to drive past one of them. "We need to clean up these streets," she'd say.

Lizabeth was a terrible representation of this. She was illiterate, perhaps, and malnourished, but I grew to realize that she was not violent or malicious at all. She was kind and innocent and slightly child-like in her desire to participate and help around the farm. She was also unexpectedly observant.

One day she approached me while I was shoveling stalls. She lolled outside one of the stalls, barefoot in spite of the cold, overalls rolled up to her calves. She liked to feel the earth, she said.

"You're a city folk," she noted, as if she hadn't already known.

I stopped shoveling and wiped sweat from my forehead. "Just me, yeah."

"Wow, aren't you worried about bringing the bitter upon them out here?"

I leaned on my pitchfork and narrowed my eyes at her. "What do you mean?"

"The Reeves are always watching," she said. "These people are like those horses out there. Someday someone will decide they're too wild and they need to be fenced in. But if they can't be found, they'll always run free." She cocked her head to the side, studying me. "I bet you've given them away already."

"They removed my tracking device when they found me," I explained. "I vomited it up."

"That's no guarantee," she said. "Not trying to throw dirt at you, it's just a fact. The Reeves won't stop until they control everyone. It's their game."

"No one cares about this place. Donna said that this area is more forgotten than The Forgotten."

She shrugged. "Possibly. Until you came along." Then she spun on her heel and left.

I speared the hay with more ferocity. What did she know? As if she had some insight into those government Reeves. She was a nobody. Just a street urchin. I scraped and scrubbed the stall until my back ached and sweat dripped from my forehead. Why did she have to bring something like that up?

A memory wedged itself into my mind. Age six. I sat in an office of leather—leather chairs, leather couch, even the desk and the bookshelves were lined with leather. Everything else was polished mahogany. If not for the tall windows behind the desk, it would have been a very dark office, indeed.

"How are you feeling, Oliver?" Dr. Makoyiwa sat behind the desk, his hands touching in the shape of a steeple in front of his chin. His face was oily, especially on the bridge of his nose and the middle of his forehead, making his skin look like leftover bacon grease.

"Fine." I swung my legs in the air under my chair, bumping them against the chair leg once in a while.

"Tell me more about 'fine.' Are you still having those dreams you were telling me about?"

I shrugged. "Sometimes."

"Do you still have thoughts of hurting your teachers?"

I stopped swinging my legs and frowned. "I never wanted to hurt my teachers."

The doctor opened the computer on his desk and studied it. "In our last session, you said you dreamed that you were hitting Ms. Sinclair over the head with a chair."

"I didn't *want* to do that. It was a scary dream I had."

He had a long, thin nose that seemed regularly itchy, because he was constantly rubbing the end of it with his bony fingers. He reminded me of a skeleton, with his sharp cheekbones, protruding skull, and glistening skin. I wished I didn't have to visit him so often.

"Dreams are a window into the soul," he said pedantically. "Although they may seem meaningless, they tell us a great deal about what's really going on in that little head of yours." He began typing.

I crossed my arms and tightened my lips into a thin line, as I usually did when I was angry.

"I'm going to advise a visit from my friend, Mr. Reeve. He works with all my most difficult cases. He can come to your house, see how school is going, maybe help you with homework." He folded his arms over each other, the long fingers encircling his elbows, and looked across the desk at me. His eyes were black. "I'm concerned for your well-being, Oliver. I don't want you to do something you regret. I've seen many cases like yours, and they always end in tragedy. I want you to live a long, healthy life, and not hurt those around you." He went back to typing. "I'm also going to advise additional medication. I'll send the prescription to your mom."

Mr. Reeve showed up a week later, if I recalled correctly. He was tall, thin and stiff. He moved as if he had been freshly pressed. He had no facial hair, and his clothing was all white, covering his entire body, even his hands. The only skin I could see was his neck, face and head, and it looked ruddy and dry, as if it had been vigorously scrubbed. He brought his own headset and joined me in my sim, but he didn't seem to do much other than sit beside me at school and follow me around everywhere. He spoke only in grunts. I got the feeling that he was mainly there to observe me, and to make sure I took my new medication, which made me feel terribly sick.

The dreams had gotten worse after that. Intense, vivid, sometimes gory dreams. I often woke in a sweat, my heart pounding, uncertain of where I was. If dreams were a window into my soul, then I had a very dark soul, indeed. I never told anyone about my dreams ever again.

Now that I thought about it, I hardly dreamt at all anymore. Ever since I had come to the caves.

"Everything okay?" Autumn's voice was like a pin against a balloon, popping me out of my black cloud.

"Just cleaning this stall." I wiped my brow and looked back at her. "Why?"

She smiled softly, her eyes kind. "That's some intense scrubbing," she said. "Want to take a break?"

I leaned on my broom, studying her. Her hair was auburn in the dim light of the barn. Her eyes were bright and full of life. She was, without a doubt, the most vibrant and beautiful girl in existence. When would I ever stop being a danger to her?

She entered the stall and put her hand on my cheek, her brow furrowed. "Oliver? Are you sure you're okay?"

I shook my head slowly, still holding the broom with two hands, as if it were grounding me. "No," I said. "I am not okay." I could tell I was worrying her, but I didn't care. I was done with the charade. She needed to know who I really was. "I am *tired*, Autumn. Tired of dark memories. Tired of the demon chorus in my head. Tired of blacking out and wondering if everyone around me is going to be okay when I wake up." I closed my eyes in disgust, head still shaking. "You think Ben Charleston is a threat?" I scoffed. "He's a child."

She scowled at me. "Stop talking like that," she snapped. "You and Ben are nothing alike. He uses violence for control."

I stopped shaking my head and stared at her sadly. She would never want to be with me after this. But I couldn't hide any more. She had to know the truth.

"I killed someone," I said. "Emer. I killed Emer."

She cocked her head to the side and shot me a perplexed look.

"Tried to. I mean, I thought I did." I took a breath. "It was on a sim. I killed her on a sim."

Her eyes widened as the meaning of my words sank in. "Why?"

I shrugged hopelessly. "I'm an evil man, Autumn. I am no good for you."

She narrowed her eyes and set her mouth in a hard, thin line. "That is a bold-faced lie," she said sharply. "I know who you are. And you ought to know that, too. You say you have demons?" She threw her hands up in the air. "Join the club!" She snorted in disgust. "When I was six, my doctor convinced my best friend to smash a toy in my face just to see how I would react. How do you think I reacted?"

I stared at her.

"I hit her so hard with my dollhouse furniture that I gave her a black eye." She choked out an angry sob. "My *best friend*, Oliver. I know now that she didn't really mean to hurt me. She was heavily medicated and under hypnosis. But at the time—consumed with rage—attacked and betrayed—I didn't even think. I reacted. And on my way out of the room, I saw them—doctors, students, psychologists—in their pristine, white clothing, standing on the other side of that one-way mirror. They were studying us. Making notes on *clipboards*. Watching two little kids beat each other up!" She wiped tears from her cheeks with an angry swipe of her hands. "To them, humans are animals. Or worse. Objects!"

She took a deep breath, walked over to me, and put her hands on my cheeks. They were soft and cool. "Look, all I'm saying is, stop trying to free fall into your regrets. It may seem easier, but it will eat you alive." She ran her hands down my arms and grabbed my hand. "Come on. Let's go for a ride."

I changed out of my muck boots and pulled on the stiff, leather cowboy boots that Bill had given me. We walked to the end of the barn and brought Ginger and Chloe out of their stalls.

I had ridden Ginger dozens of times since that day I learned to walk her. Once I got the basics down, mounting and riding her was a breeze. A light tap of my foot was all she needed to understand me, and sometimes I didn't even need to do that—she could practically read my mind. There were times when it felt like we were one person.

As soon as we cleared the barn and all the outbuildings, Autumn and I took off at a sprint. The animals had been warmed up earlier, so they went into the gallop with ease. We heard nothing except the wind in our ears and the crunch of hooves in the snow. I felt Ginger's massive strength beneath me, and we watched the world fly by. Autumn laughed. I grinned. It was like flying.

We slowed down to a trot when we reached the other side of the pasture. The mountains crowded above us, sharp and austere in their wild beauty. They threw long shadows across the snow, making it feel like it was nearing dusk even though it was only mid-afternoon. My throat burned from the cold.

"Do you see those bison?" Autumn pointed farther down the pasture, where the hunchbacked animals grazed in the snow.

Bison, I thought. *So that's what they are.* I nodded.

"When a blizzard hits, most animals run away from it. They feel the wind and take off in the opposite direction. Cattle, horses, even dogs." She shifted in her saddle. "Not bison. They run directly *into* the storm. Do you know why?"

I shook my head.

"They know that walking into the storm will get them through it quicker."

I looked out across the pasture at the fur-coated beasts. Eight big ones and two smaller ones. They were enormous animals, with small horns and thick winter coats. They ate contentedly, as if nothing could possibly bother them. "I wish I could be that fearless," I said.

"You can." Autumn looked soberly at me. "Everybody has demons, Oliver. You're not the only one living under storm clouds." She shrugged. "Maybe you just need to change direction. Decide to ride into the storm. Perhaps you'll get through it faster that way."

You're the demon, Oliver.

You'll bring the storm to them.

The voice in my head had always given me the creeps. It was like a nightmare that followed me around in real time. I had tried everything to ignore it. This time, I decided not to cower from it. This time, I listened.

You take, take, take but do not repay.

Leaches.

The world will know your crimes.

Earth parasites.

The voice was familiar. It had a sharp edge to it that grated on my nerves. When had I felt like that before?

Dreams are a window into the soul.

Leather and mahogany. Tall windows. Dark, beady eyes. A small computer. Bony fingers.

Makoyiwa!

The wolf. Black wolf. He had told me that's what his name meant. An old Blackfoot Indian word.

That was Dr. Makoyiwa's voice.

As soon as I realized it, his voice became as clear as my sim at home.

You have always been this way.
Crooked. Evil. Malicious.
You will lead death to them.
You will be the end of them.

"That's not my voice," I said in disbelief.

Autumn looked confused.

"I thought those were my thoughts, but they're not. That's not me at all!"

Abruptly there was a zap of electricity, and then silence. It was as if someone had just turned off a radio that had been playing white noise all my life.

"What happened, Oliver?" Autumn looked concerned.

Excitement boiled in my chest like a pot of oatmeal. Something had changed. I wasn't exactly sure what it was, just that I felt free. "It's so quiet all of a sudden," I said.

"You're scaring me."

I whooped and stood up in the stirrups. "Don't be scared, Autumn! Ride *into* the storm!" I kicked my heels into Ginger's sides. "I like that. Be like the bison. *Ride into the storm!*"

Autumn shook her head at my crazy and followed me as we bolted forward into an exhilarating race.

I had the strangest feeling that nothing would ever be the same.

*

"Wow, I've never eaten venison before," said Lizabeth at dinner that night. "It's really good, no joke." She chewed noisily and began licking her fingers.

Cecil nudged her gently under the table and handed her a napkin. She took it guiltily.

"We're getting low on meat," said Bill, setting his fork down on an empty plate. "Time for a hunt. It's nearing the end of the rut, so we might be able to get ourselves a buck." He leaned back in his chair, stretched, and pointed at me. "You can come with us. We've got a good spot on the other side of them hills where the elk breed."

"I don't know how to use a gun," I reminded him.

"Perfect time to learn. Man's got to be able to bring food to the table for his family."

"Can I come?" Lizabeth wiped her mouth with the napkin using both hands. "I won't make any noise."

Bill shook his head. "It's just us boys on this one, sweetheart."

Julia looked offended and signed something to him.

"Besides Julia, of course. We need her to look after the horses."

She rolled her eyes. I got the feeling she was probably a better hunter than all of them.

When dinner was over, we cleaned up the kitchen and settled down in front of the fireplace. Donna took out her knitting. The rest of us played cards.

"Texas hold 'em?" Bill suggested.

We all agreed. It was one of our favorite games. We didn't play for money, and we didn't have poker chips, so we used different sized horseshoe nails and the winner got an extra piece of Donna's pie. One of the most skilled players was Lizabeth, so she ate a lot of pie. Apparently, life on the street had been full of games, so she had years of experience. I guess that's what people did when they didn't have sims to entertain themselves.

"My grandpa was a cowboy like you all." Lizabeth liked to chatter while she played. "He told me stories about it before he died. My daddy lived on a farm until he was four, and then they all had to move to the city."

"I fold."

"I'll raise you one nail."

"I fold."

"I'll see your one."

"He said the health department told them there was disease spread by the animals. Plus the animals were bad for the environment. They were just trying to do their duty. But there was more sickness in the city than they'd ever seen on the farm. It was way dirtier, too." She laid her cards down. "Two pair, kings and nines, with a king kicker."

Cecil threw his cards down with a loud puff. "Dang it, I had a ten kicker!"

Lizabeth grinned and scooped the pot towards her. "We tied, though! The universe must be trying to tell us we belong on the same team for something, Cecil."

I was surprised to see Cecil turn as red as a lobster.

"I'll be dealer," said Autumn, gathering up the cards.

"How come you didn't move to the city, Bill?" Lizabeth drummed her fingers on the table. "Weren't you scared of the animal disease?"

I laughed. "I don't think Bill's scared of anything."

He gave me a lopsided smile. "Every man is afraid of something. Courage means carrying on in spite of it."

"So you were." She took the hand she was dealt. "Scared, I mean."

He picked up his cards. I had a feeling that his sudden poker face was for more than just the card game. "No," he said slowly. "No, I wasn't scared. I just wanted things to go back to the way they were. My town used to have street parades and farmers' markets. The high school put on a winter play in the center square every December. We had church every Sunday, even though I didn't always go. We even had the state fair visit our town one year. That was really something." He had a faraway look in his eyes, and we could tell he wasn't even in the room with us—he was visiting the past, enveloped in warm memories of the bustling town he'd grown up in. Then his face fell and he looked older all of a sudden. "Within a matter of days, it was a ghost town."

We all sat motionless, holding our cards but not playing. The air was suddenly dark and heavy, the mood somber. Lizabeth looked like she might cry.

"Let's not bring seriousness here," said Donna, looking up from her knitting. "Let's have ourselves a nice night."

As if assigned to brighten the mood, Luca piped up. "Speaking of ghost towns, do you know that Cecil has a cave ghost to keep him company back home?"

Cecil turned even redder than before (if that was possible), and the scar on his neck stood out like a thick, white rope. He shot his brother an angry look. "Shut up, Luca." His voice was hard and cold, without a trace of his usual levity.

"No, it's true." Luca was grinning, not seeming to notice his brother's animosity. "Her name is Agnes. Apparently, she's been there for years. She tells Cecil love stories."

Cecil scraped his chair back and stood, violently. He looked enormous in that cabin room. The muscles on his neck were taut and if ears could steam like they did in cartoons, his would be freight trains.

"I said shut up!" he bellowed. "When are you going to stop treating me like some immature little kid? I'm more of a man than you! I'd never leave my girl out in the cold to go deaf from frostbite."

Luca recoiled as if Cecil had just hit him. He pushed his chair back and stood, as well, and the two brothers were like giants, towering over us. He clenched his hands so hard the sinew stood out. "What did you just say to me?"

"Cecil!" Autumn scolded. "They were just kids. Julia told Luca she wanted to ride by herself. She made him go back to the house without her."

Cecil shrugged belligerently. "I wouldn't have left her, no matter what she said. It was practically a blizzard and she was only eleven years old."

Julia tapped Donna on the shoulder earnestly. It appeared she was unable to read everyone's lips in the midst of the fray. She signed frantically at Donna, who signed back what must have been an explanation of Cecil's accusation, and Julia suddenly realized what was happening. She jumped up and put her hand on Luca's shoulder.

"What is she saying?" I whispered to Autumn. Julia was signing furiously at Luca.

"She says, 'You are not responsible for what happened to me. Don't listen to this madness.'"

Luca's frown deepened and he signed back at her.

"He says he has always felt responsible," Autumn translated. "'If only I hadn't been so self-centered and oblivious. I will regret my decision for the rest of my life.'"

Julia moved herself closer to him, her intensity increasing.

"'You were ten. How were you to know what would happen?'" Autumn continued murmuring the translation to Oliver. "'It was my decision, not yours. I've always been in the habit of telling you what to do.'" Julia smiled tenderly. "'Do not assume the shackles of regret. The past is a trap as deadly as a bear snare. We have each other here and now. That's all that matters.'"

With that, Julia turned to Cecil and boxed his right ear. Shocked, he cradled the side of his head while she signed furiously at him.

"'What's your problem? Don't you know where to draw the line? Don't talk to us until you can be civil.'"

With that, she took Luca by the arm and led him out of the room. Cecil threw on his coat and stomped out the front door. We all looked around the table at each other. The expression on everyone's faces mirrored exactly what I was thinking. What had gotten into Cecil?

SIXTEEN

"*Dear Jesse,*

"*I didn't know this hunting trip was going to be so far away. We left before the sun came up this morning and we only stopped twice to eat. The sun is about an hour from the horizon, and we're just setting up camp now. Ginger is exhausted and so am I.*

"*Autumn helped me pack, so I should have enough supplies. I've never done this before. Bill gave me a rifle and it's been burning a hole in my back since I tied it to my pack. I hope I don't do something stupid, or worse.*

"*Cecil is heating up leftover stew for dinner. I don't know what's gotten into him. It's like a light went out in him. He and Luca won't even look at each other. Bill and I have done our best to make conversation, but you could cut the tension with a knife. Of course, Julia doesn't talk at all. Most of the trip was traveled in silence.*

"*Even though the journey was long and I was so tired I could've slept in my saddle, it's beautiful country and I've just been drinking it all in. I can't believe this is real life.*

"*I'll write more tomorrow, after the hunt.*"

While Cecil got the fire going and Julia set up camp, Luca and I went to find water for the horses. There was a small creek about a hundred and fifty yards from our camp, but it had crusted over with ice. We both had small shovels in our packs, so we set to work breaking up the ice so the horses could drink. We filled our flasks while we waited for them to get their fill.

Luca had relaxed a bit now that it was just us. "You see why we can't go home?" he asked. "This land is tame compared to the three-day journey back to the caves."

I took a swig of creek water, wincing from the cold on my teeth. "The horses seem to know what to do, even up those rocky trails. Couldn't we just let them take us home?"

"Horses don't belong in the caves," he said, stroking his horse along her flank. "I wish I could bring her with me, though." She brought her head back to nuzzle him. "You miss me when I'm gone, don't you, girl?"

"Why can't we all just live up here, like Bill and Donna?" I asked. "Why do we have to hide under the earth, like moles?"

Like moles hiding from the sun, burrowing blindly through their purposeless existence.

Now that I knew it was Dr. Makoyiwa's voice in my head, it didn't frighten me at all.

Luca frowned sharply at me. "I don't think you understand how dangerous it is to expose ourselves. We could lose everything."

"But we are here, and no one has come after us. Plus, Bill and Donna said that no one pays any attention to this area, so far from the city."

He raised his eyebrow at me in disbelief, like a reproachful teacher. "There are seven of us, versus eighty thousand in the caves. How would we stay concealed with eighty thousand people on the surface?"

My jaw dropped. "There are *eighty thousand* people living in the caves?"

"It's an intricate system. There are about twenty other caves like ours."

"But that's nearly half the population of the some of the cities!"

Another reproachful teacher look. "Precisely why we are such a threat to them. Even though we have no trained armies, no technology, and no interest in fighting, they know how deadly a group like ours is to their system, for the sheer fact that we won't agree." He closed his water flask. "We just want to be left alone to live according to our own choices. Is it really too much to ask, to keep our home secret?"

I shook my head with renewed understanding. "No. Not at all."

I began to understand what Autumn meant that day she told me she didn't know where she belonged. The thought of going back under the earth, living without sunlight, fresh air and all this space, made me feel a little sick. But what other options were there? Go back to the 5th City and live on the street? Try to enter one of the other cities? Going back to my old life was out of the question. So yes, protecting the caves and the lives they had all built was absolutely paramount. But would there ever be a day when we wouldn't have to hide?

"The fire is ready," said Luca. "I bet dinner is, too. Cecil's just heating up the stew Donna made for us."

I felt the rush of saliva in my cheeks. "I've never been so hungry in my life," I said as we walked the horses back up the bank.

"The mountain air will give you an appetite."

We reached the camp and tied the horses off. Snow fell down my back as I pulled on a tree branch to tie the leads to it. I shivered. I had been sweating on the journey here, but now that we were all resting, the cold that crept over me felt like loneliness.

And lonely it was, as we all ate dinner in silence. Bill was too weary to talk. Cecil and Luca sat on opposite sides of the fire and ate sullenly, not looking anywhere but the glowing center of the flames. I thought about Autumn and her radiant smile. I wished she were here.

When dinner was over, Cecil and Julia stayed at camp to clean up and Luca, Bill and I found a hollow in the hillside to use for target practice. The sun was going down and the temperature was dropping, but I started to sweat when Bill put that rifle in my hands.

I could really be dangerous now.

"This here's a Remington 700 bolt-action rifle," said Bill. "My daddy gave me this for my birthday one year. It's a good starter gun." From under his arm, he pulled out a pair of sticks bound together with twine. He pulled the bottoms apart and set it on the ground like a pair of splayed legs. "Here's your shooting stick. You'll be more accurate if you rest your gun on it."

Luca walked up to the center of the hollow and planted the target in the ground.

"I'll show you how to load it first," said Bill. "Check the chamber to make sure it's clear." He pointed.

I looked in the back of the chamber. I could smell the tang of metal. "It looks empty to me."

"Good. Now put your bullets in the chamber like this." He pulled one of the bullets out of the box and tucked it into the long, rectangular hole on top. It went in with a click. "Two more." He handed the box to me.

The bullets were smooth and cold and a lot heavier than I expected. I set two more into the gun.

"Good. Now pull the lever down and in to set the bolt, and your first bullet will be loaded."

I did exactly what he said, but as soon as that bullet dropped into the chamber, my heart started pounding in my ears. I rested my gun on the shooting stick and tried to set the sights the way Bill showed me, but I couldn't get the gun to sit still. I looked at my finger on the trigger and realized my hands were shaking.

Bill put his hand on my shoulder. "You okay, son?"

I sighed. "I've done this in video games," I said. "But I couldn't actually hurt someone with that."

Bill took the rifle from me and cradled it gently between his two hands. "You see this wood here?" He pointed at it with his chin. "It's been polished by my grandpa and my daddy hundreds of times. Can you see how much it shines?"

I looked at the honey-colored wood on the gun and realized he was right.

"And you see that barrel?" Another chin point.

I nodded.

"They taught me how to clean it myself when I was just six years old."

I raised an eyebrow. I couldn't believe someone would let a six-year-old touch a gun.

"Do you see that small lever on the side?" He turned the gun over in his hands.

"Yeah."

"That's called a safety. When it's flipped up like that, the gun won't fire."

"Oh."

"This thing is as useless as that tree over there without your hand using it." He pointed his chin at my hand. "You see that finger?"

I looked down at my fingers. "Yes."

"That finger's going to do what *you* want it to do. If you're not ready to shoot, keep your finger on the side here, like this." He demonstrated. "When you're ready, put your finger on the trigger and pull." He put the gun back in my hands. "Do you trust yourself?"

I paused. In this situation? With a weapon in my hands? I looked at Cecil, cleaning the dishes down by the river, and Julia, grooming the horses near him. I glanced over at Luca, who stood next to Bill, watching us. I looked at Bill, his weathered eyes calm. Once again, they all trusted me. I still wasn't entirely sure about myself.

"I guess so," I said.

"Then you've got all you need." Bill stepped back and gestured towards the target. "Put the butt against your shoulder, line up your sights, and take your shot."

I rested the rifle on the shooting stick again. My hands had stopped shaking. I put my finger alongside the trigger, like he had shown me, not ready to shoot yet. I looked down the barrel and got the front sight lined up with the back ones. *Someday I might need this.* I took a deep breath. *They all protect me. Autumn, Tom, Bill, even Emer. They've all saved my life. Someday I might need to save one of them.* I found the center of the target and pulled the trigger.

The gun recoiled against my shoulder and the explosion was like a thunderclap. I felt the vibration in my chest. It didn't scare me, though. In fact, it gave me a thrill.

"Not bad!" said Bill. "Not a bullseye, but you got the outer bull.

That's twenty-five points." He grinned and slapped me on the shoulder. "Not bad at all."

I smiled back. "That was a lot easier than I thought."

"Just like riding a horse," said Bill. "You never know until you try. Your ancestors had been riding horses and shooting guns for a couple of centuries before everyone got so scared of them."

"Can I try again?" I asked. Dusk was seeping in, but I could still see the target.

"Go right ahead, son."

Luca gave me a few pointers about my stance, but other than that, I took to it like a duck to water. After a few more rounds, I was ready for the morning hunt. We cleaned up just as darkness set in and the stars came out.

"So your daddy never taught you how to shoot?" asked Bill as we sat around the fire before bed. He was smoking a pipe.

"I don't have a dad. At least, I never met him." I munched on some beef jerky and stared at the flames. "I learned how to shoot on sims." I shrugged. "Pretty much everything I've ever learned has been on sims."

Bill blew a stream of smoke into the air, letting it mingle with smoke from the fire before disappearing into the sky. "I knew another boy who was raised by women. He was kind of sensitive like you, too."

I flushed. "I am not sensitive."

Bill studied me. "You're getting tougher. That's for sure."

Julia signed something and everybody laughed. I frowned, confused.

Luca translated. "She said, 'We'll see how tough you are in the morning.'"

"Speaking of which, we need to get to bed." Bill blotted out his pipe. "The deer won't wait for us to get our beauty sleep."

I sprawled out on my bedroll with my hands behind my head. The sky was an ocean of stars. "I want to learn sign language," I said to Luca, whose bedroll was a few feet down from mine.

"I can teach you," he said.

I stared at those stars until my eyes wouldn't stay open anymore.

*

Julia was right, waking up that morning put hair on my chest I'd never had. My breath was a stream of fog. Even though I had slept in my clothes, getting out of that sleeping bag was like dying a slow, arduous death. The cold seeped into my bones. We chewed some beef jerky, cleaned up our camp, and set out up the mountains.

Bill knew of a spot on high ground where we could wait for the bucks to come out. They were still in rut, despite the weather. We tied the horses to a tree, set up our shooting sticks a few yards away from each other, cocked our guns, and waited.

An hour passed. I lost all feeling in my toes. My fingers stiffened, despite the sheepskin gloves Autumn had given me. Every muscle in my body clamped down, as if I were suddenly eighty years old and riddled with arthritis. I didn't know if the others felt that way, but no one moved an inch. The forest was quiet except for a few sporadic gusts of wind.

Suddenly a set of bushes moved slightly. I swung my gun around and put it in my sights. Sure enough, a six-point buck emerged from the shrub, his antlers freezing as he listened. *Don't make a sound.* Slowly, steadily, I eased my finger over the trigger and pulled. The animal disappeared.

"You got it!" Cecil whooped and made his way over to me. Luca bounded over, too. They both slapped me on the back, and for just a minute, it was as if they had never been fighting. Bill and Julia joined us a minute later, both smiling.

"Now we'll teach you to field dress it," said Bill. "You learn quick!"

We removed the entrails and cleaned and dried the cavity, and then they helped me hoist it onto the back of the horse. I had never been so proud in all my life. I had just caught enough food for half a year's worth of meals.

The forest had been disturbed, so there would be no more hunting that day. No one seemed to mind. We were all in good spirits as we made our way back down the mountain. Even Cecil and Luca seemed to have forgotten their feud.

I turned back for one last look at the mountain we were leaving.

Trees in the mid-morning sun cast foreshortened shadows on the snow. Everything was empty and still. I wanted to etch this memory into my mind for all eternity. Until this moment, I had been a boy. Suddenly I felt like a man.

Just as I began to turn Ginger back towards the trail, I caught a glimpse of something out of the corner of my eye. A shadow moved behind an unusual rock formation on the lee side of the hill. It was gone before I could see it dead-on, but there was no doubt what I had glimpsed. The shadow was a person.

We were being watched.

SEVENTEEN

"They're back!" Lizabeth ran across the yard as we rode up, calling towards the house.

Donna and Autumn came out on the front porch, throwing on their coats, looking like they had both been cooking. Autumn wore her hair in a high bun, and it seemed redder than ever in the evening light. She wiped her hands on her apron and came running down the front steps towards us.

"God, are you a sight for sore eyes." I swung down off my horse and grabbed her by the waist. She was warm and smelled like sweet and pungent herbs. I dusted flour off her nose and kissed her.

Bill greeted Donna with a kiss and told her the trip was a success. "We had no idea Oliver was such a good shot."

Autumn put her hand on the buck that hung off of Ginger, running her fingers along the antlers. "This is your kill?" She looked at me in awe.

I grinned. "You didn't think I had it in me, did you?"

"Of course I did." Her gaze deepened. "You've changed," she said.

Cecil breezed cooly past us with his horse in tow. Luca and Julia had gone to the barn to put their horses away, and he clearly wanted to be nowhere near them. He tied his chestnut roan to the porch and marched inside.

"He's still mad, huh?" Donna shivered and wrapped her coat more tightly around herself. "Didn't you pull it out of him, Bill?"

He shook his head. "I don't have the knack you women-folk seem to have to get men to bare their souls." He threw his arm around her and looked at her tenderly. He was in the same boots as I was — it was hard to stay away from them for too long.

Donna rolled her eyes. "It's not witchcraft, Bill. Just ask him what's wrong."

"I'll do it," Lizabeth offered cheerily. "I'll make him spill the tea." She flipped her hair over her shoulder and bounded lithely up the stairs and in the front door.

"Do you suppose her parents are looking for her?" Bill asked, tying his horse to the front porch and urging me to do the same. "She's been gone nearly a month now."

"Oh." Donna looked surprised. "Don't you know? The poor girl is an orphan. Her whole family died of pneumonia. That's why she left."

Bill stood very still and closed his eyes for a moment. When he opened them, they were deep with sorrow. "It's a damn shame." He shook his head. "So much for this 'better life' in the city. 'The commonwealth of Athens is become a forest of beasts.'"

Autumn cried out in surprise. "That's from *Timon of Athens*! Bill, have you been reading the Shakespeare books I left for Donna?"

He shrugged. "Sure. Why not? They have a lot of truth to them. Some of them leave me in stitches. Not that one, though."

"No, *Timon of Athens* is a tragedy." Autumn beamed with pride. "Oliver arranged a stage performance of *Comedy of Errors*, you know, down in the caves. He directed and acted in it."

"Just what the old man wrote it for."

"It was a big hit. Everyone was talking about it. I'm sure they still are."

She was still talking about it, and that was all that mattered.

The front door opened and Lizabeth flew out of the house, stomping loudly down the stairs with tears on her cheeks.

"What happened, child?" Donna tried to stop her, but the girl was like a tornado. She tore down the hill towards the barn. "Lord have mercy. What has gotten into that boy? Maybe he needs to eat." Donna made her way up the stairs with more urgency in her step. "I have some leftover dinner, are you all hungry?"

"Yes." Bill and I said it in unison. We were tired of jerky and cold, dry bread. Warm light reached out from the windows of the cabin, like the hand of an old friend. I imagined the fire was stoked and the couch cushions had been fluffed. My aching muscles cried out for a hot meal and a soft bed.

"I'm just going to get that buck hung in the smokehouse for the night," said Bill. "We can skin and quarter it tomorrow, but I don't want to leave it out for wild animals to get it."

"Oh no, Bill, we'll do it," Autumn protested.

I nodded emphatically and put my hands on his shoulders, steering him towards the house. "Go get warm, old man. You deserve a rest."

He laughed. "I could run circles around you, kid." And he was right. But he did look grateful for the help, and he gripped the handrail with knobby fingers as he climbed the stairs to the porch.

Autumn and I untied the horses and walked them down the hill towards the smokehouse. The stars were out and they lit our way. "I can't believe you caught a six-point buck on your first hunting trip," she said, shaking her head and smiling. "You've come a long way since you couldn't even use the printing press without my help."

I laughed and groaned. "Oh God, don't remind me. What a stooge."

"Everything went fine on the trip?"

I looked over at her walking on, holding the lead loosely, staring casually at the snow-covered ground. How did she know to ask me the exact question I wanted to answer?

"I saw something strange."

"Oh?" She looked back at me with those moon-shaped eyes.

"I think someone was following us. I saw their shadow out of the corner of my eyes."

She frowned. "Who was it?"

"I don't know. They hid behind a rock before I could get a good look at them. I think they might have followed us for a while. I kept checking behind us, and I saw movement a few times. Whoever they are, they're a good tracker."

She went back to watching the ground. Her eyebrows were drawn together. "I know someone who is a very good tracker."

I nodded. "Emer. I was thinking the same thing."

"But why would she be following you? Why wouldn't she just come out in the open and join us? She knows Bill and Donna."

"I don't think she trusts me. Maybe she thinks I'm dangerous."

Autumn rolled her eyes. "I'm about done with that narrative. I've been hearing that since I first met you. The only time you were ever dangerous was when your brain was overloaded with meds."

We arrived at the smokehouse. It was a small shack with a wood stove connected to the exterior wall. The interior was empty except for a few triangular hooks hanging from the rafters. Autumn explained that they were called gambrels. We tied some twine to the buck's hind legs and connected them to either end of the gambrel (much like putting a coat on a hanger), and then we both hoisted it up to the rafters, sliding it off Ginger's back while she waited patiently. It hung upside down, spinning gently, with its antlers scraping the ground.

Just as we were locking up, a familiar sound drifted over from the barn. I turned my head to listen more closely, and so did Autumn. We both looked at each other, realizing what it was.

> *'Twas in another lifetime, one of toil and blood*
> *When blackness was a virtue and the road was full of mud*
> *I came in from the wilderness, a creature void of form*
> *Come in, she said, I'll give you*
> *Shelter from the storm.*

"The record player," she said in disbelief.

We made our way over to the barn, pulling the horses along. The volume increased as we got closer. The singer had a strange voice—rough and gravelly, more rhythmic than melodic. The bass line pulsed gently in the background, filling the barn with a warmth it had never had, as if someone suddenly turned on the lights. We brought the horses in and stood in the nave of the barn, searching for the source of the music.

Luca was seated on the floor next to the wood-burning stove. Next to him was the record player that Autumn and I had found in the caves, resting on the floor with its top open. In front of that lay Julia, her body prone, her hands pressed palm-down into the floor. She lay so still, and in such an unusual position, that I thought she might have been injured. But Luca did not seem concerned.

"What are they doing?" I whispered to Autumn.

Julia sat up and looked at us. She must have felt the vibrations from the horses' footsteps. Luca pulled the needle off the record, bringing the song to a screeching halt.

"Where did you get that?" Autumn asked.

"I took it from the shop," Luca admitted brazenly.

"Without asking Dad?"

"Yes." He squared his shoulders. "He wouldn't have let me take it."

"What are you doing with it?"

He paused and looked at Julia. She sat with her arms loosely cradling her knees. Her eyes were bright with exhilaration.

"I wanted her to feel the music," he said.

Julia signed something to him eagerly.

"I don't know what it means," he said aloud as he signed back to her. "I think it's about the shelter that women provide. I'll tell you the lyrics in a minute."

She signed again, more urgently this time.

"Okay, okay, just wait till they leave." He looked at us and grinned. "I was right. She loves it."

It felt wrong, being there. This moment belonged to them. Autumn and I put the horses away and hurried out just as Luca was putting the record back to the beginning. I glanced back and saw him signing to her while the song played, translating the lyrics. She watched him intently.

Autumn and I walked back to the cabin in silence. The sky was an ocean of stars and the night clung to the earth, coating branches and roof eaves with layer upon velvety layer. *It is so comfortable with you,* I thought. I didn't want to say it out loud, for fear of disrupting the quiet that surrounded us like a blanket.

As we approached the cabin, Autumn gave a small gasp, clutched my hand and pulled me behind a tree. Voices murmured on the front porch, but we could not decipher what they were saying.

"Who is it?" I whispered.

"It's Cecil and Lizabeth."

I frowned, perplexed. "So? Why can't we go inside?"

Autumn put a hand on her hip. "Are you telling me you had no idea?"

I gave her a blank stare.

She rolled her eyes impatiently. "Cecil has a crush. That's why he's been acting so strange lately. He's never had a girlfriend before and he doesn't know how to handle it."

Stunned, I leaned over and looked around the trunk. Sure enough, Cecil and Lizabeth stood on the front porch, their faces so close together that I couldn't see any space in the shadows. "They're kissing," I realized.

"Of course they are. This is what I've been trying to tell you."

I turned back to the opposite side of the tree, and we both slid down to sit in the snow with our backs to the trunk. I was grateful for the buffalo coat that Donna had given me. I put my arm around Autumn and she leaned her head on my shoulder.

"They might be a while," she said.

"I know." I sighed.

"I don't think we should interrupt them. They might be embarrassed if they know we saw them."

I lay my head back against the bark and sighed again. "I know." My stomach grumbled.

Autumn lifted her head to look at me. "You're starving," she realized. "And Donna has warm ham and apples fresh from the oven, and here we are just a few yards from the front door."

I groaned. "Don't remind me."

She patted my arm. "You're a good man, Oliver McNeil."

I looked down at her in shock. No one had ever said that to me. Ever. In the entirety of my life, all I had ever heard was that I didn't listen, I had a short attention span, I was too loud, I didn't care enough, I was a liar, I had violent tendencies, blah blah blah. No one had ever actually told me I was *good*.

I put my hand on her chin, pulling her face toward me gently. "Autumn Montgomery, you have saved me in more ways than one. I will love you for the rest of eternity."

She smiled, and it was as if two stars had fallen from the sky and appeared in her eyes. "I love you too," she said simply. "And I am yours forever."

EIGHTEEN

"A B, C." Luca held his hand in a fist, then he put all four fingers up with his thumb tucked in against his palm, and then he turned his fingers and thumb into the curved shape of a "C."

Slowly, cautiously, I mirrored his gestures.

"Yep. That's a start. Just practice that all day and we'll continue tomorrow."

We were sitting on the front porch with Cecil and Bill, watching the sun come up while we waited for breakfast.

"You can't only teach him three letters," said Cecil, leaning forward in his chair. "That's boring. Don't you want to learn some words and phrases, Oliver?"

I nodded eagerly. I wanted to be able to join the conversation when Julia was part of it. I didn't like being an outsider.

Cecil showed me his closed fist, then pivoted his wrist up and down. "That's 'yes.'"

I mimicked him, feeling awkward at first.

He put two fingers and a thumb together and apart in a pinching motion. "This is 'no.'"

I did the same.

He did a series of hand motions that were too complicated for me to follow. "That's, 'overbearing, arrogant brother who thinks he's smarter than everybody else.'"

"Give me a break." Luca shot him a wry look. "What's gotten into you? Sorry I made fun of your ghost, okay? I'll never do it again."

Cecil stood. "I've always been your parody. Just some idiot, tagging along after you, like a dog. Well, I won't be the butt of your jokes anymore. I know things too, you know. I know things!" He spun on his heel and marched into the house.

Luca scoffed. "What's his deal?" he mumbled.

Bill stretched his legs across the porch and leaned back in his chair. "Family feuds are common," he said. "Especially when you have history together. It's the same in a marriage. It takes work."

"What if your family feud is that your brother is just crazy?"

Bill shrugged. "He's fifteen. It's a tough age. I can assure you, it won't resolve until you can see it through his eyes. Sometimes you have to be willing to give a little and meet in the middle."

"Why should I?" Luca grumbled. "He won't give in."

Julia came up the hill carrying a silver milk pail. She was watching the sunrise while she walked, and she seemed to be in another universe. What was it like to live in a world with no sound? The sunrise was probably more vibrant for her, I bet, with no noise to interrupt her view. She seemed engrossed in it.

She looked surprised to see us as she came up the stairs. I decided to use the first phrase Luca had taught me—*Good morning*. Hand to chin, then out (*good*); left arm as horizon line, right hand hinged up (*morning*). Her face lit up. *Good morning*, she signed back.

The front door opened with a squeak and Donna called us in for breakfast. We ate heartily, then Bill and Luca rode out to fix the north fence, which was broken. Autumn stayed inside to help with the dishes. Cecil and I headed down to the smokehouse to skin the deer.

It started to snow as Cecil hung the gambrel on a tree branch. Next to the smokehouse was a rough table made from a plank of wood laid over two old tree stumps. We laid our tools out on it. "Good kill shot," he said, pointing to the bullet hole on the side of the buck. "The meat always tastes better when they don't suffer." We rolled our sleeves up and he handed me a filet knife. We set to work removing the skin.

"Can I ask how you got that scar?" I asked while we worked.

His knife paused for a fraction of a second, then resumed. His breath quickened, almost imperceptibly. "At school."

"In the caves?" I was shocked.

He shook his head. "In the city. I was seven."

"Wait, you went to a real school in the city? Not a sim?"

His tone stayed the same, but his cuts increased in intensity. "It was a government program. Some kind of social experiment. I got in an argument with another kid, and the teachers put the two of us in a room with one of those viewing windows that looks like mirrors on one side. I guess they were all watching to see what we do. Conveniently, there was a kitchen in there, containing a full complement of knives easily within reach."

"Whoa." My breath caught in my throat. "That's really twisted."

"I guess they wanted to see if a first grader could get as violent as a grown man." He looked over at me, and his eyes drooped. "They can, and they do. Both of us ended up in the hospital with multiple knife wounds."

I felt genuinely ill.

"I think that was when mom and dad started looking for a way to get out. When mom got pregnant with Jesse a few months later, they decided to leave for real." He sighed. "I started training not long after that. Ju-jitsu, boxing, weight-lifting. I'd rather use my hands to protect myself, than a knife. You can hold someone down with your hands, but your only option with a knife is to basically kill them."

The buckskin came off easily, but the head and the antlers took more muscle. Cecil set them aside for leather and tools. He then proceeded to teach me about the different cuts of meat. The back strap was the strip of meat on either side of the spine. The tenderloin was the tenderest cut. The heart could be used, too, and was known to bring health and strength to the consumer. All cuts of meat went into containers, to be brought to the kitchen for cleaning and preserving. The meat would be smoked, salted, and canned, and used in tonight's dinner.

"Can I ask you something?" he said casually while we filled containers.

"Sure."

"Once you get a girl, how do you make sure she stays interested in you?"

I shot a sideways glance his way. He had his head down, cutting the meat.

"You're talking about Lizabeth?"

He didn't stop working. "Yeah."

I thought about it for a minute. "I think you just need to make sure she knows she's important to you."

He nodded. "That's easy enough."

A few minutes passed, and we worked in silence. Finally he blurted out, "She's different from anyone I've ever met."

"Yeah?"

"I like the way she talks."

He spent most of our work period telling me about her. How she was full of questions and curious about everything. She had never gone to school, but she was hungry for knowledge. She didn't even know how to read or write. He was going to teach her. She was learning to cook from Donna, and she was pretty good. She had fallen in love with the farm and thought it was the most beautiful place in the world. She hated the city and didn't ever want to go back.

The lunch bell rang just as we were closing up the containers. "Don't tell anyone I told you all this," he said.

"No problem." I said it absentmindedly, because my attention became absorbed in something at my feet. Something familiar. I leaned down to look at it.

"What is that?" asked Cecil.

"A feather." I picked it up and turned it over in my hand. It was long and black. A raven's feather.

Cecil hoisted the sack of meat on his back. "Weird. Ravens don't usually come out this early. We still have another month of winter." Leaning forward under its weight, he set out up the hill towards the house.

A gust of wind pulled back the hood of my coat. The snow had stopped falling, and the dry air felt good against my skin, which was warm from working. I turned to look behind the smokehouse before leaving and my heart lurched when I realized that someone was standing on the hillside, staring down at me. I knew it was Emer right away. She wore a thick fur jacket that covered her hair entirely, but there was no mistaking that square jaw and sharp cheekbones. She stared defiantly at me.

"Why are you here?" I called.

"To observe you." She spoke matter-of-factly, as if there was nothing strange whatsoever about that.

"Why?"

"Evidence."

"Evidence of what?"

She just stared at me. Then she turned and walked away, disappearing into the forest.

"Oliver!" Autumn called to me from the house. "Are you coming?"

I picked up the antlers and carried it back to the house with me. She was waiting for me on the front porch. "What did you see?" she asked.

"We were right. It's Emer." I laid the antlers on the porch.

Autumn looked over at the hillside I had been studying. "Up there? By herself?"

I shrugged. "I assume so."

"Did you talk to her?"

"Yeah. She told me she was watching me, for evidence."

Autumn narrowed her eyes suspiciously. "Evidence for what?"

I shrugged. "Beats me."

We didn't play cards after dinner that evening. We were too tired. We all sat around the fire, Bill dozing on the couch and Julia and Luca curled up comfortably, watching the flames. Cecil had a simple primer book out and was introducing Lizabeth to the alphabet. Autumn played quietly on the guitar, working to learn a new song. Donna was checking my shoulder.

"The scar is still fresh, but you're healing up nicely, Oliver." She rotated my arm to check my range of motion. "Farm work has been good for you. You've grown stronger."

"I'm just glad you finally let me ride Ginger," I said, wincing when my arm reached an angle I was not used to.

"I never would have marked you as a horse boy, but you sure have proven me wrong."

"He's a natural," Bill mumbled, his eyes still closed.

"I'm as surprised as you are," I said, pulling my shirt back over my shoulder. "If you could have seen me six months ago..."

"'We know what we are but know not what we may be.'" Bill opened his eyes and yawned sleepily. "When are you going to put on one of your plays for us? Tom and Margaret get treated, but not us?"

"He was wooing Autumn," Cecil piped up.

Bill chuckled. "That's a sure way to win her over. Did it work?"

Autumn blushed and became more engrossed in her playing. I smiled.

"My mom used to take me to plays when I was a boy," said Bill nostalgically. "I still remember the smell of popcorn, the excitement when the footlights came on, the thrill of those opening lines. TV didn't even come close. There's just something about watching a story unfold in real life, with real actors... there's nothing like it." He sighed. "It's been more than sixty years since I saw one."

"I'll put on a play for you, Bill." I walked over to the bookshelf on the other side of the room and began to peruse his books. "Which one is your favorite?"

"I don't much like the tragedies," he said. "There's enough sadness in the world. If you could, choose a comedy. Surprise me."

"We used to do life-pretend, too." Lizabeth put her book down on her lap. "We didn't call it 'play.' My mom taught me it was how to stay alive. How to stay secret."

The Forgotten were known for their strange mannerisms — flailing arms, contorted expressions, jilted gaits. They wandered the streets like zombies. People caught it on social all the time. Was it all for show?

"Your own way of building caves," I realized. "If everyone thought you were crazy, they'd leave you alone."

"That's right."

I turned back to the bookshelf. *Much Ado About Nothing. Merchant of Venice. Taming of the Shrew.* All Shakespeare. Some were missing jackets, others simply dog-eared. They had obviously been read over and over again. Why did everyone think he was so great? *Comedy of Errors* had been a hit in the caves, but were all his plays that entertaining? Or did people just crave the escape a story could give them?

Well, what was wrong with escaping into a great story? It wasn't like a sim, which tried to superimpose itself on top of you, as if it wanted to replace you with fake characters and manufactured situations. No, a good story wove its tale the way reality did: it was real people who got things twisted; it was highs and lows and ups and downs; it unraveled with fervor. It knew that you were smart enough to fill in the blanks, that your own imagination was just as important as the story itself. A good story allowed you to contribute, and it added to your world, as if you were the woof and the words were the warp in the most colorful tapestry of all: life.

Tonight I realized something, I wrote in Jesse's notebook that night. *When I lived in the city, there was no future, only blackness. There was only passing the time. Every day blurred together in slow succession, like a stagnant river with nowhere to go. Now, it's as if a dam has broken. There is so much I want to do. I want to see the farm in the summer. Autumn says it is the most vibrant shade of green. I want to take Ginger and Autumn on a trip over the mountain, to a lake I found on our hunting trip. We can camp and I can try fishing. I want to help Bill with the sheep shearing in spring, when dozens of people come from the caves to process the wool for winter clothing. I want to direct more plays, and maybe even write a few myself. I have so many ideas for stories.*

I had no idea just how dead I was, Jesse, until I discovered what it feels like to really be alive!

NINETEEN

I didn't see Emer for the rest of my stay. I assumed she got her 'evidence' and went back to the caves. Another month passed. I improved my sign language to a point where I could carry on a conversation fairly comfortably, even with Julia's rapid motions. Lizabeth was learning to read, and she could often be found in the barn or wrapped in a blanket on the front porch with her nose in a book, running her finger slowly along the lines of text. She and Cecil were practically inseparable. They laughed and played games with a carefree delight I hadn't even seen in children. Cecil and Luca were still not on speaking terms.

One day in early March, I realized our time at the farm was coming to an end. I was walking back from the sheep barn, where I had been feeding Bill's flock of two hundred sheep, when I noticed a patch of yellow under a tree. Daffodils poked their bright faces out of the snow, reaching for the sun. Spring had arrived.

I didn't tell anyone at first, dreading the thought of leaving. But at dinner that night, Luca announced that the snow was melting around the horse barn. We began to make plans for the return journey to the caves. We would leave on Friday.

The mood sobered, and the rest of the meal was rather quiet. I looked across the table at Luca and Julia, whose arms touched as they ate; and Cecil and Lizabeth, who kept looking at each other like kicked dogs over their forks. As miserable as I was about going, I had it better than anyone because Autumn and I were leaving together.

"I've started plans for an outdoor theater," said Bill when his plate was empty. "It'll be built by summer. I hope you'll come back with your actors and put on a good show for us."

I held my fork in mid-air and grinned from ear to ear. "Are you serious?"

Autumn cried out in delight. "Really, Bill?"

"Of course." He laid his fork and knife across the plate and leaned back in his chair. "We could use some enrichment around here. Plus, I want you all to come back."

I beamed. "Of course, Bill. We'll be here."

"Bring Tom and Margaret, too, will you? It's been years."

"Okay, we will."

The situation seemed less somber with the promise of another visit over the horizon, but Friday still came too soon. We had everything packed and ready to go before sunrise. I made my way down to the barn to say goodbye to Ginger.

"I have to go away," I told her, rubbing the star on her nose. "But I'll be back, I swear."

She nuzzled me affectionately. She seemed to understand.

"Thanks for being such a great teacher," I murmured. "This has been the most fun I've ever had."

We set out into the forest just as the sky became flushed with pink and gold. It felt good to be leaving as an equal. I had arrived an invalid on a stretcher, but I was leaving with a full pack on my back, strong as the rest of them. Bill had given me my very own handgun, a small Colt 44 revolver that his grandfather had given him. I had refused to accept it at first, not wanting to take a family heirloom, but he was adamant that he would never let me leave unless I had a way to protect myself. "This is not the place to be complacent," he said. Donna gave me a belt and holster of bison leather, and the revolver fit comfortably in it at my hip.

We walked for three days, making camp each night. Autumn explained the way to me as we walked, and I did my best to burn the route in my memory. There was no trail, but there were landmarks. A turtle-shaped rock, a pine tree with three trunks, a barren hill. We took care to clean our camp and cover our tracks, leaving no evidence that we had been there.

At the end of the third day, as the sun was sinking towards the horizon, we came upon an opening in the hillside about seven feet high. Autumn, Cecil and Luca slowed down, suddenly cautious. "Something's wrong," she said.

"Why?" I asked.

"No sentry," said Luca.

We all took our pistols out and cocked them. Luca led the way into the cave, walking as slowly and quietly as possible. Torches blazed on the walls, lighting our way, but the tunnel was empty. It was quiet at first, but as we walked deeper into the mountain, we began to hear yelling. Then screaming. My stomach twisted into knots as the screaming got louder.

The cavern was in chaos. Tents were upended; food was strewn about haphazardly; the spice towers had been demolished. The sound of breaking glass joined terrorized voices in syncopation. People were fleeing, but the exits had all been blockaded by soldiers wearing pristine, white uniforms. The plastic sheen on their clothing made them look like robots, although I knew they were not. There were hundreds of soldiers scattered throughout the cavern. Many of them were chasing the frightened cave-goers, laughing as if it were a game of tag.

"Transport has arrived," announced one of the soldiers, his voice echoing off the rock walls like thunder. He wore a large, plastic helmet with white plumage on top, reminiscent of a Centurion from ancient Rome. "Round 'em up, boys. Everyone on the buses." He stood at the edge of the cavern, looking down on the mayhem. "Remember, we prefer them alive."

Why did he look so familiar?

Luca turned and began signaling to us in sign language. *We have to find Mom and Dad. Diana and Jesse will be with them.*

Maybe Autumn and Oliver should stay back, Cecil signed in reply.

This is a vantage point. They can cover us if we get spotted.

Luca contemplated. *If they start shooting, it'll be game over. There's no way they can kill off all those soldiers with two handguns. They don't even have enough ammo.*

You're right. Better if we stick together and try to stay hidden.

Luca nodded at his brother. *They're probably in the shop. There's a hidden escape route from there.*

We all nodded in understanding. Luckily the shop was on this side of the cavern, about a hundred yards away from us. We followed the path down into the cavern as quietly as we could, avoiding loose rocks that might fall and draw attention. It was fortunate that this part of the cave was not well lit. The cacophony continued near the marketplace, where soldiers used tase guns to stun people before handcuffing them and dragging them to the tunnels. Our tunnel was so far away, they seemed to have no interest in it.

The soldier with the plumed helmet was still barking orders. He waved his hand stiffly while he yelled, his head held high atop a perfectly straight neck, reminding me of an old British sim I had played full of pompous people at a ball. (My teacher had sentenced me to becoming "cultured.") He bent forward slightly, and he moved as if he had a two-by-four strapped to his back.

Mr. Reeve. That was who he reminded me of. Starched, robotic, silent Mr. Reeve, who followed me around in every sim. It looked like him, but it wasn't him. This soldier was slightly shorter, and plus, he spoke. The Mr. Reeve who had been sent to watch me never said a word.

Suddenly shots were fired from the north tunnels. Several soldiers fell to the ground. The others turned to face the gunfire, shooting in response. Another barrage followed. More soldiers fell. The rest of them ran for cover in the marketplace.

Taking advantage of the diversion, we sped up, running along the path until we reached the cavern floor. I could see the shop door in the cave wall up ahead. We began to sprint towards it until Autumn stopped in her tracks.

An old woman hobbled across the open floor, also heading for the shop. She wore a bright blue shawl and leaned on a walking stick. Her hair was white as snow.

"It's Mrs. Beth," Autumn whispered with intensity.

Don't do it, Autumn. Luca signed furiously. *Leave her. She will find her way.*

But Autumn was not watching him sign. She placed her hands on either side of her mouth and called out at a loud whisper, "Mrs. Beth!"

The woman turned to look her way, squinting into the shadows. "Autumn?" she called. "Is that you?"

She did not seem to understand the need to be discreet, because she called out at full volume, attracting the attention of a soldier nearby. He turned and saw her standing alone, facing the cave wall, leaning on her walking stick. "Hey, you!" he called.

Mrs. Beth turned to him slowly, a look of disgust on her face. "Hay is for horses," she retorted. "Mind your manners."

"Oh no," Autumn whispered. "This is not going to end well. I'm going to get her. Meet me at the shop."

"Wait!" I tried to stop her, but I was too late. She bolted out of the shadows towards Mrs. Beth, her hair a fiery cloud behind her.

"Hey, over here!" The soldier was calling over his shoulder now. "There's a bunch of them over here!"

There was no way I was leaving Autumn in the middle of this fray. "Get to the shop," I ordered Luca and Cecil. "I'll get them both. Just get there."

I ran out into the light just as five more soldiers joined their friend. They wore tightly-woven, white chainmail coifs that covered the entirety of their head, neck and upper body. I wondered how effective they were at deflecting bullets, seeing as how every part of their uniform appeared to be plastic, even the headpieces. But they seemed dauntless. They pulled out their stun guns and began to approach us.

These were practically clones of Mr. Reeves. No, "clone" wasn't quite right. Brothers, perhaps. Cousins. Definitely some kind of relation. They walked with the same stiff gait, lifting their knees high in the air so they could keep their backs straight.

"Mrs. Beth," I said hurriedly, rushing to her side. "I'm a friend of Autumn. May I help you?"

Both she and Autumn looked surprised to see me. "Oh," she murmured. "I suppose so. My knees…"

I couldn't wait any longer. The soldiers were only a few yards away. I leaned down and put my arm around Mrs. Beth's waist, scooping her up into my arms. She cried out in surprise. Her walking stick fell to the ground with a clatter.

"I've got it," said Autumn. "Let's go."

The three of us ran towards the shop, where Cecil and Luca stood with the door open. I could hear brisk footsteps scrambling behind me. What would we do when we got inside? They would simply break the door down. This was not a well-thought-out plan. We were cornering ourselves.

When we were approximately five yards from the door, Autumn grabbed my arm and yanked me to the side. Startled, I clutched Mrs. Beth more tightly so I wouldn't drop her. "What are you doing?" I asked.

She didn't have to explain herself, for not more than five seconds later, our pursuers tripped, fell over each other, and disappeared into a black abyss. Autumn had pulled me out of the path of an enormous, gaping hole in the ground. A trap.

I didn't have time to ask questions. We kept running at full-speed until we were safely inside the shop. Cecil and Luca shut the door and quickly locked it, bringing a wood plank down to cover everything, frame and all. I set Mrs. Beth gently on the floor.

"Oliver!" Jesse flew at me like an arrow, wrapping his arms around my waist as if he would squeeze me to death.

"Hey, buddy!" I whispered, hugging him back. "Is that your hole you dug out front?"

He looked up at me and nodded proudly. "I worked on it for weeks. Dad helped me make the cover. It had to look like it was part of the ground."

I tousled his hair. "Genius."

"We have to hurry." Tom came forward from the shadows, holding the only lit candle in the place. "Follow me."

Margaret and Diana were in the shipment room, moving artifacts aside. It seemed they were trying to uncover something. We stepped in to help. Sure enough, under the bits of machinery and gadgets was a trap door under a rug in the floor.

"We're going even deeper underground?" The thought of burying myself deeper under the earth worried me.

"It goes to the river," Autumn explained. "We can follow the stream out of the caves and make our way over the mountains."

It was a good plan. The soldiers probably didn't know about that underground river. I followed Autumn into the tunnel, feeling my way down the ladder as the darkness pressed in on me from all sides. I felt her hand reach up and grab my calf, showing me where the last rung was. I stepped safely onto the ground and waited for Tom to come down with the candle. Cecil came down next, carefully carrying Mrs. Beth.

This tunnel was narrower than all the others. In many places, I had to stoop to get through. The path wound up, down and around, until the light changed and we emerged next to the river. We were on the opposite side of the bank where we used to wash up every morning. The torches blazed cheerily on the wall, smelling of oil.

"Did you write in my notebook?" asked Jesse as we walked along the bank.

"I did. I brought it for you to read." I pulled my pack off one arm and reached around to the front pocket while I walked. "In fact, I'll give it to you right now."

He took it from me with a broad smile and tucked it affectionately in his own pack. "Can't wait."

Suddenly a voice came from up ahead in the shadows. "Well, look who's here." It was deep and rough. "Right on cue."

We all stopped. A face emerged from the darkness. He had a wide jaw, pock-marked skin, and thick, black eyebrows over beady eyes. He wore the same white helmet as the general in the cavern, its plumage a ludicrous cap over some very bushy eyebrows. Despite the prominent features and the facial hair, he was the spitting image of Mr. Reeves.

"Who are you?" demanded Tom.

"You don't need to know," the man sneered. "We are all the same to you. Commanders. You are like little children, trying to escape." He approached us slowly, lifting his knees, and as he came into the light we realized he was holding a sword. It was long, thin and made of the same material as his uniform.

Cecil couldn't help himself. He guffawed. "Is that your weapon?" he asked. "A plastic sword?"

"It is made of 2DPA-1, halfwit. A polymer two times stronger than steel, but light as paper." He glared at Cecil. "Would you like a demonstration of its effectiveness? Only if you're willing to be the test subject."

Cecil scowled and said nothing.

"Let us pass," ordered Tom, his voice strangely harsh. "We mean no harm."

"No can do, newspaper man. I have orders to take you in. All of you are in violation of the International Privacy and Information Act, International Travel Law, the Land Management Act, and a whole slew of health laws. We've been hunting you and your operation for a long time." He smirked and his eyebrows sank down over his eyes. "Luckily we had a little help from your friends. The Indian girl was particularly astute at gathering evidence."

That explained the day at the farm, when she stood watching us from the hills. That meant they knew about Bill and Donna. My heart sank to my stomach. They were alone out there, two elderly people and two young girls. Were they being raided, too?

"Are you the ones who've been killing our sentries?" asked Luca.

The eyebrows shot up and he grinned. "They were a security threat."

"What is to happen to us?" Diana asked, her voice surprisingly steady.

The soldier shrugged. "You're criminals. You'll be tried and sentenced."

Two more soldiers came out of the shadows. They wore the same polymer chain-mail, minus the helmet. They carried stun guns. And surprise, surprise—they both looked like relatives of Mr. Reeves.

"Let's not make this too difficult, eh?" He nodded to the soldiers with his chin, urging them towards us. "It will be easier for you if you come willingly."

Three of them, nine of us. I signed quickly to Autumn, hiding behind everyone in front of me.

She nodded. *I'll take the one on the left.*

I've got the one in the middle.

Cecil was watching us both. *I'll take eyebrows.*

I pulled my Colt 44 out of its holster, moved away from the group, aimed and fired. Autumn and Cecil did the same. The soldiers fell to the ground like dominoes.

Tom and Margaret were shocked. Jesse and Diana gaped.

"I didn't know you could shoot," said Jesse.

"We need to get out of here," I said, holstering my gun. There was no time to talk. I didn't care what it took, I was going to get Autumn and her family to safety.

We began to walk forward along the bank, more urgently this time. Suddenly Diana screamed. One of the soldiers had grabbed hold of her ankle from where he lay in the dirt. I jumped over to pry his fingers off of her, but they were surprisingly strong for someone who had just died. Abruptly his eyes flew open, and he looked at me with a grin.

"2DPA-1," said the leader, standing from where he had lain closer to the river. "God, I love that plastic armor."

All three soldiers were standing now.

Adrenaline rushed to my head. "Go!" I shouted. "Get out of here!" But it was too late. The soldiers had wised up and wouldn't hesitate any more. Tom, Margaret and Luca were all tased, their bodies writhing in agony as electricity flowed through them. They fell to their knees, leaving Mrs. Beth, Autumn and Jesse next in line. "NO!" I shouted, lunging forward to block them with my body.

Suddenly someone sprinted out of the shadows, took a flying

leap, and landed on the back of the plumed leader. The soldier cried out in surprise as his helmet was knocked off into the river. Ben Charleston hung over his shoulders like a deranged monkey and began pummeling the back of his head.

Cecil and I seized the opportunity and did the same, accosting the other two soldiers from the front. Cecil had his opponent on the ground in no time, but I didn't have the same fighting strength as he did. I opted for the element of surprise, throwing dirt in his face and then putting him in a headlock. The plastic fibers of his chainmail cut into my arm, but I didn't care. I would do whatever it took to save Autumn and my friends.

One of the soldiers must have dropped his taser in the tussle, because Jesse got a hold of it and pressed it into his side while I had him pinned on the ground. I heard the crackle of electricity, but it was useless against his armor. I ripped his coif up, exposing the white skin of his neck, and grabbed the stun gun from Jesse. Before the soldier could successfully twist out of my grip, I planted the taser into the side of his neck. After several convulsions, he lay still.

Leaving him there would be a liability. The stun guns only left a temporary unconsciousness. Without hesitating, I pushed his body from the side and rolled him into the river. He sank into its dark eddies and never surfaced.

Cecil didn't need any help from the taser. He could have been world champion in an MMA fight if they had those down here. One blow from him and the second soldier was out like a light. He, too, was thrown in the river.

Ben's rival did not go down so easily. He was twice as strong and ten times more stubborn. It took Cecil and Ben both to hold him down, and three tases to put him out. He followed his friends into the black water.

Stopping to catch my breath, I looked across the river at the opposite bank. Emer stood there, watching us. Her cheeks were wet with tears. *I told you not to come,* she said to me in sign language. She bowed her head in shame. *I'm sorry for everything. I thought I was acting honorably.*

I signed back quickly. *Why are these soldiers here? Did you report to them?*

You and I both did. She shook her head. *Neither of us should have come. We should have left these people alone. They just wanted to be happy.* She wiped her cheeks. *What's wrong with wanting to be happy?*

Is your dad a part of this?

She froze at the mention of his name. She stared at me for a long time, as if having some kind of internal conversation about me. She seemed to make a decision. *Whatever happens, Oliver, you watch what you say. They want your thoughts.* She paused. *Don't give them your thoughts. It's all we have left that's ours.* Then she disappeared into the shadows.

TWENTY

Ben Charleston had his hands on his knees, panting, his shaved head shining up at us.

"You saved our lives, son." Tom put his hand on Ben's shoulder affectionately.

Ben stood and faced us. "My dad thought this day would come. He said these people believe we are animals. Slaves. That we belong to them. That the entire earth belongs to them." He said his "r" sound with the same growl as before. It dawned on me that I had never seen him not angry. "I'm not an animal, or a slave. I don't belong to *nobody*."

"That's right." Tom's voice was low and steady. "You're quite right, Ben."

"Come with us," said Diana.

He frowned. "I'm just trouble," he said. "You do not want my sour face in your caravan."

I looked at Autumn, who stood behind Ben. I had expected her to be glowering at him, but instead her expression was soft and full of empathy. A conversation I had once had with Jesse came to mind: *"You city people are so… separate. Don't you know that we can only survive together?"* I remembered Cecil's explanation of kindness that day we were feeding the horses: *"We put out pieces of ourselves because someday, they come back to us better than they were before."* Autumn's face was reflecting this sentiment. Ben needed our help.

"Who's going to protect us if we get tased again?" I said, offering an olive branch. "I'd rather have you on my side during a fight, if you know what I mean."

He looked at me and shrugged. "Fine."

We walked single file along the river bank, Tom in the front and Luca bringing up the rear. Cecil and Ben took turns carrying Mrs. Beth. We ran our hands along the rock wall as we walked, to make sure we did not stumble off the edge and into the water. The darkness was thick.

I don't remember when it happened, but at some point, the air changed. The musky smell of the river disappeared, and the air felt thinner, somehow. I realized I had been closing my eyes. When I opened them, the darkness was more gray than black. I blinked, suddenly aware of the fact that I was sitting in a chair.

Do

Re

Mi

Fa

Good evening, Oliver. What would you like to do?

"What the heck?"

I am not familiar with that phrase.

My heart thudding in my chest, I reached up to feel my head. Sure enough, there was the headset belonging to my sim machine. Its speakers were embedded deeply into my ear canal so the sound would come through as if it were all around me.

"What's going on? Where's Autumn?" My hands flew out to all sides, groping for any sign of her. All I felt was the smooth leather of the sim chair.

Searching database for a character named Autumn.

"No!" I ripped my headset off and threw it on the ground. "She's not a character, she's real! She's…"

There was a squeak of metal and my door opened, pulling a beam of light onto the floor. "Oliver?" It was the quiet voice of my mother.

"What am I doing here?" I demanded, standing. The floor had

that all-too-familiar rubber material, made to grip my shoes if I was in a moving sim. "Where's Autumn?"

The lights came on, blinding me. They were harsh, white LED's. The room was entirely empty except for a twin-sized bed in the corner, and the chair in the center of the room. Every wall and the ceiling were made of computer monitors. My mom walked over and stood in front of me, studying my face. Her eyes were just as I remembered them: soft, hazel-colored, and sad. Right now they were also concerned.

"Who's Autumn?" she asked.

I snorted angrily. "Oh, come on. Stop playing me. Where are my friends? Why am I here? I want to go back to the woods."

Her eyes widened and she put her hand on my forehead, checking for a fever. "Why are you talking to me this way? I knew something was wrong with that new brain-link program. It hasn't been tested long enough."

I pushed her away and looked around the room. I was getting angrier by the second. "Where are they?" I yelled at the walls. "Where did you take my friends? Where is Autumn?"

My mom's hands flew to her cheeks and she looked at me with terror. "I'm calling Dr. Makoyiwa."

"No!" I screamed. "Keep that man away from me!"

Before I could go on, she ran to the wall and pressed a large, red button. A light next to it began to blink, and a soft alarm pulsed throughout the room. The lights went off.

"Trouble in the McNeil household?" A voice echoed throughout the room just as an image appeared on all four walls. Dr. Makoyiwa. He sat at his desk, his arms folded over each other, black eyes staring at me. "Is everything all right, Oliver?"

"He's in trouble, Doctor." My mom was wringing her hands in the doorway. "I think it's the new brain-link sim that just came out. They did say it could have side effects."

Dr. Makoyiwa put his fingers together and pressed them against his chin. "Yes, the program is linked directly to your neurons, so it makes the experience very, very real. It can take time to differentiate delusion from reality once it's turned off."

I crossed my arms and scowled. "I don't believe you." Even though I said it with conviction, a small seed of doubt sprouted in the back of my mind.

His eyes flickered. "Tell me about your experience, Oliver. What do you believe?"

"I believe that you're a lunatic trying to control me and my thoughts."

He cocked his head to the side. "And how do I do that?"

I hesitated. "I don't exactly know."

"Do you not control your own thoughts, Oliver?"

"Well, I do now."

"And what thoughts did you have during your most recent experience in the sim?"

I shook my head. "That was not a sim. That was real."

"All right. Then tell me about your thoughts from this 'real' experience."

I looked over at my mother in the doorway, then back at him. My mind was a cyclone. How did I get here? Where was Autumn, and was she okay? I had to find her. Oh, God, did I have to get out of here.

I scowled at him. "No."

He seemed to ripple with anger, but it quickly disappeared. His condescending smile remained plastered to his face. "We have the sim recorded, you know."

Dread filled my stomach.

"Your experience may have seemed real, but I can assure you, it was not. Would you like me to show you?"

I crossed my arms defiantly, but I said nothing.

The walls flickered and Dr. Mikoyiwa's face disappeared. An image of trees replaced it. Then the scene began to move, as if I were watching a film.

City Man?

Jesse's face appeared on screen.

Hi, Jesse. That was my voice.
You know my name?
Your sister told me about you. We've never met before.
What did she tell you?
She said you're pretty strong.
Jesse grinned. *Sure am.*

The scene faded and a new one appeared, this time in the caves. The image moved up and down as if someone were running. Autumn's laughter filled the room, sounding strange and foreign in this cold, modern place.

Do you want to see something amazing? she asked.
Yes.

The camera moved through the market and the crop fields, stopping at a dim corner of the cavern where the ceiling had caved in.

It's cold, in my voice.
It's winter.

The camera looked up to the sky, then down at snow falling on an arm. My arm.

Is that snow?

Blackness again, then a new scene—this time on the farm, whitewashing fences. The paintbrush moved up and down over the wood, exactly the way it would look from my perspective. Then the camera pivoted and focused on the white whiskers of Ginger.

Oh, man. My laugh. *You can't creep up behind me like that.*

The camera jiggled when the horse nuzzled me. I reached up to rub the star between her ears.

You're such a good girl.

Footsteps. A newcomer. Julia arrived on horseback.

You must be Julia.

She gave no response.

I'm Oliver. Your dad asked me to whitewash these fences. This horse came out of nowhere. Do you know her name?

My heart was heavy when the montage ended and Dr. Makoyiwa came back on the screen. I faced him in disbelief. The evidence was there, it was true. The explanation made sense. Sim technology was advancing, there was no doubt about that. But in the back of my mind, I wished he hadn't shown it to me. I wished no one had revealed that it was a sim. I wished I could have stayed in the program, being lied to about reality, for the rest of my life.

"Is this some kind of cruel joke?" I asked, wiping hot tears from my cheeks. "You watched me experience the greatest adventure of my life, thinking it was real, only to wake up and find out it was all a sim? Were you laughing while you were recording it?"

Dr. Makoyiwa looked soberly at me. "Oliver, of course not. The brain-link sim is simply a new product. It is up to you whether you use it or not." He turned to my mother. "Although, I am recommending that he stay off of it for now. You're right, he appears to be suffering the side effects." He turned back to me. "I am your friend, Oliver. I'm only here to help. I want you to be healthy in body and mind."

"Do you have something to help with the side effects?" my mom asked, still wringing her hands.

"Yes. I will write you a prescription for the antidote that comes with the product."

"Thank you, doctor."

"These sims can be very addictive," he explained. "They manipulate dopamine levels in a way that nothing else does. Oliver may experience periods of depression while he distances himself from his experience. Be sure he gets plenty of rest and takes his medicine daily."

"What about regular sims? For school?"

He waved his hand dismissively. "That's fine. I'm not saying he should separate himself from life. In fact, staying busy will be good for him. Just keep him off the brain-link products for now."

"I understand, doctor."

He smiled and his teeth glistened white. "Take care of yourself, Oliver. I'm always here if you need me. I've sent the prescription and a courier should be there right away with that medicine for you."

I didn't answer.

The screen went dark.

"Why don't you try getting some rest, honey? It's pretty late. I can give you your medicine in the morning."

I climbed begrudgingly into bed and my mom closed the door.

I lay in the dark for several hours before I fell asleep. For the rest of the night, I dreamed about Autumn.

TWENTY-ONE

My mom called me to breakfast the next morning. I was surprised, because we rarely ate meals together. I usually microwaved something and took it to my room.

The kitchen looked exactly as I remembered it. Everything was stainless steel — the cabinets, the countertops, the faucet, even the pendant light that hung over the sink. The countertops were empty, the floor pristine—not a single item was out of place.

"Coffee?" she asked, opening the cabinet next to the fridge.

"No, thanks." My tongue craved the taste of the mushroom coffee that Autumn used to make for me every morning. It was strange, how a sim could leave that taste lingering in my mouth.

I wandered over to the window and pulled the blinds back to look outside. We were on the eighteenth floor, but there wasn't much to look at other than the tall buildings across and on either side of us. The streets below were empty.

"Did you sleep well?"

I shrugged. "I guess so."

She set a plate on the counter with a soft click. I sat down to eat. The meal was dry, microwaved eggs, a small pool of ketchup, and reheated frozen sausage patties. My stomach churned in disgust.

"Dr. Makoyiwa sent your medicine," she said excitedly. She set a glass of water and two pills next to my plate.

I nodded and began to eat, chewing the eggs mechanically. They had no taste. "Can I have some salt?"

She frowned and shook her head. "The meal plan includes just enough sodium to maintain maximum health. You should never try to over-do sodium. It's bad for your heart."

I sighed and continued eating. I had forgotten about this routine. Each portion was scientifically exact, with the ratios of protein, carbohydrates, fats, vitamins and minerals that my body biometrics had indicated that morning.

We both ate in silence, hearing nothing but the sound of forks hitting plates. I looked at the two tablets next to my glass, bright blue with a ridge right down the middle. I remembered my first day in the forest, when Autumn shuffled through my vomit to find the microchip that was used to track my medication. Why would that kind of content be in a sim? The pills stared back at me like two artificial eyes, unblinking, ever watching. I decided right then and there that I would never take those pills.

Before I finished my eggs, I put the medicine in my mouth and pretended to drink it down with the water. I shoveled the last bite of food into my mouth, using my tongue to push the tablets into the middle of them. Then I stood, still chewing.

"Thanks for breakfast," I said, putting my plate in the sink. "I need to go get ready for school."

She smiled at me. "Okay, honey. Have a good day."

It was so strange to hear her say that.

Still chewing, I went to the bathroom and spat the eggs and the pills into the toilet. I flushed.

Mom was gone when I came back out. Her bedroom door was closed. I stood for a moment in the kitchen, feeling the nothingness all around me. It wasn't just silence, it was nothingness. There was no life, no interest, no action, no love. Why would anyone want to live here?

But there was nowhere else to go.

I turned and walked slowly into my room, closing the door behind me with a quiet click.

*

"How was your weekend?"

I was at the gym doing PE with my friend Carl. My shoes squeaked on the floor in my room, which moved as I ran, just like the treadmill I was on in the sim.

"Fine, I guess." I adjusted my headset, which kept slipping back while I ran. I was so aware of this as a sim. I used to be so immersed in it.

"I tried the new space travel sim. Played it all weekend. The AI is super advanced. I don't know how they create such detailed spaceships if we've never had any like that in real life."

"Someone must have a really good imagination."

"Yeah."

I wondered whose imagination had created my brain-link sim world. The characters had seemed so real.

"Can you believe graduation is in less than a month?"

I shook my head. "Nah, can't believe it."

"What're you gonna do after? Go to college?"

I grabbed a hand towel from my chair and wiped the sweat that kept falling in my eyes. "God, no. I'm done with school." I stopped for a drink. "I don't know, I'm kind of thinking of going into filmmaking."

He looked confused. "Filmmaking? Like with old-fashioned cameras?"

I shrugged. "Maybe."

He jogged for a few minutes in silence, musing. Then he asked, "What would you film?"

I got back on the treadmill, cranking the speed to a sprint. "I was thinking I'd go out on the streets. Film what it's like out there."

"What, like journalism?" He snorted. "There's nothing out there."

"The Forgotten live out there. That might be interesting to people, getting some insight into their lives."

He turned up his nose. "Not anybody I know."

I was panting by now. "Anyway, I have to find a camera... and some equipment... I'd have to have a way to edit it before publishing it online. I was thinking of going to find some of the old cities. They might have some of that stuff lying around."

Carl turned off his treadmill and mine shut down suddenly, too. I put my arms out and came to a standstill, gasping for air.

"What'd you do that for?" I said between breaths.

"Where'd you get all these weird ideas from?" he demanded. "Going outside, going to see the old cities? That's dangerous. You don't know what the air quality's like. Not to mention the water. You could carry disease back here! Do you want to go to jail?"

"Back to work, back to work." Mister Tall, the holographic droid PE teacher who was eight feet high, sailed over on rolling wheels. "Must keep going, must keep going." He said everything in pairs. I suppose the Department of Education thought students needed to hear everything twice.

"I'm in the middle of talking!" I exclaimed, frustrated. I turned back to Carl. "How do you know it's dangerous, Carl? Have you ever been outside? Ever?"

"Running is good for you. Running is good for you. Builds strong muscles. Builds strong muscles."

"No, why would I need to go outside?" Carl seemed less belligerent and more concerned, as if he had reached a danger zone. "It's safer…"

"It's safer inside? But how do you know that, if you have anything to compare it to? Are we just supposed to take everything at face value, and just accept things because people tell us it is that way? Shouldn't we observe things for ourselves?"

"Oliver, you sound crazy. Have you had your meds today?"

"Do as you're told. Do as you're told."

"No!" I ripped my headset off and slammed my hand on the touch screen on my chair. The holographic images in the room disappeared and the screens faded to black. "I will not do as I am told."

I sat in my chair for a long time, staring into the darkness.

*

"You're the demon, Oliver.

"You'll bring the storm to them."

I tossed and turned all night, falling in and out of a fitful sleep. Dreams were memories and memories were real.

"You take, take, take but do not repay."

Dr. Makoyiwa's faced sneered down at me as I slept.

"That's not my voice. That's not me at all."

He morphed into the soft, sweet face of Autumn, looking down at me tenderly while I dreamed.

"I can't believe they did this to you."

Her tears fell on my hand.

"I've learned never to discredit what I know."

Her eyes sparked with defiance.

"Everybody has demons, Oliver. You're not the only one living under storm clouds. Maybe you just need to change direction. Decide to ride into the storm. Perhaps you'll get through it faster that way."

I tried to reach her, but I only grabbed air. She disappeared into a cloud of smoke, twisting and turning through trees and over mountains. Then darkness hit, and all I heard was music.

'Twas in another lifetime, one of toil and blood
When blackness was a virtue and the road was full of mud
I came in from the wilderness, a creature void of form
Come in, she said, I'll give you
Shelter from the storm."

I awoke with a start. Sweat soaked the bedsheets. My heart was racing. I sat up and rubbed my face, surprised to find it clean-shaven, expecting to feel the four-month beard I had grown in the caves.

"It was real," I whispered. "I don't care what you say." I looked at the computer monitor that loomed over my bed. "Machine men are not capable of creating a sim like that." I pushed my blankets back and began to dress. "It was real."

TWENTY-TWO

"Where are you going?"

I paused in the doorway of the elevator. "I'm going back," I said, turning to face my mother.

She leaned against the kitchen counter, as if her body were too heavy to stand independently. "Back to what?"

"Come on." I sighed. "Enough of these lies. I know what I know."

Her eyes widened in surprise. She straightened.

"Why don't you come with me? This is no life." I gestured around me at the cold, lifeless room. "Every day is the same—we wake up, eat breakfast alone in an empty kitchen, go to our rooms to talk to people who probably aren't even real. Don't you crave the fresh air? The sunlight? Conversation? Laughter? Don't you ache for it?"

She studied me, unblinking.

I sighed and ran my fingers through my hair. "I wish we'd gotten to know each other better," I said. Then I shifted my backpack onto my shoulder and turned to leave.

"You talk about her in your sleep." Her words tumbled out anxiously.

I turned back and stared at her. She had been pretty, once. Now she had puffy, dark circles under her eyes and a permanent scowl around the sides of her mouth. I tried to see her as she had been, when I was really young and loved to touch her face.

"You must really love her."

I nodded slowly. "I really do."

Her eyes flooded. "You look so healthy," she said, and her voice caught at the end. "Your eyes are so bright."

I smiled. "Thanks."

She wiped her cheeks, shook her head, and stood a little straighter. "Do me a favor before you leave the city."

"What is it?"

"Find the Forgotten. Ask for a man named Conrad Nalley. Tell him you need his help."

I frowned. "Why do I need his help?"

"Because of the implants in your brain. The ones that make you hear things that aren't there. Tell him you and your brother were part of Project MicroTrack. He will know what to do."

"My *brother*?"

She sighed, wringing her hands. "I'm sorry. They told me you were important. Twins are uncommon. I didn't know they were going to take you from me." The tears had stopped, and now she just looked small and helpless. "I hope you can forgive me someday."

Then she turned and walked into her room.

I took the elevator down to the ground floor. The lobby was empty from front to back, without even so much as a plant to brighten the space. My shoes squeaked on the gray, stone floors. The front door opened automatically and I stepped onto the sidewalk, breathing deeply, finally free from the stale air inside.

The sidewalks were all empty. I hurried down the street, looking for a sign of the Forgotten. Every building looked the same—tall, brown, and austere, with no windows on the first story—immovable, unforgiving giants. I tried to remember the last time I had run away from home. I had a vague memory of these buildings towering above me, and the sidewalk under my feet. How far had I gotten before the police found me and returned me home?

A gust of wind swept through the street, carrying the remaining sharpness of winter. I shivered and tucked my chin into my jacket.

The sidewalks were impeccably clean, I realized, looking closely at the concrete under my feet.

Suddenly I rammed into something. I jumped back and reached for my gun, forgetting that they didn't have those here.

The wide-jawed, blond-framed, mischievous, grinning face of Cecil stared down at me.

I froze in shock. I couldn't believe what I was seeing.

He put his finger over his lips and mouthed "Shhh." He reached into his pack and pulled out a black box smaller than his hand. It had a red light on the front and a clip on the back, which he used to attach the device to my jacket. He pressed a button on it and the light turned green.

"Now you're invisible to the cameras," he said. "It scrambles the frequency. The audio, too."

Then there was a pile-up while the rest of them turned the corner, screeching to a halt behind him. Luca, Diana, Ben, Jesse, Tom, Margaret—even Julia and Lizabeth. And in the center of them all, her eyes wide in surprise, was Autumn. She smiled and it was as if the sun and the moon and the stars had all come out at the same time.

"I knew it!" we said at the same time.

Then it was chaos, and we were all hugging and laughing and jumping and my heart felt as if it would burst out of my chest. I had never been so happy in my entire life. Diana was crying. Tom thumped my shoulder. Jesse jumped on my back like a monkey. And Autumn threw her arms around my neck and kissed me all over my face.

"How did you all get here?" I asked, still in disbelief.

"When you disappeared on our way out of the caves, we knew you'd been taken hostage, but it was too dangerous to go back in," Luca explained. "We got to Bill and Donna's place as fast as we could, and Lizabeth showed us how to get here. Her friends hacked into the city database and found your address."

"Was the farm raided, too?" I looked over at Lizabeth and Julia. "Are Bill and Donna okay?"

There was a ripple of emotion, but Lizabeth said, "Bill and Donna are fine."

"How long have I been gone?"

"Two weeks," said Tom.

"Wow." I scratched my head. "They must have drugged me. I don't remember anything. They tried to convince me you were all a sim."

They laughed.

"My mom told me I should find a guy named Conrad Nalley and tell him about Project MicroTrack."

"From the Welfare District?" Lizabeth's face lit up. "I know Conrad. He brought my family food when they were sick and we were starving. He's a real genius. Probably the most advanced hacker you'll ever meet. I can take you to him."

"What's Project MicroTrack?" asked Luca.

No one had an answer.

"We should get out of here," Cecil said. "The police will probably be here soon, wondering why Oliver suddenly disappeared from their monitors."

My stomach churned. The thought of being captured and sent back to my apartment made me sick. "Let's go," I urged, and we all set off at a sprint.

Lizabeth led us through the maze of buildings, somehow aware of direction despite the identical appearance of every single building and sidewalk. After thirty minutes of walking, we passed through a tunnel under a bridge and arrived in the Welfare District.

Several sentries stood guard at the perimeter. They gave us a nod when they saw Lizabeth. She guided us through a maze of canvas tents, which had been placed in a somewhat organized fashion, with aisles between them like narrow streets. People sat on blankets outside their tents, cooked around small campfires, or milled about talking or playing cards. Children ran about the streets, playing tag and other games. Everyone stopped and looked at us as we walked by.

"This was a gov'ment project. They couldn't keep us in those high buildings, and there wasn't enough room for us in prison, so they threw us in the street. Sold us a bill of goods, they did. Made us sell our farms and our land and move to the city for a better life." She snorted in disgust. "Does this look like a better life?"

I looked at the children with their dirt-stained cheeks and the clothes that hung off their bodies like rags. I looked at the sunken eyes of people scraping the last morsels of food from their soup pots. I looked at the tent roofs patched up with duct tape and string, still caving in from years of weather. I shook my head. No. This did not look like a better life.

"'The commonwealth of Athens is become a forest of beasts,'" I murmured.

"There's my old place," she said, throwing her hand back in the direction of a ragged tent so torn it was uninhabitable. "This here is Conrad's." She led us into a tent that was cleaner and more well-kept than the others. "Knock-knock," she called. "It's Lizabeth."

The tent flap opened with a flourish and a man's face popped out. It was long and thin, with a thick crop of curly, black hair spilling over his forehead. His eyes were kind.

"Well, land sakes! My dear, you're alive!" A long arm reached out and enveloped Lizabeth in a bear hug. "What kind of voodoo is this?" he cried. "I looked for you after the winter rising. I heard about your family." He looked crestfallen. "I thought you'd been killed, too—or worse, captured by Reeves." He had the same accent as Lizabeth—fast and choppy, with the phrases slurred together—but somehow his choice of words made him sound more literate.

Lizabeth shook her head. "I snuck out past the barricades while everyone was busy fighting. I found a farm. There are people out there, living in the woods. They have food."

I began to wonder if we had made a mistake, coming here. If these people found out about the caves, they might all leave and try to find it. They would probably lead the Reeves right to us.

"You have gotten some meat on your bones!" he said, squeezing her arms. "You look wonderful. Finally had a bath, I see."

We all laughed, remembering how much she stank when she first showed up to the farm. Lizabeth grinned sheepishly.

"Who are your friends?" He turned to us, holding out his hand. Despite his tattered clothing, his hands and face were clean and his hair was combed. Each one of us took his handshake while Lizabeth introduced us by name. He had a firm grip and sincerity in his eyes.

"Please, come into my home," he said, waving us inside the tent.

It was surprisingly spacious inside. There was a small bed in the corner, and an oak chest of drawers stood next to it with candles and knick-knacks arranged neatly on top. A Persian rug covered the concrete floor. In the opposite corner was a large armchair with a footstool, and a table next to it held several piles of books.

"There's a peddler who travels to the old cities," said Conrad. "He comes to the Welfare District every five months with his horse-drawn cart spilling over with artifacts. Thank God for those scramblers—" he pointed to the device on my shirt—"otherwise the cameras would hear him clattering down the street from a mile away. Not to mention his loud singing." He chuckled. "The kids clamor for games and clothes, and the women usually want cookware. I, on the other hand, am only interested in two things: books and guns."

I looked around the room for the guns, but I didn't see any. He must have had them stored somewhere else. I wondered how far he went outside the city to hunt. There was probably only small game available until you got closer to the woods.

A piece of paper had been tacked to the tent wall next to the armchair. It had a quote written on it in big, scrawling letters:

"There are many things more horrible than bloodshed; and slavery is one of them."
—Patrick Pearse

"Who's Patrick Pearse?" I asked.

Conrad's expression clouded slightly. "He was a man who led a rebellion in a place called Ireland more than a hundred years ago."

"Did he win?" asked Jesse.

Conrad shook his head soberly. "I'm afraid not."

"What was he fighting for?" asked Cecil.

"Independence from a government that was trying to wipe out his country's identity."

I looked at the quote again. It was true, actually. Slavery was worse than bloodshed. I had been a slave my whole life, until I went to the caves. I would rather have died than go back to that.

A desk stood opposite the armchair, empty but for a small, portable computer. I stared at it dumbly. That was it? *That* was his set-up? The most advanced hacker in the city? Maybe he really was a genius.

"Can you help me?" I asked. "My mom told me to find you. She said I'm supposed to tell you that I was part of Project MicroTrack, which has some kind of mental effect on me."

His face fell. All trace of joviality in his eyes disappeared. He glanced down at the device that Cecil had clipped to my jacket. "Don't take that scrambler off, whatever you do."

"What's Project MicroTrack?" asked Autumn.

"It was an experimental government program." He went to the chest of drawers and started rummaging through the top drawer. "Fully accepted by the public, of course. Voluntary at first. Your mom must have offered you as one of the first lucky candidates. All in the name of science." He pulled a silver, dome-shaped device out of the drawer. It had two handles welded to the sides, which he used to carry it over to me. "Once they've primed your brain, implanting you as an infant, subsequent injections will be more easily absorbed—and then it is *very* difficult for your body to push them out." He had me sit down in the chair, and he placed the dome on my head. It went through a series of electronic beeping sounds, and then I felt a flash of static, which jolted me out of the chair.

"What is that?" I asked angrily. "I felt that from my head all the way down my arms and legs!"

He pulled the device off my head. His lips were set in a long, thin line. "They're in your brain, your arms and your legs."

"What are?"

"Microchips the size of atoms. Only these don't speak the usual language. These chips contain magnets, which reverse polarity in their own version of 0's and 1's. It makes them more powerful despite their microscopic size. It also makes them really hard to find."

An arm and a leg.

And a brain.

The last pieces of the puzzle clicked into place, and everything began to make sense. The voices in my head. The raid on the caves. The recording Dr. Makoyiwa had when he tried to convince me it was all a sim. The syringe before I was pushed off the back of a van. They must have injected me with microchips so they could spy on the caves.

"Why would my mom volunteer me for something like that?" I muttered angrily.

"It's being promoted to parents as a way to keep their children safe. If they ever go missing, they'll be able to track them down within minutes."

"Like dogs," said Luca.

Conrad nodded. "Like dogs."

My heart sank to my stomach. "I'm not going back there," I said vehemently. "I'd rather die."

"How do we get it out of him?" asked Autumn.

Conrad returned the metal dome to the chest of drawers. "It's a risky procedure, but it can be done. We've performed two successful extractions."

Two! "How many were unsuccessful?" I asked.

He sighed. "We lost thirty-seven. It depends on how deeply into the brain tissue the chips have embedded themselves. We have to judge how deeply we can go during the surgery, but without proper medical equipment, that is difficult."

Those were not the odds I was looking for.

"What is the procedure?" asked Margaret.

"We make several small incisions, and then we use a machine with magnets to pull the chips out. The arms and the legs won't be a problem. It is only the brain that is a concern. If we cut too deep, the body will not make it."

We all looked at each other as we realized the magnitude of this problem. I wasn't going to continually endanger my friends, but I meant what I had said. I would rather die than go back. It sounded like I had my choice.

"When do I start?"

TWENTY-THREE

"All right, Oliver, you'll feel a small prick for the anesthesia, and then you'll have a nice nap while we get these chips out of you."

I lay on a wooden table in the medical tent. Autumn stood next to me, her hand on my arm, and the surgeon stood over me with a syringe in his gloved hands. Everyone else was waiting outside.

"Hold on," I said. "Just give me a minute." I turned to Autumn. Her eyes were brimming with tears and she was biting her lip. I grabbed her hand, feeling her smooth fingers, those small hands that had somehow lifted me onto her gurney of pine branches that day she found me in the woods. Words tumbled out of me like mountain rockfall. "If I don't make it back, I want you to know that you have been the best thing that ever happened to me."

She put her fingers on my mouth, hushing me.

"No, I have to say this, just in case." I kissed her palm and pressed it between mine. "No matter what happens, I want you to know that I'm grateful for every minute of it. Even death, even pain, even the guilt and heartache and loss. I wouldn't trade it for anything, because it meant that I got to spend this time with you. I am so, so grateful I got to spend this time with you."

Her tears were falling now, shamelessly spilling down her cheeks in two endless streams. She pinched her lips together and nodded. "Me, too," she said, patting my hands tenderly. "Me, too."

Suddenly there was a commotion outside. The canvas door flap pulled back and Conrad entered the tent, stooping to get inside. "Is his scrambler still on?" he demanded, checking the small, black box that was clipped to my shirt. The light was still green. "Reeves are here. They want to search every tent. I think they're looking for him."

I sat up. "Should I hide?"

He shook his head. "We've got to get those chips out of you, or you'll never be able to hide anywhere. We're going to have to stall them. Autumn, I need you out of here."

"Wait—"

But it was too late. The surgeon plunged the syringe in my arm, and I couldn't even finish my sentence. Everything faded to black.

*

You have to get up. It was her voice. She looked down at me, silhouetted with the trees in the moonlight. *I can't believe they did this to you.*

> *... 'twas in another lifetime*
> *One of toil and blood...*

Dad, the guy's a live wire. You'll put everyone at risk.

> *... When blackness was a virtue*
> *The road was full of mud...*

Your air and water are sterile, and yet you city people are always sick. You have endless knowledge available at the push of a button, but you do not think or imagine or create. Do you not question any of this?

> *...I came in from the wilderness,*
> *A creature void of form...*

I've been wanting you to do that for the longest time. Her laugh. The sweetest laugh. *You're a good man, Oliver McNeil.*

...Come in, she said, I'll give you
Shelter from the storm.

"You'll drown in memories if you keep doing that." A woman's voice filled my mind.

"I can't see anything." It was true. Everything was black.

"It happens." She didn't really have a voice, now that I thought about it. Concepts seeped into my mind like rainwater filling a dry pond. "Once you decide where you're going, you'll see things, one way or the other."

"I get to decide where I'm going?"

"Well, kind of. If you die, you can't really change your mind at that point. I've been trying to out-stubborn death since 1913."

"So I'm not dead?"

"Not yet. I guess that's what everybody's trying to sort out."

"Who are you?"

A pause. "My name was Agnes. Now, I am Nobody."

Why was that name so familiar?

"Well, you're talking to me, so you must be somebody."

Another pause. "I suppose you're right."

"I can't die. I need to make sure Autumn is okay."

"Then don't die." There was a conceptual shrug, as if she was suggesting the simplest thing in the world.

Don't die. It faded to a whisper.

"Agnes," I said, remembering the name just as I began to fade out. "Cecil's ghost..."

Don't die.

I can't live without you.

Please come back.

"Oliver. Please come back to me." It was Autumn's voice again, but this was not a memory. This was real life.

I opened my eyes.

Her hands were on my cheeks, her tears were in my hair, her smell was all around me. I reached up to feel her arms, her back, her head. She was real. She kissed me, relief washing over both of us like a tsunami.

"Did it work?" I asked, sitting up. My arms and legs were wrapped in bandages. I felt my head and found it wrapped in gauze.

"There's no time," she said quickly. "Reeves are searching every tent. They're looking for you." She thrust a pile of clothes in my arms. "Put these on. We have to go."

Suddenly I realized that she looked different. Her teeth were black. Her cheeks were smeared with mud. Her clothes were a patchwork quilt of rags. She hardly looked like herself.

I did as she asked, donning a tattered pair of pants and a long-sleeved shirt that was frayed around the edges. The small, black device was no longer clipped to my clothes. "No scrambler?" I asked.

"You don't need it anymore. We're getting out of here." She put a hat over the gauze on my head. "The others got a head start. We'll meet them in the north woods, about five hours from the city."

"We're wearing costumes?" I asked.

"In case we get caught."

I could hear the murmur of voices outside the tent.

"Quickly," she whispered. "Out the back."

She pulled the tent flap up in the back and we both ducked through. We ended up wedged between a stucco wall and a long line of tightly packed tents. The voices had moved inside, so they must have just entered our tent. Autumn put her finger on her lips and motioned for me to follow her.

We tiptoed slowly along the narrow patch of concrete behind the tents, doing our best not to step on the tent lines or accidentally shake them. Clouds moved in overhead, blocking the sun and sending a chill down to coat the tents and penetrate the holes in our clothing. I shivered. We found a patch of dirt behind one of the tents, and Autumn rubbed it on my face with spit. She led the way down the row of tents and we came out at the entrance of a tunnel on the other side.

Everyone is waiting for us— she began to sign, but she stopped in mid-sentence. Three figures emerged from the tunnel, blocking our way out.

We turned the other direction, but a line of Reeves stood at attention.

We were trapped.

One of the men stepped forward and my stomach churned as I realized who it was. Dr. Makoyiwa.

Autumn turned to me with intensity in her eyes. *This is to be your greatest performance ever,* she signed. *Whatever you do, do not speak.*

"Where are you off to?" Dr. Makoyiwa asked. The corners of his mouth curled up ever so slightly. "Don't you know we're performing a health inspection? We have numerous reports of an infection in this area."

She crossed her arms and faced him. "We are not infected with anything."

"Well, aren't you spunky," he said, raising an eyebrow. "I have declared a state of emergency in the Welfare District. I am the city's senior health inspector. I have full authority to detain you if you disobey my orders." He came closer to us. "I don't recognize you," he said to Autumn. "Have I examined you before?"

She squared her shoulders defiantly. "No."

I stepped forward and stood next to her protectively. Our difference in size was practically caricaturistic. His forearms were half the size of mine.

He looked up at me and his sneer deepened. "Now, you, I recognize. You've tried to run away again, have you, Oliver?"

"His name is not Oliver." Autumn's face was expressionless. "And he cannot hear you. He is deaf."

His eyes flickered. "What are his biometrics?" he asked one of the figures in the tunnel. "Name, identity?"

One of the Reeves stepped forward, holding a computer tablet. He was staring at the screen with a confused look on his face, his finger shuffling through data. "He has none, sir."

"What?" Dr. Makoyiwa turned to the soldier and yanked the tablet out of his hands. His finger flipped through the data angrily. "Why not?"

"We don't have biometrics on the Forgotten, sir. Hackers keep wiping it out, and the federal budget hasn't allowed for its replenishment in several years." He shrugged. "It's a big project."

Dr. Makoyiwa snorted in irritation. "This kid is *not* one of the Forgotten. He is my patient. He belongs in building 202. His mother is worried sick."

"You are confusing him with his brother," said Autumn.

Realization flooded the doctor's face, and his expression changed completely. "That's right," he said, looking at me in awe. "I nearly forgot. We gave one of the twins away."

Autumn rolled her eyes. "You mean you threw him away. A baby. You threw a *baby* away and left him to *die*."

He ignored her. "The likeness is uncanny," he said, studying me. "He's a little bigger, perhaps, but the facial features are identical. Different colored eyes, I suppose." He shook his head with regret. "I would have loved to have studied them. Such an anomaly. But the law does not allow for multiples."

"Unless they're Reeves, of course." Autumn's voice was thick with irony.

He frowned, seemingly confused by her bitterness. "Of course. Reeves are genetically perfect. Cancer does not grow in them; illness is nonexistent; they reproduce effortlessly. They are the approved race." He continued to stare at me in awe while he spoke. "I would say you're lying; but if he has no biometrics, then he can't be Oliver. Saved by the Forgotten, eh, kid?"

I backed away from his scrutiny. At the same time, the third figure emerged from the tunnel. She was a thinner version of Dr. Makoyiwa, but there was no mistaking the raven-colored hair and prominent cheekbones. It was Emer.

"Come here, child." The doctor pulled her over by her arm. "You studied Oliver extensively. This is the long-lost twin of Oliver McNeil. Do you see the likeness?"

Emer stood before me, her shoulders bent forward, her eyes heavy and tired. She seemed smaller than I remembered her. "Yes," she said quietly.

Her father's expression changed again, turning cold as stone. He grabbed her arm and yanked her closer to me, so that our noses were almost touching. When he spoke, he almost snarled. "And do you see any *differences* between this person and Oliver McNeil?"

Emer blinked. She did not move. She stood staring at me in that position for many minutes. I could smell her skin and feel her breath on my mouth. I did not back away, for fear of looking guilty, but I was certain she could see into my soul.

She was going to give me away.

Then she put her hand on my chest and pushed me back, wrinkling her nose. "This is a half-wit who smells like he hasn't had a bath in ten days."

I gaped at her. Without a doubt, she was lying. She knew it was me. I don't know why she did it, but part of me wondered if this was some form of an apology. I remembered her expression that day in the sim, when she saw me running toward her, when she begged me to let her explain why she had humiliated me. Maybe she did regret it. Maybe there was more than one side to her, too.

Dr. Makoyiwa narrowed his eyes. Before he could speak, however, a loud shouting erupted from the other side of the tents. The line of Reeves standing guard over us suddenly scattered, yelling, "Get down!" Then a barrage of gunfire exploded from somewhere within the tent city.

Terrified, the doctor dove behind the soldier holding the tablet. "Real guns?" he cried. "Who gave them guns?"

The barrage lightened, and dozens of Reeves came running, their boots clicking on the pavement in uniform rhythm. At the center was a general, his head plumage slightly smaller than the one who had led the raid on the caves. They all stopped in front of Dr. Makoyiwa.

"Permission to leave the Welfare District, Sir!" The general gave him a quick salute.

The doctor still stood behind his bodyguard, although he straightened, trying to regain his composure. When he spoke, his voice trembled ever so slightly. "Permission denied! You are to go back and disarm those people at once."

The general seemed to be in pain as he balked at his orders. "We are unprepared, sir. We did not bring enough weaponry."

"Why the devil not?" shrieked Dr. Makoyiwa, his face glistening with oil and sweat.

"We thought they were invalids."

Gunshots broke out again, this time closer than before. More Reeves clip-clopped over to the battalion that stood before the doctor, looking expectantly at him. I looked over at the tunnel, realizing that it was the only way out and would soon be jammed with people. I had to get Autumn out of there.

The Reeve with the tablet looked up from the monitor, his eyes round. "Sir, the system is down. The police cars are inoperative."

Dr. Makoyiwa's face turned ashen. "God help us," he whispered.

Autumn's dad had spoken of the "stampede effect." It was something that happened when groups of people became frightened. Fear was more contagious than a virus, he said, and when it spread throughout a crowd, they became a herd of sheep galloping in a mad frenzy off the side of a cliff. Only when they were in the air, falling to their death, did many of them realize that they should have turned back, away from the herd. The most dangerous sheep never even considered it at all, not even when their bodies lay bloodied and broken on the rocks below.

The stampede effect overtook the battalion of Reeves faster than a tsunami. I grabbed Autumn's hand and pulled her into the tunnel, trying to out-run the soldiers, but we were too late. We were swallowed up in a sea of Reeves as we all plunged into the darkness of the tunnel.

I gripped Autumn's hand as tightly as I could without crushing her bones. Bodies pressed in on all sides, jostling us as we tried to keep moving forward. I lost track of which way was out. The air was thick with hot breath and the smell of sweat. My foot came down on a hard, plastic boot and I stumbled, caught myself, and began to walk more carefully.

Suddenly bullets fired in heavy staccato from behind us. I pulled Autumn in front of me and we hunched over, continuing to push forward through the throng of panicked Reeves. Bodies began to fall around us. I could hear bullets ping off armor and walls and tear through flesh with muted thuds. Space opened up as Reeves fell away, and we clamored over them, suddenly heartened to see light up ahead. The gunfire stopped momentarily and we finally reached the empty streets on the other side of the tunnel.

The sun had set and the streetlights cast eerie shadows on the concrete, but the air was fresh and cool. Stray Reeves scattered across the street, their footsteps sharp drumbeats that echoed in the silence. I pulled Autumn around the corner of one of the buildings, seeking asylum in the darkness.

"You never answered my question," I whispered. "Did the surgery work?"

She looked up at me in the dark and her eyes were like stars. "Yes, Oliver. It worked."

"The chips are all gone? Every single one? They can't track me anymore?"

"Every last one." She smiled tearfully. "You're free."

Free. For the first time in my life, it was true. My thoughts were my own. I could go where I wanted. And I was not a danger to anyone. I was myself, and nothing else.

The chaos mounted around us, as revolutionaries poured out of the tunnel behind the Reeves, mad with the gluttony of war. Starving, debased and forgotten by their government, they had reached their boiling point, and they were not cooling down. When guns didn't work, they used their bare hands, tearing armor away and cutting flesh from bone with hunting knives.

Autumn and I hastened along the sidewalks, away from the fighting. Street lamps thinned and then disappeared as we reached the edge of the city, but the moon was full and its silvery light flooded the valley before us. The woods spread thickly across the landscape, its wildness calling to us like an old friend. The border between city and forest was unmistakable, for not a single tree grew in this concrete jungle, and the timber seemed to turn its back scornfully where it did take root, reminding me of a gang of school kids pointedly ignoring a bully.

"Dad said he'd leave a message for us under the roots of that large cedar tree," said Autumn, pointing to an evergreen that towered above its border mates. "Everyone left to find Bill and Donna after you went down for your surgery."

Dread hit me in the pit of my stomach. "What happened to the farm?"

She looked over at me, her gray eyes sad in the moonlight. She shook her head hopelessly. "Reeves took it all. The sheep, the pigs, the hens. They burned the house to the ground."

The wind came out of my lungs with a loud puff. Bill's childhood home, gone? But he was meant to live there until the end of his days. How were we going to keep the caves fed? I realized how nonsensical that thought was. The caves had been raided. The people were gone. There was no one left except us.

The next thought hit me with dark dismay. "What about the horses?"

"We have them," she said, her tone of relief reflecting my sentiment. "Bill, Donna and the girls hid them in the woods. Donna gave them Valerian in just the right doses to put them to sleep. They lay with them until the Reeves were done and gone." She put her hand on my arm. "It could be worse, Oliver. Let's go find the message."

We made our way down the hillside into the valley. Crumbled concrete and gravel faded into wet soil and the soft, whispering grasses of early spring. Sagebrush and juniper glimmered in the moonlight and scratched gently against our legs as we moved through them. The world was quiet.

We reached the forest edge when the moon had moved two fingertips across the sky. Autumn explained that that was roughly equivalent to four hours. She taught me about the stars as we walked—how the constellations move around the sky all year, some even disappearing over the horizon for a little while and then reappearing as they traverse the sky in a circle. The north star is the center of their universe, which she showed me how to find using the Big Dipper. This is how slaves found their way to freedom a long time ago, she explained. Finding and following the north star.

"How history repeats itself," I murmured.

She nodded in sober agreement.

The cedar tree had roots like enormous, gnarled fingers. Autumn knelt on the ground and felt around them, pushing pine needles aside and digging under bark until she pulled out a small roll of leather tied with twine. She unfurled it and we both peered at the letters carved into the hide.

Grandfather Rock at East River. North to Reed Hollow. End at Holly Hill.

I didn't understand the directions, but Autumn nodded and stood, pocketing the leather. "We're crossing the river at Grandfather Rock because it's shallowest there. Can you swim?"

I cringed and shook my head sheepishly. "Not against a real current."

"We'll use my rope. The water will only come up to your chest at the highest point, but it's strong, and I don't want you getting carried off downstream."

I added "swimming" to my mental checklist of skills to learn.

The darkness deepened as we made our way into the woods. While many of the trees were still bare skeletons from the fading winter, conifers like fir and pine stood tall and bushy, blocking out the moonlight. Our eyes adjusted quickly, and we both cocked our guns and kept alert for bears and wildcats.

"Do you still wish you lived in the city?" I asked cautiously while we walked, afraid of her answer.

She looked at me in surprise. "Not at all."

I breathed a sigh of relief. "That's good."

She ruminated for a moment. "I don't know if I ever wished for that," she went on. "I just didn't know my place in the world. I was tired of hiding under the earth like a worm. What was I to do? Take over my dad's print shop and do the same thing every day until I die? Marry Ben Charleston, who hates the world and would make me hate it, too? There was not much future for me. Not much future for any of us."

"Well, now, I don't know about that," I said. "I guess life is what you make of it."

She gave me another look of astonishment. "That's true," she said haltingly, her inflection full of wonder. "'It is not in the stars to hold our destiny, but in ourselves.'" She looked up at the pieces of sky peeking between the trees, and her long, white neck caught a stray beam of moonlight. God, she was beautiful.

"You know, I've been thinking about Shakespeare," I said.

"Oh?" She looked at me with the corners of her mouth turned up, as if I amused her.

"He was a good storyteller, but I don't think that's the only reason he was so popular. He's immortal because his words are truth," I said. "No matter how the world changes, truth is forever. That's why evil men lie. I don't mean little white lies, or lies that save the people you love. I mean convincing the whole world that black is white, that up is down, that nature is bad and that true happiness can be found in a video game. And once the whole world believes it, no one considers anything else. At that point, they are all slaves." I hoisted my backpack up higher and dug my heels into the dirt as I walked. "Evil men lie because truth is forever, and they want forever all to themselves."

I was met with silence. It was a long, thick silence that seemed to hang in the air in front of us. Had I made her mad, somehow? I looked over at her again and was startled to see that her cheeks were wet with tears.

"Are you okay?" I asked in consternation.

She nodded, keeping her eyes on the ground in front of her. I wondered if she was embarrassed to be crying, being the tough, impenetrable girl she was. But she did not wipe her cheeks, and the tears fell to the ground like raindrops.

"Why are you crying?" I asked.

She swallowed, attempting to collect herself. Then she turned to look at me with those deep, clear, universe eyes. "There never was a truer statement, Oliver McNeil," she said. "And I'm going to tell you a truth that is very, very important. I may have saved your life that day in the barbed wire, but you have saved mine and changed me in the most inexplicable, profound, and permanent ways. You are my future and *you* are my forever. Even if the whole world disappears, I am yours until the end of time."

I stopped and kissed her then, pulling her into me gently, feeling her wet cheeks and tasting her tears. She wrapped her arms around my neck and somehow they were wet, too. Suddenly there was a loud swelling around us, and I realized our hair had a layer of moisture on it.

"It's raining," I said.

It was not just raining, it was a spring monsoon. It came upon us in a mad rush. Thunder rumbled and lightning crashed while the rain came down in torrents. We pulled on waterproof jackets from our backpacks and continued our trek through the woods.

We were shivering uncontrollably when we reached Grandfather Rock. The boulder stood more than ten feet high on the bank of a river, its north side leaning over the water in the shape of a hunched old man. Sheet lightning lit up the river valley and Autumn and I both gasped in horror.

The river was a rushing, churning, violent thing. There was no way I could cross that as an inexperienced swimmer.

"It's the melting snow from high up the mountain, mixed with the rain," Autumn yelled over the storm. "The river's blown out. It's going to be worse everywhere else, though. This is the only place to cross." She crouched down and unhooked a bundle of rope from the side of her backpack. "Help me tie this rope to that aspen tree. I'll bring it across and attach it to one of the tall firs on the other side. You'll have to swim when you get to the middle of the river—it's too deep to walk—but whatever you do, don't let go of that rope."

"What about you?" I hollered, wiping rain out of my eyes. "That current's too strong."

"It slows down where it's deeper." She grabbed a long, thick tree branch from the river bank. "I'll use this to push against the current while I'm walking." Her face softened and she came over to put her hand on my cheek. "I'll be fine, Oliver. I'll see you on the other side."

We tied the rope tightly to the tree trunk and she hung the loop of rope over her shoulder. The water was brown and murky where she waded in, pushing her walking stick into the river bottom downstream and moving slowly against the powerful eddies. The water rose to her knees, then her waist, then her chest as she moved toward the middle of the river. The sound of rushing water was deafening.

Another flash of lightning illuminated a cluster of boulders sticking out near Autumn. What luck! She grasped the top of one of them and kicked forward, her shoulders disappearing under the water as she began to swim. A roll of thunder crossed the sky as if competing with the sound of the river. One last flash of lightning flooded the valley, and suddenly I spotted an enormous, craggy log barreling downstream, heading straight for her. "Look out!" I cried, but my voice was lost in the wind, and it was too late, anyway. The log hit her on the back of the head and she disappeared, sinking like a stone under the dark, turbulent water.

My mind exploded in alarm. I didn't think; it was more primeval than that. My body was consumed by a single impulse—*Save Her!*—and it responded with a ferocity I had never experienced. I charged into the river, pushing past craggy rocks and stray logs as if they were mere pebbles and twigs. The water was icy, but I hardly noticed it as I plunged into the murky rapids, searching frantically for Autumn.

I went down again and again and came up empty every time. I pumped my arms through the water towards the boulders in the middle, grabbing hold of their craggy sides and feeling around for her body, her hair, her backpack—*something*. "Just give me something," I begged the river. "She is not yours. She is mine." I dove down again, circling the rocks, my fingers raw and bleeding from digging into their sharp crevices to hold on.

Just when I had begun to look downstream, wondering if the current had carried her somewhere I wouldn't be able to reach, my leg hit against something softer and more forgiving than a rock. My heart lurched and I reached under the water, overcome with relief when I grabbed a fist full of hair. I pulled her up to me, clutching her limp body in my arms, forcing her mouth upward into the air. "Breathe," I commanded. But she was limp as a pile of clothes, and her mouth did not move. "Breathe!" I shouted again, shaking her. Her face was gray and her lips and eyelids were purple.

I had never done CPR, but I had seen it plenty of times in movies. I didn't have time to get her to the river bank, so I had to do it in the middle of the stream, with one arm holding on to the rocks. I draped her body over my free arm and brought her face up to mine, tipping her head back as I had seen it done. I wrapped my fingers around her face and pinched her nose closed. I covered her mouth with mine and breathed out slowly, watching her chest rise and fall. *One, Mississippi. Two, Mississippi.* Wait. I knew I was supposed to pump her chest, but I couldn't. I tried again. *One, Mississippi. Two, Mississippi.* Rise, fall. Rise, fall. Wait. Repeat.

Thunder rolled in double time as I began to panic. This wasn't working. Why wasn't she responding? It always worked in the movies. I had felt her presence all around me as I focused on giving her my breath, but now all I was aware of was the rushing river and relentless rain.

"You are my forever," she had said to me. "I am yours until the end of time." I could hear her voice in my head. Well, she was *my* forever, and I was *not* going to live without her. I looked downstream at the rushing rapids. My fingers loosened their grip on the rock. If she was gone, then I was going, too.

I looked down at her face one last time. The rain had let up and the clouds parted, bathing her in moonlight. Her hair floated in the water and she looked strangely peaceful. I leaned down to kiss her one last time.

Before my lips touched hers, there was a choking, gargling sound. I opened my eyes to see her convulsing and vomiting water. "Oh my God," I exclaimed, pulling her up so all the water came rushing down her chin. The color returned to her cheeks and she looked at me with round eyes. "Oh my God." I pulled her in to me and wrapped my arms around her. "I thought you were gone."

She clutched my shoulders weakly. "I want to get out of here," she gasped, looking around in confusion. "Take me away from here."

"Okay, let's go." I hoisted her onto my back, wrapping her arms around my neck like a scarf, and pulled myself around the cluster of boulders. I kicked and yanked my arms through the water until my feet found solid ground in the rocks at the river bottom.

"Wait, what are you doing?" she whispered in my ear. "You can't swim."

"I can now," I said, wading toward the bank so ferociously that I dragged river rocks out of the water with me, kicking them from my waterlogged shoes. I lay Autumn gently on the ground and collapsed next to her.

"Did I die?" she asked breathlessly.

I stared up at the night sky, panting. "Almost."

"So you saved my life again."

I laughed. "Can we be done with this trend?"

She rolled over and lay her head on my chest, shivering against me. "Thank you," she said.

I ran my hand over her wet hair. We lay like that for a while, sharing the warmth of our bodies and slowing the rhythm of our breath. The moon moved half a fingertip before we decided it was time to go.

"North to Reed Hollow," I said, quoting Tom's note as I helped her up. I found the north star and pointed in the direction I thought we ought to go.

"That's right." She rubbed her arms for warmth. She still looked a little pale.

"How did you know that I have a twin brother?" I asked as we made our way back into the deep woods.

"Had." She kicked the dirt with her boots. "My dad has a friend in the city who works in cyber security. Dave. They knew each other in college. He was the one who told us about the caves. Anyway, my dad sent him an encrypted message when you first came to stay with us, asking him to look into you." She looked over at me. "We may be backwards, but we're not stupid."

"How does your dad send encrypted messages without a computer?"

"He carves it in leather, like this one." She patted her pocket.

"He sent one of the paper boys to bring it to him. They know how to get past the cameras."

"And what did your dad's friend find out about me?"

"Your mother birthed you as part of the 2065 population program. The government had spent decades suppressing reproduction in its fear of population growth, and fertility and birth rates were reaching near-extinction levels. By 2060, humans were an endangered species. The program took people who were in fairly good genetic shape and allowed them one child, and one child alone."

"Who was my father?"

"Oh, the program only permitted artificial insemination."

I shuddered. For some reason I was reminded of the plastic-tasting packaged eggs my mom served me for breakfast every morning. Fake food, fake kitchen, fake family.

"Dave had to look deep into the dark web for the actual medical files, but he found them and discovered that your mother had birthed twins. Quite an anomaly in today's medical world. Her doctor followed all the protocols and sent the second child to the solid waste facility."

I looked at her in shock. "Solid waste? You mean trash?"

She pursed her lips. "That's exactly what that means."

We walked in silence for a long time. I felt heavy, weighed down by a darkness I had never felt before. I didn't want to ask exactly how children were disposed of in such a place. I imagined what my brother would look like if he had been permitted to grow up. I wondered what made them choose me over him.

"Why is this place so horrible?" I asked, running my fist into a nearby tree. The shock of pain was better than the cold, empty ache that had enveloped me.

Autumn caught my arm as it swung back. She ran her fingers softly over my knuckles, giving me a reproachful look. "Don't do that," she begged. "I know better than anyone what it means to be consumed by hate, but it'll eat you up before you can do anything about it. You can't change the past. The future is untamed land, though, and you said yourself that life is what you make of it." She took my hand in hers. "Don't look behind you. Look ahead."

She was right. I knew she was. But I mused on it as we walked on, as the sky lightened and the birds began to serenade the dawn. I would do something about that darkness, I thought. I would change the world somehow.

"City Man!"

I looked up at the crest of a hill, where twelve figures were silhouetted among the trees. A herd of horses stomped and snorted beside them. The smallest shadow waved and jumped excitedly.

I waved back. "I'm not a city man any more, my friend!"

They all laughed.

"Thank God for that!" Bill called.

I had a strange sensation, which I tried to understand as Autumn and I hiked up the hill toward them. There was electricity in my spine, light in my head, and fire in my chest; but it was not pharmaceutical, or artificial. It was the realest thing I had ever felt. It was a fiery blaze that no one but I stoked and mended; a herd of wild horses chasing the sunset; a flock of meadowlarks circling the sky. It was elation; it was excitement; it was adventure. It was *life*. And it was all mine.

END

BOOK CLUB/ LITERATURE SEMINAR

DISCUSSION GUIDE

1. We live in a world of rapidly-advancing technology. How do you imagine the world will be in ten, twenty, or thirty years? Consider medical advancements, education, the arts, entertainment, and general lifestyle. How do you think it will it be different from your life today? How will it be similar?

2. In *The Boy Who Learned to Live*, a section of society decided to remove themselves entirely from the modern world of technology. A group similar to this today would be the Amish community. Imagine what it would be like to live that way, removed from all the comforts you are used to (no cars, no electricity, no Internet or TV, no washing machines, dishwashers, etc.). Do you think it would be difficult? Would you be able to do it?

3. If we lived in a completely digital, AI world, do you think we would ever need to interact with other human beings to survive? What would be the pros and cons of this?
Autumn describes being on drugs as feeling like "a block of wood." What do you suppose she meant by that? Do you think she would be aware of that state if she hadn't stopped taking them?

4. Throughout much of the book, Oliver believes that deep down, he is evil. Is he? Why or why not?

5. At the end of chapter 8, Emer tells Oliver, "Simulated murder is still murder." Is that true? Do people on the Internet or in video games always behave the way they would in real life? Discuss.

6. When Oliver realizes he will never be able to watch a movie again, he is devastated. Later, he realizes he can put on theatrical performances to achieve the same end: telling stories. Discuss the differences and similarities between theatre performances and movies or television.

7. In an end-of-the-world situation, do you believe that people would still desire to tell stories or put on shows? Do you agree or disagree with Autumn that "stories give you back pieces of yourself"?

8. Consider the title of the book. Do you believe that Oliver "learned to live" in the end?

9. What does it mean to you to truly live your life to its fullest? Provide specifics.

ACKNOWLEDGEMENTS

This book would not exist without the help and encouragement of many.

I'd like to thank the late Dave Wolverton, whose teachings helped me take this story from a mere spark of an idea to a fiery blaze that consumed me until it was all out on paper.

To my mother-in-law, Janet, who always wanted to know how the book was going, and who was one of the first to read it. Thank you for your interest in my imaginary universe.

To Cori, for the lessons in horse-whispering. Thank you for your patience with this very green cowgirl.

Enormous gratitude to James, the cover artist, and to Susan, my editor.

Thank you to my children, who allowed me to bounce ideas off them and never balked at my strange hypothetical questions.

And lastly, to my husband, who listened patiently to my jabberings on about Oliver and his adventures over dinner or during our evening walks. He was the first to read and love this manuscript, and thus, he helped me bring it to life.

www.ingramcontent.com/pod-product-compliance
Lightning Source LLC
LaVergne TN
LVHW042251070526
838201LV00110B/331/J